RIDE SOUTH TO PURGATORY

JAMES C. WORK

SAGEBRUSH
Large Print Westerns

Copyright © James C. Work, 1999

First published in Great Britain by Gunsmoke
First published in the United States by Five Star

Published in Large Print 2015 by ISIS Publishing Ltd.,
7 Centremead, Osney Mead, Oxford OX2 0ES
by arrangement with
Golden West Literary Agency

CIP data is available for this title from the British Library

ISBN 978–0–7531–5371–0 (pb)

Printed and bound in Great Britain by
T. J. International Ltd., Padstow, Cornwall

Foreword

This story is fiction. Many of the details, however, are true. Late in the 1870s, in the high plains cattle country, many men still preferred their old Civil War vintage percussion revolvers over the newer 1873 Colt. The .44 Winchester rim-fire was being superseded by the center-fire model, but was still an impressive possession. In southern Colorado there really is a river named the *Purgatoire*, or Purgatory, which early cattlemen called the Picketwire. "Uncle" Dick Wooton operated a toll road over Raton Pass from 1865 until 1878. And as merchants and farmers began to settle the land between the Cherry Creek gold fields and Santa Fé, the last of the Spanish dons were losing their power and their Spanish land grants. The railroad era was being born while the great sprawling ranches known as *haciendas* were becoming extinct.

Some will say that I have my facts mixed up when it comes to the Ghost Dance religion, commonly associated with the Great Plains tribes. However, it was a Northern Paiute named Tavibo who came out of Nevada in 1869 to preach the new religion. One of his disciples, Wovoka, also a Paiute, continued to spread the message after Tavibo's death. In 1889 it reached the Great Plains, leading ultimately to the tragic Wounded Knee massacre in 1890. Ghost shirts which were believed to be bulletproof are found in museums today.

Gangs of rustlers still roamed parts of the Kansas Territory, generally seizing stray cattle or stopping trail herds to claim ownership of unbranded or poorly marked animals. The gold country of Colorado was known for its lawless and rough men, most of whom lived a desperate hand-to-mouth existence. The fort that Pasque takes care to avoid, late in the book, was notorious for the crude and violent men who lived in and around it. The site is near present day Fort Morgan, Colorado, but in its operational days it was known first as Camp Tyler and then as Fort Wardwell.

Did the Keystone Ranch ever exist? For one brief era sandwiched between the end of the Civil War and the final defeat of open range ranchers in the Johnson County Wars of 1892, the high plains of the West knew a loosely-organized society of cattlemen reminiscent of the feudal kings of medieval Europe. They commanded armies of mounted men, administered vast acreages, built sprawling ranches, and had their foremen, ramrods, *segundos*, and lieutenants supervising cattle ranges larger than some Eastern states. Most of them were honest and capable and Christian gentlemen, ready to help settle the territory.

Such a ranch was the Keystone.

No matter how many facts they may have, storytellers throughout history deal in imagination. Sometimes the imagination makes the point better than the research. Early day yarn-spinners created stories of gods and demigods. Others took peasants and made them into princes and princesses. Some even tried to make their point with fables in which animals talked and acted like humans.

My way is to paint a picture in the imagination, walking a very fine line, indeed, between what the reader might agree to believe in and what the reader will find too preposterous. It is the way of legend, the traditional way of myth-making. It is an old story, this tale of a young man who learns the penalties of revenge, of haste, of poor judgment. The idea of using winter to represent a time of death and rest, and the idea of spring as a time of rebirth and new growth — those are also old notions. Pasque is a player, an actor in an ancient fable. His costume includes the sage-battered chaps and the dusty Stetson of the American cowboy.

James C. Work
Fort Collins, Colorado

CHAPTER ONE

The Rustlers' Iron

After two months on the trail, Pasque was back on the Keystone range again, ready for a soft bed and a good hot meal. One of Mary's roasts, with baked potatoes. Uncle Art had done well when he hired Mary to cook for him. Nobody could turn out a better roast, or better biscuits for that matter.

He trotted over a ridge, heading down toward the Kathy Fork. There was a cabin there where some green homesteader had once tried to raise beans and corn — in deer country. The homesteader had starved out, and riders from Uncle Art's Keystone Ranch now used the place as a line cabin.

A whiff of wood smoke rose in dying wisps from the chimney, but there was nobody home. The weather-beaten wagon had come a long way on its worn-out wheels. Poking out from under the tarp was a horse collar, some hames, a shovel handle.

Inside the cabin, the stove was still warm from breakfast. Pasque figured three men were staying in the place — their bedrolls were on the bunks, their extra gear hung on pegs. There were only two slickers, pretty well-worn. A couple of tote sacks of groceries hung from the log rafter near the stove.

Out back, there were new horse droppings in the corral dust. There was fresh water in the horse trough. Pasque made a circuit around the cabin, which brought him back to the wagon. He peeled back the tarp to look for something with the Keystone brand on it, like a grub box or maybe a tool chest. But all he found was a tangle of old wire, a canvas bag of fence staples, and a branding iron. The brand was an oval with a cross inside it.

Pasque pulled the tarp over the wagon bed again, the way he had found it, then ran to his horse, and hightailed it for the nearest timber as fast as the pony would go. It was not until he was deep in the trees that he finally pulled up to take stock of his situation. Three men, somewhere right around the cabin. The Oval Cross brand. And here he was all alone, six hours' ride from any help.

For that whole six-hour ride to the Keystone, Pasque never relaxed. He hardly ever took his hand off the butt of his Colt. He avoided riding into any gullies where he couldn't see who might be there. He rode out of his way to avoid ridge lines where he might make an inviting target. When he stopped to water the horse, he checked in all directions before letting the horse put its head down to the water, and he did not dismount. Even when he finally saw the sombrero-shaped redstone bluff that marked the main ranch and then saw the hayfields and the faraway figures of men and horses, he still felt a tight, crawly sensation up and down his spine. Oval Cross riders had shot both of his brothers. In the back.

At last he trotted toward the corral by the barn.

"Well, *there* he is," the hostler said, coming out of the tack shed to open the corral gate for him. He gave Pasque's cow pony a quick look-over as Pasque swung down from the saddle. Pasque couldn't tell whether Pat was talking about him or the horse.

"He OK?" Pat asked him. It was the horse.

"Yeah, just fine," Pasque said. He took the bedroll and grub sack off, then loosed the latigos and the cinches, and pulled the saddle free to toss it onto the top rail. Pat picked up the saddle blanket from where it had fallen.

"You been gone a while," the old man said.

"Clear to Montana," Pasque replied. "Had to get a new set of shoes up there, too. Old ones got so thin I sold 'em to a peddler to make reeds for jaw harps."

Pat snorted and hoisted one of the horse's hoofs, examined the Montana horseshoer's handiwork with one eyebrow raised in disapproval, said — "Hmpph." — and put it down again. "Just have to do 'em over, I guess."

Pasque threw his saddlebags and grub sack over his shoulder and picked up his bedroll and Winchester.

"Pat," he said, "you hear of anybody staying at the old cabin up on the Kathy Fork there?"

"Sure. You know your Uncle Art was winterin' some of that rangy old Texas stock up there. He hired him a couple of new men to see if they could round 'em up. Nothin' but a bunch of thick-hide tangle-tails, but he

7

wanted 'em collected for some reason. Never listens to me about them things. Sent Tim along, too."

"These new men. Don't suppose they came from Kansas?"

"Matter of fact, I believe they did."

"What outfit?"

"Don't know as they ever said."

"Anybody know who they are?"

"Big one's called Link somethin' or other. He seems to be the boss. Me, I don't like him much . . . seems to be all mouth. Mebbe he's as good as he says he is, mebbe not. And he keeps an eye on Missus P. too much to suit me. Reminds me of that old stud rooster strutting out to impress the hens."

"The other one?"

"Calls himself Moore, or somethin' like that. I stay out of his way, too. He's one of them Southern boys that don't know the war's over. Got himself a problem about the color of my skin."

Pasque hunkered down and used his finger to draw a big oval in the dust, then drew a line lengthwise through it, and another line through it crosswise. It was kind of lopsided.

"Either of 'em sporting that brand there?" he asked Pat.

Pat pushed his hat back, scratched at his hairline, and studied the drawing. "What do y'call that?" he asked. "The Window Sash brand?"

"Nah." Pasque drew a rectangle and put a cross in it. "That's the Window Sash. This one here is more of an oval. Ever see it? Maybe on one of those guys' horses?"

8

"No . . . 'course, they came in on a wagon, and the horses that was pullin' it was pretty well busted down. Don't guess they was ever worth brandin' in the first place. But there's somethin' . . ."

"What?"

"Well, give me a minute. Saw that mark somewhere. Yeah, I know. One of 'em . . . Link, I guess it is . . . he's got a version of that brand burned into the fender of his saddle. Fancy outfit. Center-fire rig. Pretty important to you, is it?"

"Might be," Pasque replied, turning toward the bunkhouse again. "Might be a good idea to forget I asked, too."

"I heard that," the hostler said.

And then Pasque turned again, like something else had just occurred to him. "Hey, Pat!" he yelled back.

The hostler's face peered around the corner of the shed. "What?" he said.

"Did you say Missus P.?"

"Yeah," Pat replied. "The boss's new wife. Came about two weeks after you left to go north."

"Oh, that's right. I nearly forgot that was goin' to happen," Pasque said. "Well, that's somethin'. Things'll be different around here from now on."

"I heard that, too." Pat grinned.

"So," Pasque went on, "does that mean Mary ain't cookin' up at the big house any more?"

"No such thing," Pat said. "Her and that worthless husband of hers, Lou, hell, they're permanent fixtures in the place. I guess Missus P. has taught her some new

9

dishes is all, and Lou, now he wears clean shirts to loaf aroun' the house an' garden."

"Well," Pasque said, "I guess I'd oughta get cleaned up and find a fresh shirt before I go and meet my new aunt."

"Don't need to bother," Pat replied. "She took a buggy and drove herself to town for a week of shoppin'."

"Herself? All alone?" Town was almost twenty miles to the east, and with Oval Cross back-shooters roaming around out there, it was an especially risky trip for a woman to take by herself.

"Oh, yeah," Pat said. "That's a woman who is tough-minded, besides bein' young and pretty. I told her to take a couple of the boys along, or at least a scatter-gun, but she wouldn't hear of it. You don't tell her what to do. You'll see. An' I wouldn't bring it up with your Uncle Art, neither. He figures whatever she says is the good Lord's own gospel. He won't hear no arguin' with it."

"Whatever happened to the old West where men run things?" Pasque asked as he started to walk away.

"Damned if I know," said Pat.

CHAPTER
TWO

A Bear in the Bush

Art Pendragon was in his office at the back of the big main house. At the sound of footsteps coming across the living room, he swung his boots down off the oak desk, put down the book he had been reading, and began rolling a cigarette.

"Glad to see you back," he said as Pasque walked into the office. "Have a good trip? Weather OK all the way? What did those boys in Montana have to say for themselves?"

"Well," Pasque said, "most of 'em ain't that keen on tryin' to raise any quality beef that far north. Other'n that, I had a dry trip and no trouble."

"Didn't like the idea of buying our breed stock, eh? What about longhorns?" Art asked.

"A couple of 'em said they'd buy a few and give it a try, or else sell 'em for beef. The others didn't think Texas stock had a chance in hell of makin' it through the winter. They say they need a tougher breed to stand up to blizzards."

"I guess we'll have to start small, then, and see what happens. What about the Indians?"

"The agency said they'd buy all you can send, provided they arrive in good condition. All kinds of government rigmarole and forms to fill out to get a contract, though. I got the stuff in my saddlebag. But lookin' at the beef they had standin' in the corrals at that agency, they ain't real picky about what the Indians get. But listen, I want to talk to you about . . ."

Art walked over to his liquor cabinet and poured two healthy shots of bourbon. He handed one to Pasque. "What's on your mind?" he asked.

"It's about those new waddies I hear you hired."

"Who's that? Oh, yeah. Link and Moore? What about 'em?"

"On the way down, I swung by Kathy Fork. Figured I'd just check in there and see if anybody was around. Nothin' there but a wagon, though."

"They were staying there, along with Tim. Rode back here today to pick up supplies and see what I want to do with that range stock I've got up there, what with winter coming on and all. Fact is, they rode in just a few hours before you did. They must have been right ahead of you all the way back. I don't think I'll send them back up there, though. They were only able to put together a small bunch. Tim and maybe Walt can drift that herd back toward the main ranch by themselves."

"Where they from, do you know?" Pasque asked.

"Who, Link and Moore? Kansas. They're out of Kansas."

"That's kind of what I was figgerin'. It was Kansas rustlers that killed Jim and Chris."

"And you think these new men know something about the rustlers? Big place, Kansas," Art said.

"I don't know how to say this, except straight out," Pasque said. "I think they had somethin' to do with it."

Art sipped his bourbon and looked Pasque straight in the eye. He had been hoping to see Pasque forget some of the anger and pain of that murder, but in those eyes he saw the cold determination that had been there ever since Pasque came riding in to the Keystone, a very young cowboy with no family left in the world except him.

"But your brothers were killed by a bunch of phony trail-cutters, I thought. Somewhere on the Shawnee Trail, wasn't it? What leads you to this idea that Link and Moore had a hand in it? They just don't seem like range bums or rustlers to me. They came in pretty shabby all right, just about starved and at the end of their string. But they know their business. That Link is a real top hand. That's why I could send 'em to the Kathy Fork on their own."

Pasque sipped his whiskey and stared out the window. "All I know," he said, "is a gang of riders came in on the herd Jim and Chris was with. Pretended they was trail-cutters for a big Kansas ranch. That's how they got into the herd. They stuck with the cattle for two days, makin' like they needed to look at this brand and that, gettin' a feel for the drovers' routine. Then early that mornin' in the dark they shot Jim and Chris and that other kid and stampeded the herd.

"Some of the drovers said these trail-cutters had a brand they said they was lookin' for. A cross inside an

13

oval. Pretty handy brand. They could point out a Window Sash or a Goose Egg or a blurry 101 or damn' near any old haired-over burn on a steer and claim it was a Oval Cross. A few days of arguin' over every brand, and everybody would start to ignore 'em. Any cowboy gets tired of ropin' and throwin' steers ten times a day just to study the brand."

"You still haven't said what this has to do with Link and Moore," Art said.

"Like I told you, I stopped at the Kathy Fork cabin. Went pokin' around in the wagon to see if it came from the Keystone, and guess what I found?"

"Couldn't imagine," Art said.

"A brandin' iron. Not an old one, either. Been used, but not much. Oval with a cross inside it. That don't mean they shot my brothers, but it does mean that they know somethin' about it, and I aim to find out what it is, even if it takes bendin' a Colt barrel over their heads."

Art made another little trip to the bourbon bottle.

"Take it easy," he said. "Don't want you gettin' hurt. You're all the family I got left, you know. And you don't want to be calling Link out. He looks like he could fight as good as he can rope."

Pasque brooded a while, but he was thinking that Uncle Art wasn't all that interested in this discovery of his. Could be he had other things on his mind. Wouldn't hurt to change the topic anyway.

"I heard that family thing's changin'," Pasque said.

"Hey? Oh, you mean Gwen!" Art said. "Oh, yeah. I told you I'd been writing letters to her. Funniest thing.

We hadn't thought about each other since I was your age and she was in pigtails, and then I ran into a fella who knows the family, and we start writing. Sure is a nice lady. You got yourself an aunt *and* an uncle now, so there's all the more reason to take it easy on turning yourself into judge and jury. I don't want to boss you around, Pasque, and God knows I want those murderin' trail-cutters found and hung. But I have to ask you to just lay off for a while. They're good workers, and I'm shorthanded. You starting up a fight is the last thing I need right now. Just let it drop, at least for a week or two. Could you do that for me? Treat them like any other cowhands and leave them alone?"

"Art? How the hell can I do that? You mean just work alongside 'em, and pretend I don't know they had somethin' to do with it? I don't know. I stood there by my folks' graveside and promised two things, Art. I promised the folks that somehow I'd get Jim and Chris back there to Illinois and put 'em in the family plot, and I promised I'd see them murderin' sons-of-bitches hang. And here's two *hombres* that know somethin' about it."

"I know it's goin' to be tough. OK, if it'll get that damn' wild look out of your eye, I'll get the two of them up here, and we'll talk it out like civilized people."

Pasque snorted. "Yeah, and have 'em vanish in the mornin'. I got a better idea. We'll keep things quiet and nice for a while, like you said. Until they get kinda used to me. Then why don't you send the three of us out on a job somewhere. Check the windmills on the east range. Once I get 'em alone and away from the ranch,

I'll get the story out of 'em. Might come back alone, too."

"I can't do that, Pasque. There's not much law around here, but, if I go letting you . . . or anybody . . . be a self-appointed judge and jury, it will just get worse. Nope. Can't do it."

"Listen, Art, all I want is . . ."

"No! You're always jumping the gun. Here I am, trying to keep the last member of my family alive, trying to keep peace in the territory around here, and all you want to do is go off and swap lead with two men at a time. And I might add that you don't even know how good they might be with the gun. Dumbest thing I ever . . ." Art fell into scowling silence, surprised at his own outburst, but not entirely. "I'm eager to do right by Chris and Jim, too, God knows. But they're dead, and that won't change. Link and Moore might or might not know something about it. And it's *my* job, not yours, to find out what it is. This damn' vengeance idea of yours, taking two men out into the sage to shoot it out, this won't do anybody any good, not your brothers, not you, not this ranch."

Pasque stood, scuffing the rug with the toe of his boot. His face was hot, and he was squirming a little to get away, but he knew he had to stand there and take his uncle's verbal drubbing.

"They're not going anywhere for a while, and, if they do, you know I've got plenty of men here who could track them down again. And friends all over the territory, besides. I've worked hard, mighty hard, building up the Keystone reputation, and there isn't a farmer or a whang-string rancher out there anywhere for a hundred miles that doesn't owe me a favor.

"If Link and Moore had anything to do with that murder back in Kansas, and, *if* they run off from here, you can bet your year's wages that they won't get far. But dammit, Pasque, if you turn hothead on me and go off and kill them, there's no way I could protect you from the federal marshal. And you know I wouldn't, even if you are my nephew. Nobody would ever trust the Keystone or anybody who works on it, not ever again, if I was to do that."

Art put the bottle away and slammed the liquor cabinet shut, then turned again to Pasque.

"Now I want you to get something to eat from the kitchen, if you're hungry. Clean up and just relax. Link and Moore are down there at the bunkhouse, and I want you to be nice as pie to them until I find out their whole story. You start in on them about this branding-iron business, and I'll send you packing for another trip. And this time it'll be so far north that you'll think you're a fence rider for Santa Claus.

"Now then, when you stopped off in Montana to talk to the Army about buying some remount studs from the Keystone, did they give you any idea what prices they were offering?"

"Yeah," Pasque said, head down. "Got their bulletin in my saddlebags. I'll go get it."

"No, you go eat something and cool off. I'm going to get myself a cigar and go outside for some air myself. I'll wander on down to the bunkhouse later on and pick it up."

There had been nobody there earlier, when Pasque had dropped off his bedroll and saddlebags on the handiest empty bunk, but now most of the crew was back from the cook shack, picking their teeth with wood slivers and getting ready to settle in for their evening of cards and pulp novels. Some had already started to repair their riding gear or were oiling their boots.

The one called Link, kind of tall and slick-looking, listened while Walt and the Pinto Kid got Pasque to tell about his trip. But after a few minutes of Pasque's stories of places he'd stopped and things he'd seen, Link started to look bored and changed the topic.

"So you're the boss's nephew we heard about," Link said. "Well, that explains why you thought you ought to plunk your gear down on my bunk like you own the place. Didn't see you at chuck, though. Headed straight for uncle's house, did you?"

"Had to check in," was all Pasque replied.

"I'll bet," Moore put in. "Check the new livestock while you was at it?"

"Huh?"

"Missus P. She's a nice filly. Built for speed, I'd say."

"Didn't meet her." Pasque glared. "Don't know you, neither. Don't much like hearin' anybody talk about any woman like that, I can tell you that much. Let alone talkin' about my uncle's wife."

Link put in his two cents' worth. "That's a woman worth talking about, though. So, you didn't see her?"

"Nope."

"Well, sir, you hang around the south side of the main house there sometime about bath and bed time. Might get a good glimpse for yourself, if those curtains aren't drawn exactly tight." He grinned around at the other men as he spoke. "'Course, you being family and all, you could walk right in on her, I guess, and have a nice long look."

The Pinto Kid looked up from the monte game spread out on the bunkhouse table. Mac looked up too, both of them starting to rise from their chairs to see if they could head things in another direction.

"How's about a little stud poker, Pasque?" the Kid said. "You must have saved up your whole summer wages while you was out on the trail."

Pasque turned to him and tried a thin smile. He had almost lost control there for a minute. "Anybody winnin' that crooked game of yours?" he asked. "Got enough for your own spread yet?"

"Nah," Pinto Kid said. "All the money went out o' here with Bob's bunch. These here waddies are broke flatter 'n a fresh cowflop. Playin' for buttons and matches, now."

Link seemed to want to change the conversation, too. He sat down on the bunk and patted his stomach. "Cook rustled up a pretty good stew tonight," he said. Then he looked at Pasque. "I guess you get all your suppers up at the big house, though," he said.

"Sure," Pasque said in reply. He was doing his best to keep his voice calm and sociable, but his eyes had that cool, steady gaze to them. "Just us family. Always have pie for dessert and everythin'."

"Missus P. will be back pretty soon to serve you that pie, too," Link said.

"Yeah."

"I wonder what she wears to supper," Link went on. "Probably that little checkered dress, the one that fits kind of tight across" — he cupped his hands in front of his leather vest — "or maybe that dark red one that's cut down so low in front?"

"Guess it won't be none of my business to notice." Pasque kept calm.

Moore was up from the table now, as if he was just looking around for something else to do. This conversation had an edge to it that made a sensible man want to stay out of it. He never had liked Link's way of speaking sometimes, his kind of half-sneering talk that made everything sound like a challenge. Or dirty. Link was a good man, but, when he felt a fight coming on, he turned real cold and deliberate. And nasty.

"Oh, you'd better notice," Link went on. "Won't be able not to, you see."

"You know that, do you?"

"Hell, yes. I watch her, every chance I get. What man wouldn't?"

"Let's drop it, Link."

"Ah, don't you want to hear how I was out having myself a smoke the other night and happened to be looking up at that window . . . over in the big house . . . and she was gettin' ready to have a bath. Boy, I saw them . . ."

"Shut up, Link." Pasque's words came through clenched teeth.

"Now, kid, a man can't help getting a little hot over the sight of a pretty woman."

Link saw the punch coming, and he turned, but, in turning, he caught Pasque's driven fist right in the rib cage and belly. He groaned as the air burst out of him.

Pasque followed with a plank splitter to Link's chin, and the sound of his knuckles, hitting jawbone, echoed loudly in the small room. Link shook off the dizzy blur and punched back, trying at the same time to put up his left arm as a guard. Pasque side-stepped to the right, and, when Link swiveled around to see where he'd gone, he let go with another powerful slam to the guts.

Link went backward, hit the wall, grabbed the back of a chair, saved himself, and took another sledge-hammer hit in the face that seemed to whirl his head clear around.

Mac was up on his feet now, and he and Ward and the Pinto Kid were frantic to seize Pasque's flying arms and put a stop to this. Moore was moving toward the line of pegs beside the door where four gun belts were hanging; Pasque tore himself free of the grabbing hands, slammed Link out of the way, and lunged at the gun belts just in time to get hold of Moore's hand.

"No!" It was Link's voice. "No!" He words rasped hoarse, like one of the blows had mashed his vocal chords. "No, Moore! No gun play!"

Pasque clubbed Moore across the teeth with his forearm, feeling the pain as Moore drooped back against the door frame. Pasque gained control of himself and studied the two men. Link wheezed in the middle of the room, hanging onto the chair for support, trying to get his head clear while he used his sleeve to mop blood from his mouth. Moore, holding his face with both hands, had slid down the door frame to sit on the floor.

Pasque pulled Moore's cap-and-ball revolver from its holster and aimed it toward Link. "Why no gun play, Link? Why no gun play?"

Link only groaned. They could all hear his breath wheezing.

"Maybe you and Moore here can't afford the attention, maybe? Might be that a shooting would bring out the marshal, and he'd know something that maybe we should know?" Pasque felt his confidence growing like somebody had pumped fresh air into his chest with a blacksmith's bellows.

He pointed the pistol at Moore. "What do you say, Moore? Maybe while Link there gets his breath, you could talk to us about trail-cutter brands. Like a kind of oval with two lines running through it. What do you call that, Moore? Oval Cross? Goose Egg, maybe, with a cross?"

Link stopped mopping at his mouth. His breathing seemed to stop, too, for a second, as he stared at Pasque.

The door burst open, and Art came into the bunkhouse, moving fast, taking two strides to Pasque before Pasque could even turn around. His hand came down on the old Colt and ripped it away from Pasque's hand in one, long, smooth stroke like a loose corral pole falling across his wrist.

"What the hell is goin' on here?" Art demanded. And he didn't listen for an answer. "You all right?" he said to Link and Moore collectively, seeing them mopping at the blood on their faces. They nodded, sort of sheepish.

Art didn't address his nephew by name, or look at him directly. Instead, he included the whole bunkhouse in his anger. "Let's get this place straightened up," he said with clenched teeth, "and while you're at it, I want those damn' cards out of sight, and I want to see gear stowed away and the floors cleaned up. Place looks like a damn' pigsty. Moore, Link, you see if you can manage to get your butts on over to the house. I'll talk to you in my office."

Art looked at the Colt, which he had been holding by the cylinder. The grease-plugged chambers showed it was loaded, but there were no caps on the nipples. "Picked yourself a dandy gun to get into a shoot-out with," he said for Pasque to hear. "Some cool-headed killer you are. Damn' near got yourself killed." He thrust the gun into Walt's hand. "Take care of that," he growled.

Back at his office, Art poured himself a bourbon. And himself only. But Link was the first to speak.

"What's wrong with that nephew of yours?" he demanded. "We were just having some fun with him about being related to the boss, and he goes crazy. Started yelling about branding irons and egg brands and trail-cutters. Crazy kid."

Art sat on the edge of his desk, looking over the rim of his whiskey glass at the two men who were standing on his carpet. "He was talking about a branding iron he found in your wagon, up at the Kathy Fork cabin. And right now I want you to tell me all about that iron. I want to know where it came from. And I mean exactly where it came from."

Link told most of the story, with Moore throwing in such details as he thought Link had missed. Art sensed right away that they didn't mind talking about it, like guilty men might. And it was a simple story. They had been drifting up from Texas, getting away from a bankrupt ranch where a year's work had netted them next to nothing. Sometimes they rode the grub line, sometimes got a little work for a day or two. Then one day in Kansas, in a saloon, a cowboy at the bar started buying drinks and struck up a conversation with them.

He was looking for men to ride for a trail-cutting outfit, he said. Men who didn't have any ties to particular ranches, men who could stay out on the open range for maybe two months at a time, men who could ride at night, if need be.

This trail-cutting outfit, according to this cowboy, had a contract with half a dozen ranches. The outfit would wait out on the range for trail herds to come by, during the herding season, and then check each herd to see if cattle from the ranches they represented had drifted into the trail herd and were heading for Montana with it. Might be a dozen different brands of ranch cattle in a herd. They'd cut them out, then hurry them back to the ranch, or get them to a holding place.

24

Then they had to make tracks back to meet the next trail herd.

They had to be careful, the cowboy said. Had to kind of sneak up on these herds, since the drovers weren't really anxious to stop a drive of two or three thousand steers for a couple of days just to cut out a few strays. Some trail outfits were known to cut out the ranch brand animals themselves and hide them in a draw somewhere until the trail-cutters had gone.

"It was about the end of that first month," Link went on. "They had me and Moore here driving that old wagon with the branding irons and some bedrolls and food in it. Outfit had a chuck wagon, an' used this wagon for tools and wire and such.

"Anyhow, we were sneakin' up on this one herd, pretty late in the afternoon, coming in from the west with the sun behind us. The foreman, he told us to hang 'way back with the wagon because of the dust we raised."

Moore spoke up. "I was kind of suspicious . . . well, we both was . . . because some of the cutting crew had been gone for nearly a week, and we'd been told they were already with this herd. But now we were sneaking up on it. It just didn't smell right, did it, Link?"

"Have to agree with you," Link said. "So we got in this arroyo and were loafing along, you know, and all of a sudden we heard gunfire. *Pop, pop, pop,* off over the rise, like firecrackers. I ran up a hill, and all I saw was our boys, riding in the other direction, and a bunch of trail drovers after them, guns blazing. The herd started to mill, too, and I could see a couple of waddies with Winchesters, scouting around for more of our outfit.

"So, me and Moore, we turned and flogged those old bangtails as hard as we could and got the hell out of there. After hiding out most of the night, we finally found a little ol' ten-shack town where we figured to wait for the crew. If they were still alive."

Moore cut in again. "Yeah, but we didn't hang out there for long, lemme tell you. People were talkin' about a bunch of rustlers passin' themselves off as trail-cutters, talkin' about callin' in the marshal from Dodge City."

"That was us, see?" Link resumed. "So we just left town real quiet, and drifted west to get out of that country. Ended up about half-starved right here at the Keystone. You know the rest."

Art paced the floor in front of his desk, rolling a cigarette, and smoking it down to a stub before he spoke again. He looked at the men's faces, where the blood had caked and dried to give them the look of prize fighters.

"Well, it was OK before Pasque got here. But having the three of you on this ranch just isn't going to work out. Got off to a real bad start, and Pasque is a hothead. You don't help matters much, either.

"OK," Art went on. "Made up my mind what to do here. First of all, you two head back to the Kathy Fork. And I mean tonight, right now. I want you off this place, until I can get my nephew calmed down some. Meanwhile, I'm going to contact a friend of mine. He's marshal at Republican Crossing out in the Kansas

Territory. Then I'll send for you. And if I decide to believe your story, we'll see if you'd agree to go out there and help posse down those trail-cutter friends of yours. That's the only way I can figure to get you settled right with my nephew. You help the marshal look for them, get that straightened out, and I'll see about some long-term jobs for you here at the Keystone. That way I'll get some hands, we'll do some good for the law, and maybe Pasque won't have this damn' revenge thing on his mind all the time."

"I still don't get it," Moore said. "What revenge thing?"

"Pasque had two brothers with that herd. That, or some other herd your friends tried to steal from. All Pasque knows is that they were shot in the back, and the shooter was with the Oval Cross brand. The brand he saw in your wagon. That clear it up enough for you?"

"Clear enough," Moore said. "I'm happy to steer clear of that crazy *hombre*."

"Just one thing," Link said. "We might have been drifters, but we wouldn't have stolen no cattle, not if we'd known what was up. I can't speak for Moore, but I'd be glad to help your marshal friend catch up to those rustlers. I aim to settle down out here somewhere, and can't have people associating me with crooks."

"Me, too," Moore said.

"Fair enough. Now you two get your gear and hit the trail."

"What'll we tell your nephew or the boys at the bunkhouse, when they see us packin' up?"

"Tell 'em nothing," Art said. "Tell 'em you're going back to Kathy Fork to bring back the rest of those bony old range steers before the snow hits. Just get moving."

Early the next afternoon, Bob Riley came over to the new corral where Pasque was busy busting out post holes with a rock bar. Pasque stopped working, took a drink from the canteen, and eyed the foreman with as much amusement as he could muster.

"How are you and that pickle fork gettin' along?" Bob asked.

Pasque regarded his hands, where a blister was forming in spite of his leather gloves. "I'm gettin' the hang of it. You know, when I said it would be good to have a job that didn't involve ridin' for a while, I wasn't exactly thinkin' of post holes."

Bob looked down the line of post holes, each with its own pile of dirt, and nodded approvingly. "Good job," he said. "I think you're a natural. Want to take a break?"

"What you got in mind?" Pasque asked.

"Art wants us to ride out an meet Missus P. She's due back from her trip to town today, and Art thought she'd appreciate some company for the last couple o' miles or so. Give you a chance to meet her, too."

"OK with me. Just lemme wash up first."

Bob and Pasque were about ten miles from the Keystone, when they found her buggy standing in the middle of the dusty road. She wasn't in it. A lead rope had been clipped to the horse's headstall, as if she had intended to tie the horse or lead it, but it was dragging the ground now.

"That don't seem right," Bob said, pulling his saddle carbine out of its scabbard.

"Bad place," Pasque said, looking around.

Where the horse and buggy had stopped, a small creek encouraged a dense thicket of chokecherry and wild rose bushes. A line of cottonwoods screened the opposite bank of the creek, and beyond that was another quarter acre of chokecherry, most of it high enough to hide a man on horseback.

"You look around here for tracks," Bob said. "I'll ride back up the road, in case she got thrown out of the buggy, or something. If one of us fires two shots, it means for the other one to come runnin'."

"Right."

Bob rode off. Pasque dismounted and tied his horse and the buggy horse to a sapling by the road.

Pasque didn't have his rifle, but he drew his Colt and checked the cylinder before he started studying the ground. Somebody in small boots with high heels had stepped off the buggy, for sure. And — he looked behind the seat — her luggage and packages were still there. The situation looked peaceful enough. The small tracks led on down the dirt road a few steps, and Pasque could see where they went off into the chokecherry bushes, and not too long ago — the grass was still bent down.

"Ah." Pasque grinned, embarrassed. "Just, ah . . . probably a . . . call of nature."

He could fire a shot to let Bob know that he'd found the trail, but it would startle the lady. And he wasn't about to go walking into the brush to see what she was up to. So the polite thing was to go back to the buggy and act natural until she came out of the bushes again.

That's where Mrs. Art Pendragon found him, standing next to his horse. He had his head down, pretending that he was fixing his stirrup. When he heard her footsteps, he lifted his head enough to see the pair of boots coming at him, peeking out one at a time from beneath a full, fawn-colored skirt as she walked. He slowly lifted his eyes a bit more, lifted his hat brim casual-like while he dropped the stirrup, and saw the snow-white shirt with its puffed sleeves. He got ready to say — "Afternoon, ma'am." — and stood erect and saw the wide-brimmed hat. Under that hat brim he saw a pair of eyes that sent his heart racing and his blood pumping up into his face, and he forgot what to say altogether.

Finally, as she stood there smiling inquisitively at him, Pasque managed to stammer it out. "Art sent me . . . sent us. Bob, I mean. He's gone on back up the road because we thought that . . . Art sent us both. To meet you, I mean. Your horse wasn't tied, and we thought maybe he wandered down here and left you."

"Well," she smiled, "I'm glad Art sent you. That was nice of him. I'm sorry about the horse. I tied her to that branch over there, but the knot must have slipped."

30

Pasque studied the branch that she pointed to, and studied the ground some more. "Yes ma'am," was all he said.

"Are you in a hurry to get back to the ranch, then?"

"No, ma'am. No hurry at all. We just came to keep you company . . . I mean, Art sent us."

"Yes. So you said. And who is with you?"

"Oh. Bob. Bob Riley. Uncle Art asked him to ride out to meet you, and Bob asked would I go along."

"I see!" She laughed. Her laugh was like spring water bubbling over stones. "And you said Uncle Art, so you must be Pasque?"

"Yes, ma'am."

"It's such an unusual name," she said. "Since it rhymes with task, is it spelled the same way? I know I've heard that name somewhere, but I just can't recall where."

"It's like the flower," Pasque said. "French, I guess. It's just kind of a nickname, 'cause I pick those little purple flowers in the springtime. Always have, ever since I was a little kid."

Her eyes brightened, if it were possible for them to be any brighter. "Of course!" she exclaimed. "The wild anemones. Those are the very first ones to blossom. Beautiful flowers. Well, Pasque, that's a lovely nickname. In the spring, perhaps we can go looking for pasque flowers together. I love flowers. Oh, and that reminds me! Do you happen to have a spade with you?"

"A spade? You mean like a shovel? No, ma'am."

"I found some young rose bushes back there." She indicated a thicket on the other side of the tiny creek. "I wish I could dig some and take them back to plant at the ranch. I love rose bushes."

Pasque searched under the buggy seat where he found a wheel wrench and some baling wire wrapped in an old feedbag, but no shovel of any kind. "I've got my sheath knife," he said. "I've used it and the tin plate from my mess kit to dig firepits on the range. Maybe that would work."

Bob came riding back, having found nothing, and volunteered to stay at the buggy and whittle and hold the horses, while Gwen Pendragon and Pasque went off to grub rose bushes out of the sand. Gwen was soon busy at it, down on her hands and knees, using Pasque's knife to dig a trench around a wild rose plant. Pasque had gone to his saddlebags to get his work gloves, so he could carry the thorny bushes to the buggy.

He was on his way back, pushing through the chokecherry thicket, pulling on his heavy gloves, when he heard the scream. He busted his way through the branches, ignoring the scratches, as they whipped his face and arms, cussing as they tangled his chaps. When he burst into the small clearing, Pasque saw a scene that was afterward burned into his memory like a tin-type photo. Gwen was on her knees, one arm raised like a shield, and she was screaming at a bear. The bear, showing its yellow teeth and growling, had reared up on its hind legs and was swatting the air above the terrified woman's head.

"Roll!" Pasque shouted. "Roll out of the way! Get clear!"

As Gwen continued to scream, the bear made a hoarse-throat, rasping bellow. She dropped the knife and rolled far enough to give Pasque a clear shot. His hand went to his holster, and he felt the heavy glove clawing awkwardly at the revolver's butt and realized that the thick leather fingers wouldn't go in the trigger guard. The Colt slipped out of his hand and into the dirt.

Without thinking, or thinking only of the woman who was up against the chokecherry bush, half sitting, still shielding herself against the teeth and claws coming at her, Pasque charged the bear.

His first blow was a wild haymaker, the gloved fist catching the surprised sow on the side of the face right between her snarling upper lip and her bloodshot eye. She snorted and shook her head. He punched her again, as hard as he could, this time on the side of her nose. She dropped to all fours and turned away from Gwen. The bear was now facing her new attacker. She started to rear up into her fighting stance again.

But Pasque moved faster than the bear. The only thing he could think of at this point was to get the sow by the head, like throwing a steer or like twisting a bucking horse down, and try to hold her while Gwen ran. Or maybe Bob would get there, if he had heard all the commotion.

Pasque got one of his arms over the thick neck, like he would if he was bull-dogging a steer, and got his elbow crooked around the strong, slobbering jaw. With his other hand he grabbed a handful of fat and skin and fur, and used the bear's weight to pull her down. He had the bear, for a moment. But the bear also had him, too; her weight crosswise on top of him was pinning him to the ground and crushing the air from his chest.

Then two shots rang out, the sound of a .45 Colt, echoing like a field cannon in that tiny clearing. The bear went into a panic, shaking her head violently to get loose from Pasque's grip, her weight grinding down hard. He felt one of his ribs snap, and then she tore away from him and was gone. Pasque groaned as he rolled over and got to his knees. His ears were ringing, but he could still hear the bear, tearing away through the brush. It must have been Bob, he figured. Bob must have heard the commotion and got there just in time.

But it wasn't Bob, who was still cussing and crashing in the chokecherry thicket, trying to find them. It was Gwen. She stood there with Pasque's Colt in both of her hands, smoke rising from the barrel.

"You should have seen it," Gwen laughed, passing Pasque's plate to Art for another slab of prime rib. "First, that poor bear didn't know what to make of it, when Pasque ran in and started hitting it with his fists, and then I fired two shots practically in its ear."

Pasque laughed, and then winced at the sharp pain in his side. "I don't know about the bear, but my ears are still buzzin'." He smiled and winced. "I didn't know what to make of it, either. Matter of fact, I didn't really know what I was doin' in the first place."

34

Art held his fork high in the air like a king making a royal pronouncement. "You saved a damsel in distress, Pasque. You threw yourself into the jaws of death for the woman I love. We are forever in your debt . . . name your reward!" Art liked to read old stories of chivalry and romance.

"Name my reward, huh?" Pasque said. "How about no more post holes?"

"Done! No more post holes. Next week you can start ditching the south hay pasture, instead."

"Art!" Gwen said in her best tone of indignation, "what kind of reward is that? Digging ditches! Pasque deserves a vacation, at least."

"Vacation!" Art exclaimed. "The man was doing his job, that's all. I sent him down to help look after you, and he did. Like the poet said . . . 'Do your duty, and leave the rest to heaven.'"

"Oh, hush." Gwen rose to her feet and picked up the carving knife, which she wiped clean with a napkin. She stepped around behind Pasque's chair and laid the blade of the knife on his shoulder.

"For chivalry toward a lady," she said solemnly, "and courage in the face of a great beast, I do dub thee Sir Pasque of Keystone."

"Well," Pasque replied, trying not to let himself laugh because it hurt so much when he did, "if I'd been that chivalrous, I wouldn't have let you dig those bushes yourself in the first place. That wasn't real polite."

"Ah, but I insisted! You are still my knight in shining armor."

"Some knight," Art said. "More like a crazy buckaroo in worn-out chaps. Now, if that bear had been a big rogue male, instead of some dumb fat sow, or a grizzly, instead of a little ol' brown bear, I might be impressed."

"Never mind," she replied. "I still think you ought to reward Pasque. Maybe you could give him a special position at the Keystone."

"I will," Art assured her. "By the time he finishes his ditch digging, the boys will have all the new fence posts set on the south pasture. Pasque's new title will be Sir Wire-Stretcher and Lord Staple-Whanger."

Pasque looked at Gwen, and Gwen caught him at it. Her eyes were beautiful in the soft light of the oil lamp. A little red in the face, Pasque began pushing at his mashed potatoes with his fork, making them into hills and valleys alongside the prime rib.

The more Pasque got used to eating supper with his uncle and his beautiful new aunt, the more he liked it. Even the teasing of the other ranch hands about it couldn't keep him from looking forward to each evening, and it wasn't just because Mary could cook a whole lot better than the bean-wrangler they had down at the bunkhouse.

"Pasque," Gwen said one night as the men were polishing off the last of an apple pie, "I'm so glad to have you eat with us. I'm sure that your Uncle Art would get bored, having no one but me to talk to during supper."

Bored? Then Uncle Art must need spectacles. Strong ones. Either his eyes were going dim, or he had gone numb south of his belt buckle. A man who'd find Gwen boring could sit on a hot cook stove and not feel it.

But Pasque didn't say so. He didn't know much of anything to say, to tell the truth, so he just said: "Yes, ma'am."

"Call me Gwen," she insisted.

"Sure," he mumbled.

Art took a fiendish delight, watching Gwen give Pasque some lessons in civilized dining. There was a clean tablecloth every evening, china dishes, silverware, water goblets, and cups with saucers. They had soup before the main course, and dessert and coffee afterward. During the whole event, Gwen also expected conversation. A typical one ran something like this.

"More of the pie, dear?"

"Oh, no!" Art said, patting the exact spot where the last two pieces now resided. "Couldn't eat another bite. Sure is good, though." Then Art grinned at a mischievous thought he was having. "Did you ask Pasque what he thought of your dress?"

"Why, no, I haven't. How *do* you like this dress, Pasque? I bought it on my trip to town. Art thinks it's too tight. What do you think?"

Pasque looked over the rim of his cup, close to choking on the coffee, and tried his level best to look like a man who was going to give an objective, serious opinion about something. But he looked like a cowboy, estimating the weight of a heifer at an auction. The bright red dress was tight in the waist, full-skirted, with long sleeves. It was cut low enough that he could see the beginnings of the valley between her breasts. A little locket hung there from a gold chain, drawing even more attention to that delicious division of her assets. Well, he'd had his look. Now what the hell was he expected to say?

"It's sure pretty."

"Too tight, do you think?" Gwen was enjoying this.

"Is it kinda uncomfortable when you eat a lot?" he said.

Art's deep-chested chuckle escaped and went rolling across the room. Pasque fixed his uncle with a look that held a promise of future mayhem. He looked back at Gwen, who was trying to keep a straight face.

"A little, I suppose," she said. "Maybe I'll let it out some, before I wear it again. Not to change the subject, since Art seems to be having quite a good time with it, but I also bought some new books. One is a novel by Mister Hawthorne, although I said I would never read him again after that horrible *Scarlet Letter*. And I bought a book of poetry I think you'd like."

"Me?" Art said.

"Well, I suppose you would. But I was thinking more of letting Pasque read it. It's from England, by Mister Tennyson . . . *Idylls of the King.* Wonderful adventures of the knights of England. I'll get it for you after we've finished our coffee."

From dresses to literature, from politics and philosophy, to news of the ranch, every evening Gwen cheerfully kept the two men lingering at the table and talking. Both could remember the nights they spent at a poker game in the bunkhouse or toasting their socks and nursing a cigarette in front of the fire. Gradually, with patient persistence, Gwen was making a civilized home at the Keystone. Someday, she secretly hoped, there would be a cowboy in every chair at her dining table, each one a credit to Art's ranch, with Art presiding over it all.

Gwen Pendragon had no way of knowing the future. Someday, to be sure, the hard and violent ways of the old West would be gone forever. Law and order would be commonplace, and Mr. Colt's justice would be out of date. But before the life of guns and leather would give way to crystal and linen, there was going to be one last test, one event to prove that the range cowboy had a sense of courage and honor and chivalry that no amount of civilized living could soften. Gwen Pendragon could not know that the taming of the West would come with a high price attached to it. And it would be Pasque who would be chosen to pay it.

CHAPTER
THREE

The Months Before Christmas

September slipped away from the high plains, taking with it the deep green of grass and cottonwood groves and leaving behind the dry colors of brass and yellow. Pasque did his work and brooded about Link and Moore. Art had been moving them, and him, like chess pieces. They took a long, long time getting that pitiful little herd of cull steers down from the northern hill country, he thought, and then Art sent them off again, toward the east edge of the Keystone range.

Meanwhile, he had ridden into town with Art so his uncle could send a telegram to some friend of his in Kansas Territory. They waited two days for the answer to come back, and then Art had to answer that one, and wait for another.

"Pasque," Art said on the way back to the Keystone, "this friend of mine is a Kansas lawman, Marshal Bob Roberts. He's the one who sent the news about Chris and Jim. We didn't know what had become of you, then, but, of course, you were out tearing up the range this way and that, looking for the trail-cutters. Bob's been a good friend for a long time. His telegrams tell me two things, and I believe 'em both. One is that he's still looking high and low for those killers. He hasn't given up. The problem has been finding someone who knows what they look like and where they called home. One trail drover looks pretty much like another one, you know.

"The other thing is that he's pretty sure Link and Moore weren't involved in the murder. The trail crew that drove off the cutters that day never saw two men in a wagon, and a foreman from a herd that had been hit earlier in the season didn't know anything about a tall, slick fellow like Link."

He still wore the brand on his saddle, Pasque thought silently. And someday, he told himself, he'd find a way to get either Link or Moore or both of them alone, away from the ranch, and have it out with them himself. For now he had to go along with Art and wait. Better proof might come along, if a man waited. Meanwhile, he'd make it clear that he didn't like either one of them. He wouldn't drink with them, wouldn't joke with them, and, if Art ever made him work alongside of them, he wouldn't speak to them.

Each evening after work and before supper, Pasque took his Colt and some tin cans down to the creek and fired six rounds as fast and as accurately as he could. Then he reloaded and fired six more times. A lot of cowboys didn't practice and couldn't shoot worth a damn, but it was mostly those who still carried the old cap-and-ball revolvers that had to be hand-loaded with loose powder. Most of them were relics of the war.

Oats for the horses were kept in the barn, hanging from the rafters in gunny sacks so the mice and rats couldn't get at them. Every time Pasque went into the barn, sometimes several times a day, he stopped and drove his fists into those hard burlap sacks, putting all his weight behind each punch.

October blew out of Wyoming on the back of a snow flurry that lasted overnight and vanished again, making the dry range seem all the more dry afterward. Pasque began to get restless. He had been sitting around the ranch too long. The new corral was finished, the green riding stock was broke, the new pasture ditched and fenced. Even his practice with the Colt was getting stale to him — he could send a tin can dancing and put all six shots into it no matter where it bounced. He could reload faster than most men. Punching the oat sacks had made his knuckles callused, and with either hand he could send them thumping against the barn wall. Most of all, he was tired of waiting to do something about Link and Moore and that Oval Cross branding iron.

Mary had returned to the dining room, carrying the buttermilk pitcher and a steaming bowl of red vegetables. After refilling Pasque's glass, she set the bowl in front of him. "There's your milk," she said, "and there's the rest of the beets, still nice and hot." She sensed Pasque's almost imperceptible grimace. "Better enjoy them," she admonished. "Lou was able to keep them under straw in the garden until now, but he says the frost has finally got into the ground. You won't see anything but root cellar carrots and potatoes and canned beans for the next six or seven months."

Pasque dutifully forked a helping of the boiled beets onto his plate and passed the serving dish to Art. Art sniffed the vegetables, and then passed the dish to Gwen, who gave him a tiny, scolding look.

"Well," Art said, pushing his plate away from him as if he had turned down the beets so he could discuss business, "I guess Bob and the boys will be finished with their sweep of the Greener range by now. Should be heading almost a thousand head toward Ogallala right now."

"I imagine so," said Pasque. "Kind of a gamble for you, ain't . . . er, isn't it?" Gwen was trying to break him of saying ain't.

"Oh, sure. But it's going to pay off. Johnson will keep 'em on grass another month or two at Ogallala, if the weather holds. Then he'll feed them until the spring grass is up. And when the agency in Montana sends word that they want beef, our herd will be at least a month ahead of those Texas steers."

Pasque nodded and finished his meal. When Mary's husband, Lou, came limping in to clear the table, Gwen rose and led the way to the sitting room.

Pasque, walking behind her through the dining room and into the sitting room, admired the way her straight back and slim waist moved without swaying, her full skirts whispered in stiff silk tones, and, instead of walking, she seemed to flow across the room. Being in the house with this woman made his need for vengeance start to weaken. It made his fists relax and his muscles feel at ease. But that softening was at war with the hard-eyed feeling he got from the kick of the

Colt in his hand or the crunch of his fist, driving against the grain sack.

"Art," she said, just to make conversation, "when are you going to let Pasque try his hand at being foreman? You give him all kinds of responsible jobs that take him all over the territory. Can't we find him a foreman's job of some kind right here? You know I love having family at supper, but I can't, if our nephew is always off on some errand for you."

Pasque could have added something that Gwen hadn't seemed to notice, namely that Art also had a habit of sending Link and Moore off on errands. But instead of saying anything, Pasque just went on watching the way she walked across the room. Link was right about one thing: she was good to look at. She had two kinds of walking. When she readied herself to go riding and wore her leather breeches, her walk was different. There seemed to be a pivot right on her back, right under her wide leather belt, giving her hips a polite, sweet little swing.

Art went to the mantle, where he opened a humidor and fussed around, filling his pipe. He gave Pasque the apologetic look that men use when a woman asks them about such things. Cattlemen were not much given to talking about promotions and raises and such. Sometimes a particular cowboy had a kind of natural skill and was better at his job than most other men. Everyone recognized it, and he just naturally got a few dollars more because he was worth more. Or, a man might be a leader, have a good head on his shoulders, and he'd just naturally get a foreman's job, when one came open.

Art knew that Gwen was right about Pasque's state of mind. He was a man who was keeping something bad inside. He had a right to, of course. The kid had gone through hell, losing his folks and then his brothers, and then thinking he had found part of the gang of killers, but being kept from doing anything to them. He had a right to be restless. Art had to agree with Gwen about the possibility of promotion, too. Pasque was not only his nephew but a good worker with a good mind. Still, whatever was gnawing at him was close to the surface. No telling when Pasque might fly off the handle. Art lit his pipe and tossed the match into the fireplace.

"I guess Bob would like to hold onto his job a while longer," he said between puffs. "And this time of year we sorta pull things in and get ready to sit tight for the winter."

"Besides that," Pasque added, although feeling self-conscious about it, "Art can't just promote me 'cause I'm his kin. And I wouldn't want it that way, you see. The men around here expect a fella to earn his spurs, so to speak. I'll get my chance. Don't you worry."

Mostly for the sake of changing the topic, Art gestured toward the dining room. "I'll tell you what you *can* worry about, Missus P.," he said with a smile. "You and Mary . . . and Lou . . . need to get together with that new bunkhouse cook . . . what's his name? . . . and make sure the winter supplies are going to be enough.

45

Need to fill that root cellar, and figure out what we need to buy in the way of potatoes and sugar and canned tomatoes and such."

"Of course," she smiled. "I suppose Mary and Lou have a good idea what we need?"

"Oh, sure. Mary would probably like it, if you helped her make some preserves, too. And then there's the party to plan for."

"Party?" Gwen asked, looking up from the needlepoint she had picked up from the footstool.

"Every year for the past five, or maybe six years, Keystone has thrown a big Christmas shindig. We build tables out of planks and sawhorses the whole length of the big room, and have three or four days of eatin' and dancin'. Everybody's invited. Heck, we see neighbors that we never see otherwise!"

"Well, that sounds like fun!" Gwen smiled widely, her face beaming at the idea. "How many will be coming this year, do you think?"

"Hard to say. Fact is, I never bother to count! We just keep the food flowing, and people come and go and have a good time. And it seems like every year, something special happens. I get to expecting it, in fact."

Pasque patted his flat stomach and stretched his arms. "Hate to interrupt," he said, "but after that good meal I feel the need of a little walk. Then I need to hunt my bunk . . . been a pretty long day."

He started toward the door, then turned back again. "Say, Art," he said, "about Link and Moore." He knew that with Gwen in the room Art would have to give him the real information and make it look like a natural conversation. "They goin' to be back in the bunkhouse this winter? Seems they've been gone a good long time."

"They'll be back pretty soon," Art said. "But then I'm thinking of sending them over into the Green River country to see if they can scare up some decent horses for us."

"You say you knew 'em pretty well?"

"Not especially," Art replied. "But Link is a good hand. Knows his animals. In fact, I'd say he was better than any man on the ranch when it comes to a rope. Moore isn't that good, but he works hard." It was clear that Art hadn't told Gwen anything about the argument and Pasque's suspicions. "He was even up here at the house a few times before you got back, and seemed to be a real polite fellow. Gwen liked him, didn't you, honey?"

"Yes, he was quite pleasant." She did not look up from the needlepoint.

That seemed to end the conversation, even though Pasque was hoping to let it build up enough to ask if Art had any idea how soon he could confront them again about that Oval Cross brand. So he said his good nights, stuck his head through the kitchen doorway to thank Mary for a good supper, and strode across the big room and out across the wide porch. A soft cool breeze touched him lightly with odors of stable and corral. The same breeze carried faraway reminders of sage, dry now that winter was almost on top of them, and whiffs of pine forests on the blue-black dark mountains to the west.

He came to the road leading out to the main gate and walked it at a slow, relaxed pace while drinking in the smells and sounds of the night. By starlight, the road was only a dim strip of light-colored earth in the dark brush. Off in the black distance a coyote yipped; next to the starlit track, a rabbit or a night-foraging bird made the dry undergrowth rustle. Behind him, Pasque could hear a faint clatter of pots and pans in the cook shack.

Foreman, Gwen had said. Hell, he would never be a foreman, here or anywhere. He had watched all kinds of foremen, good and bad, and he had seen his own shortcomings by comparison. For one thing, he was too quick to get into trouble when he could just as well wait and see. Except sometimes he waited too long, and things built up inside him until he felt like exploding. He had found a can of beans, once, that was all swollen up because the beans had gone bad, and so he used it for target practice. The slug hit the can, and the can flew into pieces, just blew up. He felt like that, sometimes, from sitting and doing nothing about the murders of Chris and Jim.

He should have waited by the line cabin, up there on the Kathy Fork, to get some answers about that branding iron. And done the shooting, if he didn't like the answers. Or, after he talked to Pat about the brand, maybe he should have gone straight after them, instead of talking to Art. What the hell was he afraid of? Even now, right now, he could go up to Art and demand to know where they were. But he wouldn't. He was a man who had either to start shooting or just ride off; once he got to thinking about other options, he got confused.

That was a second reason he'd never be a foreman. He was quiet and liked to keep it that way. He was no good at arguing with another man, face to face, without letting it get down to curses and fists. A good foreman, now, he had to stand right up to a cowpuncher who wasn't doing the job and tell him to get the slack out of his string. A good foreman couldn't afford to raise his voice, and he sure couldn't run an outfit with his fists, not for very long.

Pasque's steps had brought him to the crest of the ridge where the wagon road dropped down again into the black night shadows. There he turned and looked back at the tiny squares of light, the windows of ranch buildings that were like toy houses tossed into the brush. He turned to look down the road into the inky darkness, and he looked up into the sky all carpeted with stars. Somewhere an owl hooted.

Where the hell was he going? There he stood, on a road made of dust, a road that came to a dead end in a big house where he would always be the orphan relative but never anything else. Where the road led in the other direction, he thought he knew — to other places, other ranches, other jobs as a forty-dollar-a-month buckaroo until he was too old to climb aboard a cow pony.

And in the middle of that road, somewhere between an owlhoot and a smell of horse manure, he stood.

But, by damn, not for long. Somewhere out there in the wide waste of land between the mountains and the

Missouri River there was a pair of biscuit vultures who knew something about the deaths of his brothers. And it was time to quit kicking dust off his own boots and find out what it was.

CHAPTER
FOUR

The Visitor's Game Begins

It took Art Pendragon nearly twenty years to make the Keystone Ranch the biggest in the territory. Along the way he had earned a reputation as a fair man and a friendly man, a man who shared whatever he could. He was particularly famous, in the territory, for his Christmas parties. Art had always loved Christmas, and, whether he had a good year or a bad one, or was living in a one-room line shack or a big sprawling ranch house, he rounded up some food and cut himself a Christmas tree and had the neighbors in.

Making a success of the Keystone meant many things to Art, but the best thing to him was being able to open his big house to neighbors and strangers alike, some of whom came from the far corners of the region to feast on roasts and steaks and cauldrons of venison stew and more kinds of bread and pie and drink than you would imagine possible. Guests brought more food, or they brought hand-made presents like embroidered handkerchiefs or pot holders for Mary, fancy wooden bootjacks or whittled puzzles for Art, polished cedar animal figurines for the mantel.

These humble Christmas presents were tokens of greater debts. Some pioneer families owed their start to the Keystone because Art had loaned them their breeding stock or winter hay. Art had hired pioneer kids to be cowboys, when the family needed cash to keep the homestead going. His Keystone riders helped other ranchers open snow-clogged roads, or tracked down a calf-killing lion, or had gone out of their way to deliver a bit of mail. More than once, Keystone men had run off suspicious-looking range bums that had been lurking around.

This Christmas was better than ever before, because this Christmas there was Gwen. When he was courting her, Art hadn't given much thought to the way she might change the annual Keystone Christmas get-together. After more than two years of writing back and forth, they had gotten engaged by mail. And then he went to St. Louis where he wooed her, won her, and wed her. He had seen his future with her as a sort of big, rosy glow, and hadn't paid any attention to such particulars as Christmas.

There was another reason that Art was glad for Christmas to be coming. There had been a brief telegram a month earlier from Link and Moore, saying that they were joining up with Bob Roberts's posse and hoped to have the trail-cutters rounded up before long. But then weeks with no more news. And with little else to do, Art had been letting it bother his thoughts too much. Pasque was very edgy, too. He kept waiting for the two to return, when he wasn't arguing with Art about going out to look for them. Christmas would be a big relief. Everyone could settle down.

As Art looked around the big house at all of Gwen's decorations, he smiled to remember how plain and simple it used to be. He and his men would put up the Christmas tree and hang a few boughs here and there. Mary would see to it that there was lots of food on the table, and that was it.

That was before Gwen. The new mistress of the Keystone soon put Mary to work as a decorator, along with her husband, Lou. She went down to the stables and enlisted Pat, who up to that point was the hostler, farrier, and blacksmith. Together, the four of them turned every corner of the house into a scene from a Christmas card. Lou gimped up the ladder a hundred times to tie sprigs of holly and swags of evergreen along every rafter beam. Pat brought his hammer and half a keg of horseshoe nails, driving them into the log walls wherever Mary or Gwen wanted to hang a wreath or a spray of juniper.

The whole house was a Yuletide world of ribbons and wreaths, of long evergreen swags and kinnikinic berries, and paper chains and popcorn strings. There were two Christmas trees. Gwen had put one on each end of the head table, so that guests coming through the double doorway would be greeted by two long tables of food and drink and two symbols of Christmas celebration.

"And won't Art look wonderful," she said to Mary as they arranged the tablecloths and candles, "sitting right here in his new jacket, the center of the head table, facing his guests as they come in? Just like a lord in a castle!"

Mary agreed, even though the lord was making himself conspicuously absent and leaving the house decoration up to his lady. When he did appear, it was only to stand in the center of the room, smoking his pipe, while looking all around and grinning.

Art and Bob and the ranch hands had plenty to do outside. They scrubbed out the main barn and hauled in fresh bedding straw. Many of the neighbors would throw down their quilts and buffalo robes there and stay a night or two. For the older kids, Art and Bob scrubbed out a couple of adjoining sheds — one for the girls, one for the boys — and filled them with knee-deep straw. There was always a rough-and-tumble fight in the boys' barn at Christmas time, and sometimes a tussle or two in the girls' shed.

Among other preparations, like making sure there were enough stalls for buggy horses and enough feed and water available, was the matter of fixing a place outside the back of the house for the bench.

The bench was where the whiskey keg would be. Except for a little sweet wine with dessert, there would be no liquor allowed inside the main house. But during the evening, the men would find moments to slip away, saying that they were going out to sit on the bench and have a smoke, and soon there would be a dozen or more of them standing around a small bonfire, sipping whiskey from thick clay cups.

The bench was placed out of the wind, in a corner formed by one wall of the house and one wall of the kitchen. As it happened, the fireplace was on the one wall and the kitchen ovens backed up to the other; not only were the walls warm to lean against, but in that angle of the house there were no windows. In other words, if a wife was curious to see what her husband was up to, she had to go clear outside and all the way around the building to find out.

None of the wives ever bothered.

On the second night of Christmas, Art was feeling pretty full of himself. He was getting used to sitting at the head table — as Gwen called it — laughing and talking along with his neighbors, watching to see that the serving dishes were always full and that people had whatever they needed.

Pasque was on his right, at the first table of the right-hand row. Facing him, at the left-hand row of tables, sat Pat and the Pinto Kid and most of the other more or less permanent hands. Art liked having them there, all of his reliable cowboys.

"Pat," Gwen said, catching the hostler as he passed behind her seat with his plate of second helpings, "I wonder if you could open the doors when you get a chance? It seems to be getting awfully warm in here."

"Yes'm. Just let me put this plate down, and I'll do that."

When Pat swung open the high double doors, they made a picture frame for an early evening that was changing from purple-blue to gray. Art could look down between the two rows of tables and out the door and clear across to the foothills beyond. Deep, long shadows were blurring into darkness. Scattered patches of snow gleamed white under the last light of the clear, cold sky.

"Been lucky with the weather," he said to Gwen, who had to lean toward him to hear him over the din of other conversations. "Paul Nielsen . . . that man sitting there with the two grown boys . . . he tells me that the wagon road was blown clear of snow all the way to the Scotch crossing."

"I hope it holds," Gwen replied, laughing, "because I don't think we could feed your friends for very long, if they got snowed in here. In fact, I don't think Mary has enough plates left for even one more guest!"

"Well . . . ," Art said, "it looks like she'd better find some." He gestured toward the open doors. "Here's some more company," he said.

The conversations stopped. Little children fell quiet; people with full mouths continued chewing silently. Women stiffened against the backs of their chairs, glanced at the faces of their husbands, and looked again at the figure in the doorway.

Art's Keystone riders eased their chairs back away from the table, took the napkins from their laps or out of their shirt fronts, and quietly laid them beside their plates. More than one of them let his right hand slide down along his thigh, only to remember that his gun and holster were hanging from a peg in the bunkhouse or were stowed in his saddlebags. You didn't bring a gun into Mrs. Pendragon's house, just like you didn't drink whiskey in her presence, or wear spurs when you stepped on the polished floors.

But the huge rider was carrying guns on his saddle. And the saddle was on a huge horse of some massive breed that no man there had ever seen before. No one seemed to have heard the horse's hoofs on the polished wood floor, but there he stood in the doorway just the same.

The rider's wide-brimmed hat was dark blackish-green; a buffalo coat covered him from his neck to the tops of his boots, and it covered the saddle and the back of the horse as well. As many cowboys did while riding in winter weather, he wore a scarf across his face. Only his dark eyes could be seen above it. It seemed to be made of silk, the deep green color of kinnikinic leaves.

In front of him, in holsters attached to either side of his saddle horn, were two antique revolvers. They looked like old percussion models, probably Walker Colts, too heavy to be worn on a belt and so were carried on the saddle instead.

Art was the first to stand up. He addressed the giant man in a calm, matter-of-fact tone, as if such sights came riding through his door pretty much every time he sat down to supper.

"Maybe one of the boys could stable your horse for you," Art said.

No one moved.

The stranger did not answer. His eyes took in every part of the room, slowly and thoroughly. They seemed to linger particularly on Pasque, then moved on to take stock of the other rows of men sitting at the tables.

57

He undid the clasp of his buffalo-hide coat, and lowered the silk bandanna, and swung down to the floor more gracefully than you would expect such a large man to do. Even standing on the floor, he still seemed to fill the whole doorway. Later on, Pete Niles, who was sitting nearest the door, would say that the man's head was actually the same height as the horse's. Pete also described the saddle: it was built along the lines of those old Spanish jobs, with a tall, curved cantle and a wide, flat saddle horn like a big rawhide pancake. The holsters were tooled leather and set with silver, made to be carried on the saddle.

The stranger raised a gloved hand and pointed to Art. "Pendragon." It was not a question. Afterward, there were people who said he was looking at Pasque as he spoke.

"That's right," Art said.

"We have heard of you, even south of the Arkansas. There are stories about people who owe their peace and quiet to you. Other stories say that you are responsible for ridding the Wyoming range of villains and outlaws. You, and your riders."

"I suppose that's right." Art had not moved from his place, nor had he smiled. "Care to sit and take supper with us?"

The big man shook his head slowly. "I think not." He looked around again, slowly. "Besides," he finally continued, "I appear to be a bit late for the main course."

"There's still plenty," Art said, his voice warming just slightly. "Maybe you'd take some dessert with us. Why don't I just get one of the boys to put your coat some place and take care of your horse . . ."

The horse began to back out of room, in that careful way that big horses have of placing each hoof deliberately, until it had only its head in the light.

"Later, perhaps," the stranger said. "First, since I have nothing with me in the way of a Christmas gift for your fine house, allow me to offer you some Christmas Eve entertainment." He paused and looked around again as if making a challenge. He spoke again. "According to the stories I have heard, you have certain *vaqueros* who still live by the gun, in these days of law and order." He fixed his eyes on the Pinto Kid, who had crippled a rustler named Stephens last fall, and then on Bob, who had outdrawn two gambling slickers and wounded one of them during a visit to town. And he then looked into Pasque's eyes.

"I propose," he said slowly, "that we step outside, now that you have finished your suppers, and have ourselves a little sport. You might even offer me a taste of that whiskey you have in the keg, sitting on the bench behind the house. In turn, I might show your *vaqueros* a thing or two about fancy shooting. I presume that none of them are afraid of gunfire . . . for sport, of course."

There wasn't a man in the room who lacked nerve. But these were men who also had managed to stay alive in hostile country, thanks to common sense and a good feeling for the odds. And at this moment, without a gun among them and looking at a giant of a man who had two cap-and-ball six-shooters on his saddle and

59

probably one or two more guns under that thick coat, the odds were bad enough to make anyone hesitate.

Art saw that the big man was challenging him, but he didn't really have any choice except to see if he could get this game — or whatever it was going to be — outside, away from the women and kids.

"Sure," he said, taking his coat from the back of the chair. "Bob? Pasque? Any of you men want to see a little shooting for sport? We'll wait for you out at the bench."

The dancing light of the bonfire and the yellow glow of the lanterns flickered against the log walls. The men stood in silent postures, looking like a still-life engraving. Some had their heads down, hands in pockets; others crossed their arms across their chests and watched with open curiosity. A few had more of a foot-forward, chin-out stance to show that they were not intimidated by this tall stranger.

Art and the giant stranger stood near the bench, and each took a cup of whiskey. Art studied the stranger carefully, but Pasque noticed that Art was relaxed, as if he had already figured out who the dark rider was and why he had come to the Keystone for Christmas.

"New to the territory?" Art asked.

The stranger sipped his whiskey. "No, not really," he said. "I seem to get up this way whenever the first winter snow falls."

"I see. And . . . from what you said in the house there, I take it you don't exactly favor the way the Keystone watches out for its neighbors?"

"You know that's not it," the stranger replied. "That's not it at all. The truth is that I was preparing to return to my winter home south of the gold camps and just across the Picketwire. But then I recalled having heard about the Keystone, where cowboys still stood for courage and chivalry like the knights of old. And for skill with weapons as well. Naturally, I could not pass by. Each year it becomes more and more difficult to find men willing to play my game." He again seemed to be looking at Pasque. And Pasque knew it.

The stranger went on. "They look quite young, these knights of yours. They have the appearance of men who have solved life's puzzle. I wonder . . . do they understand death at all?"

The more Pasque studied the big man, the less he liked him. He could only come up with one reason that an armed stranger would be riding into a ranch with a chip on his shoulder, and that was that the man was looking for a fight. He had come from the north, he said, which was the direction Pasque thought Link and Moore had gone. Maybe he was some friend of theirs, or a member of their gang, and he was here to see about getting rid of the kid who had seen the branding iron and who had taken a dangerous interest in their movements.

"What I propose," the stranger was saying to the group of men there in the lamplight, "is to see if you, Mister Pendragon, or any one of your riders, is courageous enough to shoot at me and then let me shoot at him in return. As I said, it is a game I like to play, and these days I find fewer and fewer men who will play it with me."

The silence of the group finally broke, and all the men began to mutter. Not one man spoke directly to the stranger, or directly to Art, but they hurried to tell each other that they, by God, would be glad to accommodate. Just take a minute to duck down to the bunkhouse and get a gun, and there would be some, by God, lead flying. But still, in all the murmuring and cussing, no man stepped forward.

"Pretty risky game for you to be playing," Art said. "Most of these boys are pretty good shots. I wouldn't want anybody to get hurt swapping lead, 'specially on Christmas Eve. But I guess we could set up a target . . ."

The big man interrupted him with a laugh that seemed to make the lantern flames dance. "Target! This round-table assortment of fire-eating buckaroos, these gentlemen who can outdraw any outlaw and who wrestle bears before lunch? A *target!* Decline my game if you will," he said, "but let's not have anything so tame as shooting at a target."

The muttering grew, but still there was no man who stepped forward. Finally, Art spoke.

"Well, if you feel that way about it, since it's my house and my Christmas party, I'll just step inside and get my Colt."

"No need!" the big man roared. "I will make you a present of one of mine! If someone will just go to my horse there, in front of the house, and get one of my saddle pistols, we'll get on with our contest."

Art took a step, but Pasque was ahead of him. "No, Art! I ain't gonna let you do it. I don't know what this crazy *hombre* wants, but I think it has somethin' to do with me, and I know it ain't got nothin' to do with you. I'll want to be the one to take him up on his little game." Pasque looked at the other men. "You boys don't think we oughta let Art fool around with this lunatic?"

The boys now stood mute, but consent was written on their faces. Pasque was every bit as good a shot as Art, and he wasn't married. It was decided.

Pasque took long strides around the corner of the house and quickly came back, and he had one of the saddle pistols, an enormous old Walker Dragoon Colt. Men seldom carried them these days, since they were so long and heavy, but they still had enough power to stop a charging bull dead in its tracks. Pasque spun the cylinder, checking each chamber for a load, and inspected the percussion caps.

"Where do you want it?" he asked the big man. And his eyes were cold and steady.

The stranger raised one hand. "Have patience. There's a bargain we need to make first," he said. "And I'll tell you what the bargain is . . . I will allow you three shots, and, if you hit me, you keep that pistol. A gift."

"Fair enough."

"And bring it back to me by next Christmas."

"Bring it back?" Pasque blinked.

"And I will use it to shoot at you. That is the game. You must come find me, and, when you do, you allow me to shoot at you."

Art stepped in. "Have I got this straight?" he said. "You expect Pasque to shoot you three times with that horse pistol, and *then* you're going to ride out of here? And then the kid has to play some kind of hide-and-seek game with you next year?"

"That's my proposal. He doesn't have to continue, of course, now that he knows the procedure. I would not force anyone to play against their will. We can share a bit of your whiskey, and I'll take my leave of you. It won't be my fault, of course, that the Keystone didn't quite measure up."

"Give me that Colt," Art said, laying a hand on the gun that Pasque held.

"Nothin' doin', Art. This is my play now. I'll drill the son-of-a-bitch for his Christmas present, if that's the way he wants it. If this cannon actually works and he walks away, I'll follow him all the way to hell for the showdown."

The giant's laugh rang out again. The stranger walked to the log wall and took a wide-legged stance, hands on his hips, arms holding the thick buffalo coat open. He stood there mockingly, waiting for death with a smile on his face.

Pasque raised the pistol, then turned and aimed out into the darkness where the lantern light was glimmering faintly on an old milk bucket. The Walker Colt roared; a yellow stab of fire flashed out in the gloom. The men saw the bucket fly into the air, split nearly in half by the heavy lead ball, spinning off into the night. A cloud of sulphurous smoke rose over the firelight.

"Thought maybe you packed this thing with blanks," Pasque said. The stranger went on smiling at him, taunting him. So Pasque took aim at the big chest, thumbed back the hammer again, and again there was an ear-splitting roar and flash and cloud of smoke. Through the haze Pasque thought he saw the huge figure move slightly, but the figure did not fall, and so he cocked the weapon a third time, and for the third time the hammer came down on forty grains of gun-powder and sent a .44 caliber ball smashing into the body standing there in the haze.

Three shots. Pasque lowered the smoking revolver, his hand still tingling from the recoil.

Laughter, deep, full laughter came out of the thick gray haze. "That was good shooting, my young friend!" the stranger laughed, turning to walk away. "You have nerve and a steady arm. I hope you do try to find me again, come next year at about this same time. When we meet, will you gamble with your life, or will you gamble with your death? I suggest you spend the year discovering which. Come earlier, if that suits you better!" And he laughed again.

No man moved. They could only stand frozen, a collection of carved figurines of cowboys hardly breathing, until they heard the pounding of wide hoofs on the frozen ground and the ringing of laughter disappearing into the night.

The echoes finally stopped, and the smell of sulphur drifted away, and the men — except for some who had hurried indoors to tell their wives about it — clustered around Pasque to look at the gun.

Bob poked into the chambers with an old nail he had picked up. "Three rounds fired," he said. "Three still loaded." He scratched at the grease. "There's lead in here, all right. Unless he forgot the powder, or just had waddin' in those first three chambers, this Colt could kill him."

"Wasn't no waddin'," Pasque answered, flexing the fingers of his gun hand. "I guess I can tell the difference between shootin' a ball and shootin' a blank."

Several men had taken a lantern and gone to the wall. They reenacted the scene, sighting along their outstretched arms to determine the angle of Pasque's shots.

"Probably missed him," one of them said. "That's the only thing I can think of."

"Oh, yeah?" Pasque replied. "Well, then tell me, Lem. Would *you* have missed at that range? And did I miss that old bucket?"

"Hell, no," Lem said, "and I ain't never seen you miss at that range, neither. So what's your answer?"

"Damned if I know. The barrel could be bent so I'd miss, but I still hit that bucket out there."

Mac suddenly called to them. Holding a lantern high, he was peering intently at the wall. "There's your bullet, at least one of them," he said.

Two inches to the right they found the other hole. No doubt about it at all. The surface of the wood was caved in, indented, as if hit with a ballpeen hammer, and in the center was a half-inch hole. The holes were about the height of a man's head, just where they would be if Pasque had fired from shoulder level at the chest of the tall man.

Lem stood where Pasque had been, and Bob stood in the stranger's place, and there was no doubt about it — if there was lead in those holes, it had gone right through the stranger.

Bob took out his knife and began digging at the log. Some of the boys drifted to the bench for a cup of whiskey. Others passed the giant's revolver among themselves, sighting along its barrel, examining the loads. Two stood apart, smoking cigarettes and looking off down the road where the stranger had gone.

"Art," Bob said.

Art walked over to the circle of lantern light.

"Look." Bob carefully placed two lead balls in Art's hand, and Art held them close to the light.

"Pasque," Art said, "you'd better see this."

What Bob's careful carving had excavated from the log were two .44 caliber balls, only slightly flattened from the impact. They were both stained, but whether with pine pitch or with blood it was hard to say. In the grooves made by the barrel rifling were stuck some strands of unmistakable curly hair. Buffalo hair.

"I'd say I didn't miss," Pasque finally said.

"I guess not," Art said. "And somebody has to go after him, and not next year. Now. He's out there wounded, like an animal. We gotta find him."

Art Pendragon and the Keystone riders searched until daybreak. Some of the men tried to track the big horse, which was next to impossible on frozen ground criss-crossed with livestock tracks. Some rode to high spots, hoping that the wounded man had built a campfire that they could spot. Bob and Pasque made long zigzags, back and forth, across a line leading roughly north, then began a series of widening circles, and still found no sign of him. Or did any kind of rider, for that matter, although, once beyond the fence, they came to place after place where a rider would have left tracks in drifted snow or loose gravel, but not a track did they find. Not a single drop of blood, not on the ground or in the snow or on the bushes.

All the other searchers reported the same thing as early morning found them sitting around the big table in the festive hall, eating breakfast with wolfish appetites. No one had seen a track made by that horse. No one had seen a campfire anywhere for miles. No one had heard a sound other than the wintry night breeze, rustling dry old leaves among the yucca. The big man and his big horse had vanished. And for days afterward, Pasque rode and searched for sign and found none. The man was gone as if he had been a dream, a ghost, as if it had never happened. And yet Pasque knew that he had been there that Christmas night, just as he knew he had to find him and finish the shoot-out.

He remembered the night he had stood in the middle of the road and wondered what kind of life lay ahead of him.

CHAPTER
FIVE

Death in the Snow

January and February were death months that year.
Pasque rode out almost every day, sometimes with the
Kid or with Mac, most often alone. And it seemed,
wherever he rode, he found death. One day it was
a frozen steer, lying in crusty snow at the bottom of a
ravine, its hide ripped open by coyotes. Another day it
was a rabbit, still warm, tracks in the snow telling the
story of panic and struggle; a hawk circled overhead,
waiting for Pasque to ride on.

The weather had turned very cold after Christmas,
and within a week every stock pond on the main range
was frozen. Most of the creeks froze. And no matter
how well they stoked the bunkhouse stove before
turning in, the cowboys woke to find a skim of ice on
the water bucket.

The snow was colder than usual. It was not the thick
blanket snow that would come down in big flakes and
pile up three feet deep all over the territory. Instead, it
came across the open land in the teeth of the north
winds, horizontal flints of ice, stabbing into the
shivering flesh of men and animals, driving itself
through the tiniest cracks of a wall, shrieking down the

chimney. But in spite of the cold and the blowing snow that hit his back like buckshot, Pasque would still ride out, even if it meant packing himself into layers of long johns and clothing and coats and gloves until it was all he could do to get into the saddle.

He checked the whole west fence of the main ranch, from south to north. He rode to the line camps at Willow Creek, Spenser Mountain, The Dutchman's Mine, and Kathy Fork. At the Kathy Fork cabin he once again felt a shiver crawl up his back. He felt the anger, too, and kept looking around, hoping to suddenly see Link and Moore. They were long gone, of course. But he imagined it all, finding them, challenging them, gunning them down. And for some reason he felt that they had gone north. Just as the cold blizzards and killing sleet came out of the north, north seemed the direction to go.

Near Dutchman Flats he came across the carcass of a horse, and got down to turn it over so he could study the brand. He was hoping to find an Oval Cross, but then recognized it as an old mare from the Keystone string. She'd probably strayed and then died in the cold with no grass to eat and no water except for what snow she could eat. He looked down at the frozen body, and then looked northward.

He looked north again when he found a deer with its neck broken, lying at the foot of a cliff. Another death. Out on the east range he surprised an antelope dragging a broken leg. His Winchester released its running spirit from its crippled body, and, before the shot's echo had died away over the rolling hills, Pasque looked north.

When Pasque was back at the main ranch, the boys in the bunkhouse noticed the same thing that Gwen had begun to notice: his face seemed to sag more, dragging down the corners of his mouth, and wrinkles had appeared at his eyes. He looked grim and troubled.

Nothing made sense to him any more, especially death. Out there in Kansas his brothers were buried, but so were thousands of other men. And what had killed all of them? First there had been Indians living all over the plains, Pawnee and Lakota and Cheyenne, Kiowa and Arapaho and Ree and Crow, and they had killed each other. Then had come settlers and cattlemen and cavalry, and they had killed the Indians and brought cattle to shove out the buffalo, and plows to tear up the ground. Then the whites had range wars and killed each other. Nobody, except maybe the Indians, could claim natural rights to the land, but they all killed to keep it. Others killed to take it away.

What did that stranger in the old buffalo coat say? *Do you understand death at all?* And that other thing he said, after Pasque had shot him twice. *Do you gamble with your life now, or with your death?* What the hell was that supposed to mean?

And what did all this stuff with Link and Moore mean? Here came two men who needed killing, two men he probably had a right to kill, and Pasque had let them ride away. He didn't have to listen to Art. He could have gone after them and gunned them down, and then he could have just gone west. Or north. Somewhere nobody knew him.

Then came a stranger nobody knew, and he had stood right up and asked Pasque to kill him. He had treated death like a big joke, and Pasque had fired at him point-blank, but couldn't kill him. What had the huge stranger been after, anyway? Just a crazy lunatic, the boys had said, fooling people by using a trick gun or maybe wearing some kind of armor under that heavy buffalo coat. Pure loco. The West was full of crazy lunatics.

A winter of death. Two men had run away without shooting, and one man had been shot and had ridden away, laughing. Pasque began to wonder if the death of anybody or of anything ever mattered. To him, at least, it didn't seem to. He was beginning to feel indifferent to the deaths of his brothers. He hated himself for it, but some days it didn't trouble him any more than finding a rabbit frozen dead in the snow. He took himself to task, angry at his indifference. He told himself he'd lost all his feelings. It wouldn't matter if Old Buffalo Coat really did shoot him dead. Might be better off that way.

It took a mountain lion, one cold March day, to change his mind.

Pasque had decided to ride to one of the remote line shacks. He told Art and Bob Riley that he would be looking for heifers that might be ready to have early calves, but what he was really after was some sign that Link and Moore were still living somewhere on the range. He set out in good weather, with a few days' provisions in his saddlebags, but then that north wind turned on him and brought down a heavy snow.

Pasque rode on to the line shack anyway, a cabin called the Old Barnes Place, where he expected he would find some provisions cached. It was a long way back in the foothills, and by the time he got there the storm had built up two feet of snow. The Barnes' cache, however, turned out to be as empty as a whore's Bible box.

He started back for the main ranch. His own grub had run out, and there would be more snow coming. He could maybe shoot himself some meat, but he hadn't seen a live animal since leaving the empty line shack, and that was three days ago now.

He found a place to sleep where the wind had blown most of the snow away from the grass — kind of exposed, but mostly dry. Pasque built himself a fire, gathered up a night's worth of wood, and rolled into his blankets. He chewed on a handful of rose hips he had found and decided that he was going to make it. With luck, he'd be back at the main ranch before dark tomorrow. His stomach complained some about having gone two days without real food, but there was always a chance of venison or at least rabbit tomorrow. He curled into the warmth of the blankets, covered his head as best he could with the collar of his sheepskin coat and his Stetson, and slept.

When he woke, there was a weight pressing down everywhere on his body and something ice-cold against the exposed part of his neck. He stirred, and the snow that had been falling on him for the past three hours cascaded down around his neck and got inside the coat collar against his bare skin. He turned the other way and more snow slid down inside against his back. He stopped trying to shake it off and just lay there, figuring. He might get a hand free and brush the stuff off of himself, then sit up. Or he might sit up very carefully and gradually slip out from under the white blanket.

"To hell with it," Pasque said. He threw off the blanket and got up to dance around, getting warm, while he shook snow from his coat and brushed it from his pants and tried to dig it out of his collar. It was fluffy snow, cold and dry, covering everything in sight. Across the wide park at the foot of the pass, up over the high ridges, up and down the length of the park, all was stark white except the shadowy groves of spruce trees where he should have slept the night. There was a slight dip in the white nothingness where a creek ran. Sage clumps had turned into little white mounds. There was no wind at all, and under the overcast sky there was a silence as deep as a grave.

Pasque dusted the snow from the saddle blanket he had been using as his ground cloth, and then used the saddle blanket to sweep the powdery snow from his saddle. Automatically, from the habit of hundreds of nights on the open range, he looked around for firewood and cussed himself for not laying a good fire stack and covering it the night before. Then he laughed at himself, the sudden sound breaking the still silence.

"Fire?" he said to the snow-mounded sage bushes, "hell, what would I cook, anyway? Got no coffee, nothin'."

So rather than waste his time gathering wood and starting up a useless fire, Pasque saddled up and moved on. Riding would warm a man better than a fire, and, if he was lucky, he might cut some fresh game tracks along the way. No point in staying still. None at all.

By day's end he was across the southwest ridge and had broken out of the trees again. He found himself in another park, another wide-open, snow-blanketed, little prairie in the middle of the hills. He had seen deer tracks, but they headed away from his line of travel. From a tree squirrel's cache, he stole enough pine nuts to fill the big pocket of his heavy coat. The nuts were tiny things, but he ate them anyway as he rode along, gingerly cracking them in his teeth and using his tongue to separate the pinhead-sized meat from the broken shell. Gave his mouth something to do, at least.

He crossed creeks that had been opened by an earlier March thaw and found plenty of water. Water could fill the belly. He thought about catching fish, but figured the effort of doing it bare-handed would use up more of his strength than he could get back. Better to keep riding. Better to move in the general direction of the Keystone and trust to luck that he would find game, or a ranch or trapper's cabin. Even a trail, right now, would make the stomach feel more hopeful. He was quite a way from his familiar territory. Farther than he thought. He wouldn't make the ranch by nightfall.

* * *

That night the light of a half moon lit up the shimmering snow and gave the ghostly mountains an unreal purity. There was an unsettling silence over everything. Pasque got under the drooping branches of a giant spruce where he built a cheerful, little stick fire on the dry ground. He tied his horse under another tree nearby, then wrapped himself in the blanket, and went to sleep.

In the early morning hours, there was a scream. Pasque woke to full consciousness immediately, but at first he didn't know why he had come suddenly awake, sat up, or was listening. Gradually, his mind remembered that scream. Part dream, part real. Maybe it was *all* dream. The icy air was dead still. Wispy smoke of the fire's few embers drifted up into the spruce branches. The silence was deep and eerie. Beyond the trees, in the snow, nothing had a shadow. Nothing made a sound. Only the shuffling of the horse nearby kept Pasque from believing that he had gone deaf in the night.

A scream. He pulled on his boots and slid the Winchester from the saddle scabbard. He wrapped his blanket around him, over his heavy coat, and stepped into the open where he could see up and down the long park. Nothing moved. Just white and more white, and his own tracks. Pasque turned and walked the other way, back into the forest. Some sense, some feeling beyond anything he could hear or see, seemed to tell him that he was not the only living thing out here; whatever company he had, he would find on the other side of the trees.

He came to the clearing on the other side of the trees, and it was a hundred yards to the next bunch of spruce. There it was. A cat. Lion. Not a particularly large one. Just a mountain lion. And it was dragging something big. A deer. The lion tugged the carcass like a dog, pulling a blanket across a floor, trying not to step on it, keeping its head as high as possible, struggling to get it to the shelter of the trees. The snow slowed it down as much as the weight.

"Well, friend cat," said Pasque under his breath, as he levered a shell into the Winchester's chamber, "I think I'll just let you give me a piece of that venison for breakfast."

The cat heard the sharp click, turned toward the sound, and caught sight of the man standing there. It saw only a dark silhouette against the snow, almost part of the dark shadows of the tree branches. Nothing but a vague shape, unmoving, silent except for that harsh, clicking sound. The cat had probably never heard a Winchester shucking a shell home; for that matter, the cat had probably never seen a man. And still for some reason known only to a spirit that lies beyond the understanding of either cats or men, it feared the dark shadow. It forgot the warm deer meat, and it froze, focusing all of its concentration toward that dark shadow and that single sound.

Pasque, sighting down the barrel, felt the effects of hunger. His hands shook; the front sight was blurry. He couldn't even estimate the distance. He blinked his eyes and then squeezed them shut again, hard, and opened them suddenly into the snow-glared light, but it did not help. He held his breath, but the barrel of the rifle went on weaving around and dipping up and down with a mind of its own.

"Well, hell," Pasque whispered, "I don't need to kill you, cat. I just need to scare you off, so I can cut me a steak or two for breakfast. You'll hardly miss it, and then I'll be gone out of here."

He aimed high and pulled the trigger. The lion gave a jump; it screamed into the sound of the rifle, and was gone.

Pasque thought he was running as he hurried toward the freshly killed doe, but he was actually limping a little and stumbling a lot; a person watching the hunger-weak cowboy would have thought it looked like a man who was moving and falling forward at the same time, and only the dragging forward of each foot prevented each fall. But he was moving, that was the important thing. Moving toward venison. Breakfast!

The lion remembered that he had cocked his ears toward a small sound, and just before the air exploded in a sharp, cracking blast, his muscles had instinctively tensed up for a leap. Before, after, or at the same time as the crack of sound, something had hit him. His body had suddenly jolted sideward, both hind feet thrown out from under him in the snow, all of him dragged backward and down. His breath was gone, knocked out of him as if he had fallen from a tree or from a ledge and had landed hard on a rock flat on his side, and his breath would not come back no matter how desperately he tried to draw air into his lungs.

78

As he found his hind legs, or maybe without finding them, he made a leap for the shadows, his front legs pulling strongly toward the nearest trees, his back legs suddenly weaker but still moving. To the first tree, past it, onward, instinct taking him up the hill, not down, up toward the rocks, through the clear space above the trees to the rocks, to the rocks . . .

Pasque got to the carcass of the doe. There were no marks on it, except for a little blood near the neck where the lion had dragged it. It must have died of a broken neck. Now Pasque looked around him. The right thing to do would be to hang this meat properly, clean the guts out, let it bleed nicely, and maybe skin it to save the hide for something.

He took out his knife and began to cut the belly. No strength for the niceties, now. He'd get that breakfast steak, maybe some of the ham for lunch and dinner, and get on his way. After all, that lion was probably hungry, too. No point in eating up everything the host had, leaving nothing. Just isn't polite. So he stopped slicing the belly open, wondering why he had started to do it in the first place, and went to slicing himself a leg. That would do. Nice roast of venison there.

That's when he saw the other blood. He had just put a bit of the raw warm meat into his mouth to chew on while he finished his butchering, when he saw the blood. It speckled the snow on the far side of the deer. The light brown of the deer and the deep red of the blood made a stark, unreal contrast to the white of the snow. There were signs that the cat had thrashed around and tracks weaving away, tracks that looked like the front legs were leaping and the hind ones were dragging.

"Well, damn!" said Pasque, his mouth automatically continuing to chew on the raw meat. "I hit him. Damn! Didn't want to do that."

He returned to his cutting, and looked again at the tracks, limping away. He finally wiped the blade on the hide, put it back in the sheath, and picked up his Winchester. As he set out, following the tracks of the lion, Pasque could feel the snow in his boots and the cold air against his sweating forehead. He was aware of the way the icy air made his nostrils seem to stick shut, and of the crunching noise he made. He felt the weight of the rifle and marveled at it as if he had never hefted it before. After days of steadily becoming numb to the feelings, he was aware of their return. Some men would say that it was the meat that brought the vitality back, but they would be wrong. It was a sudden awareness of life. In all that dead and frozen stillness, life announced its persistent presence to the man who had forgotten about it.

He threw a backward glance toward the place across the park where his horse was still tied, and shook his head.

"Dammit," he repeated. "Far to go back, far to go on."

The tracks led him out of the trees. They marked the lion's ascent of the mountain, toward the far pile of rocks. Pasque plunged on through the snow, tasting the bit of venison in his mouth, feeling the rifle's weight in his hand, talking to himself, and hearing his words interrupt the quiet of the mountain.

"Just breakfast, that's all. In the air, in the ground, hell, I could have shot anywhere or just maybe yelled and run out there, but no! I gotta shoot close, I guess. Dog-gone the damn' thing, when a man can't even miss on purpose . . ." And he went mumbling on up the hill, much like a small boy who has just broken a window and is on his way to face his father's wrath, imagining his father's speech and rehearsing his own lines as he goes.

The lion made it to the rocks, and, when it attempted to jump to the top of a boulder high enough to be a refuge, or at least higher and, therefore, safer, it slipped. The back legs stopped working altogether, the lungs could not fill with enough air, and it slipped and went down hard, falling flat on its side, feeling the hot and searing pain, now that the shock had been run off, and the lion went down in the trough of snow between rocks high on either side.

The sky was clearing — blue openings of infinite depth now came to view between clouds that were thinning out into separate floating islands of white. There were the gray, granite walls rising on either side of him, the soft cool snow beneath his body's burning side. There were the drifting clouds. There was the endless blue.

And then that other animal put its head over the edge, intruding between the blue and himself lying there, and it looked down and made noises.

"Ah, dammit, there you are. Listen, friend, I just feel terrible. I mean, this is your range, and I come here and steal food and then shoot you up like this. Now, if you were down on *my* range, stealing calves and such like, why, I'd sure go after you in no time. But this . . . this just ain't right."

The lion seemed not to hear him, even though the green eyes were looking straight at him. There was pain in those eyes, the quiet and intense pain of the strong. In the end, it is those who do not fear pain who feel it most; it shows in their eyes, no matter how strong they are.

"Thing to do, see, is that I got to finish you off now. Don't want to, but it's the thing to do here. So, well . . . I'm sorry about it."

One echoing crack of the rifle. It was sharp and short, yet seemed to Pasque to bounce forever down and over the rocks, seemed to echo back from the depth of the pine forests and spruce forests below. After the echo stopped and his muscles stopped shaking from the climb up, he shimmied down to where the lion lay and moved it out onto a slope where the broken rock was scattered like talus. There he cleared a space of snow and put the lion's body on the bare place and began laying up a cairn of granite. He made it very thick, the tops and the sides triple layers of heavy flat rocks that he dug out of the snow, all the while telling himself that it would keep the coyotes away.

Although he did not know it, Pasque was not really protecting the carcass. He was paying tribute to the spirit of the wild predator, making a memorial to remind himself to remember, saying with each carefully laid stone that something strong had died here. Men have built such monuments to fallen heroes and to fallen horses on summits of high mountains and low prairie mounds. A year earlier, Pasque could have gone after a predatory lion and killed it and left it, or skinned the carcass to make a rug or a pair of gloves. That was a year earlier. This year, it was different. This year the idea of bringing death for no reason, of violating an unspoken code of hospitality seemed wrong. To come here and shoot this wild thing was an act that seemed to trouble the very mountains themselves.

Pasque finished his cairn of rocks. "There," he said to the cold, stiff thing that now lay within the dark cold tomb, "that'll keep the varmints off you for a while." But the thought did not make him feel better. He turned away, and, going back down the hill toward where the venison lay freezing in the snow, Pasque did not look back. Death and life. Life and death. He shook his head at it all. It had all become too damned important, all things considered.

The doe was not heavy. Pasque hoisted it to his shoulders, the half-severed leg dangling, and made his way back to his sheltered camp. He hung it there in a tree, did a proper job of it, even though it was half-frozen, left most of the innards for critters who would appreciate a meal, carefully butchered the meat, and packed it into his saddlebags. He did not eat until he had done the thing right. The guts were in a careful pile, away from the little fire circle he called his camp, as was right. The meat was cut and packed, save for the piece he wanted for breakfast. The blood on the ground was covered up with snow and duff that he kicked around, and the hide and hair tufts were buried in a crevice between tree roots.

The smell of the meat roasting over the slow fire made Pasque's appetite rage, but he made himself have patience and roasted it well. He heard the sound of the fire and the sizzle of dripping fat, falling into the flames. He could hear tree branches dropping loads of snow with that *whumpf* sound as the afternoon sun brought a little warmth to the air. He heard the horse pawing away the snow and ripping off clumps of the dry grass stems. When he ate, he ate slowly, cutting each piece with his knife and chewing it thoughtfully. And once, in mid-bite, he realized that he was sitting in just the right place to look back at the mountain, at the dead lion's cairn, while he ate.

Many years afterward, some cowboys, riding roundup, followed their strayed Herefords up a forested slope and across an open bit of ground and into a rock outcropping. They discovered an old stone cairn, almost square, heavily built. They wondered what or who might be buried in it, and why it was there.

"Indians didn't build it," one of them said. "It must've been some old pioneer or cowboy who was passin' through here, I guess. Maybe he lost a partner, or a relative or somebody, an' he buried 'em here."

"Well," the other one said, "whoever he was, he built 'er good. Like it was his partner, or maybe his wife. A man wouldn't go to that trouble for just anybody."

They rode on. "Y'know," the first one said, "it puts me in mind of an ol' story we heard back in school. There was this warrior, one of them Saxons, and this other guy was his worst enemy. He hunted and hunted for him, and finally caught up to him and killed him. Then he went and collected a buncha rocks from all over and built a monument to him. Them two hated each other, and he built him a monument."

They came to the forest's edge, and, just as they rode on into the pines, one man looked back up the mountain. And one did not.

CHAPTER
SIX

The Medicine Wheel Blacksmith

"Looka that now, would ya?" Mary's husband, Lou, held out a chunk of potato impaled on the tip of his knife, so Pasque could look at it. Pasque looked and went back to his coffee.

"Wouldn't think a shriveled-up thing like that would grow a new plant, would ya?" Lou was at the kitchen table, cutting old potatoes into chunks for planting. "That's what I love about a garden. Take these here potatoes, been sitting in the cellar for . . . what? . . . nine months almost? . . . and stick 'em in the ground and you got new potatoes."

Pasque nodded. "I guess so," he said.

The day was sunny and cold. He was sitting in the kitchen with Mary and Lou, having coffee, while he waited for Art. The kitchen was warm with the sweet smell of bread baking.

"Or take that corn," Lou went on, pointing his knife at a sack of dry yellow kernels. "Stalks come up green an' full of life. Why, it's one of the biggest thrills in the world to see them first little shoots in the spring. Then in the fall, you come along an' rip off the ears, knock down the stalk, keep the best kernels. Them little dry dead things turn into sweet corn plants again next year. It's a miracle."

Pasque nodded again. Even old Lou had to keep reminding him. Death and life. He remembered the lion and the venison. He wondered where Link and Moore were by now.

The back door banged open, and Art came in, pulling off his heavy mittens and opening his sheepskin coat to the warmth of the kitchen range.

"'Morning, Mary," he said. "Pasque. Lou. How're things?"

Art shook his coat out and brushed his Stetson, hung them on the peg by the door, checked his boots for mud, ran his hand through his hair, and hitched up his belt. He poured himself a cup of coffee. Pasque had seen all these gestures before, and knew the signs — Art had something on his mind.

"You wanted to see me?" Pasque said.

Art studied his coffee for a minute. "Well, yes. We noticed . . . me and Gwen . . . that you're gettin' pretty antsy these days. Don't seem like your old self. Don't seem like the kid who used to wear flowers in his hatband."

"No flowers this time of year," Pasque answered.

"You know what I mean. You oughta get away from this place for a while. I told Jonas Robbins you'd do a favor for him."

Jonas Robbins had a ranch southeast of the Keystone, out in the arroyo country. One corner of his range ran clear to the Platte, but even with all that acreage he hadn't done too well the last couple of years. This year he was running his place shorthanded.

"What's the job?" Pasque said.

"Jonas talked to a drifter, a cowpuncher lookin' for work who came up along Crow Creek. Said he saw a squatter out there. This squatter looked to be puttin' up a shed, and he had a forge goin'. Accordin' to the drifter, it looked like the start of a blacksmith shop. Might be this squatter is expectin' more settlers. Sometimes we get foreigners who can't read a map or don't know to hire a locator, and they think they're on some section that's been platted for a town site."

"So Robbins wants me to run him off?"

"The rule is that he gets a warning first. I thought maybe you'd ride out that way, see if you can find him, and sort of urge him to move on. You'd better take a pack horse and one of the tents we use on trail drive, too. The weather could turn out nasty in that country."

"Sack of grub and an axe and maybe an extra blanket oughta do it. Tent just makes a nuisance. The extra horse might come in handy, though. Yeah, I'll ride out there and see what's up. Get started first thing in the morning."

It was just beginning to look like April the morning that Pasque set out on his ride to the camp of the Welsh blacksmith, Evan Thompson.

On the high prairie just east of the Rockies, April can be a discouraging month. The bright blue mornings usually begin with frost and don't seem to get any warmer even though the sun keeps rising toward noon.

Riding the lee side of a slope that shelters him from the breeze, a man might feel warm enough to unbutton his sheepskin. But then he moves to where the breeze can hit him again, and he's glad to be buttoned up.

Some April days hold the promise of rain, when scattered clouds gather low over a swale on the far horizon. But instead of giving the land a nice spring drench, they turn to gray drizzle and make a cold, damp blanket over the range. Or they let down heavy snow, the wet and thick kind like new plaster slapped on a wall. It flattens the dry bunchgrass left over from summer, buries new green shoots out of sight, bends the cedars that grow alongside the draws. Even the stiff bayonets of yucca plants sag under the soggy weight.

On other days, the sun has some warmth to it. The air holds the heat. The ground starts to thaw. On days like that, a man wants to strip off his shirt and long johns and get down to bare skin. He gets an urge to lie in the sunshine and let his pony out on a long picket rope to search for the tender clumps of young grass.

Evenings lengthen in April. After supper, it's good maybe to ride or walk to a rise of ground and watch the evening come down. Coyotes show up an hour before dark, hurrying down arroyos and slinking over the hills. Antelope stand and look around. And when the light finally slides down behind the blue-black range of mountains far to the west, the stars seem brighter than they have been all winter.

Winter, though, isn't ready to give up. It might be that there are yellow flowers in the new grass. The pincushion cactus might be swelling up into bud, ready to bloom. Cottonwoods in the draws might have the beginnings of leaves, and some of the prairie antelope and whitetails and cattle may have dropped the early fawns and calves. But winter doesn't care.

Great, towering, gun-metal clouds come up from the south on a freezing wind, or roll down from the north like wet, dense-smoke billows. As they pass, concho-size flakes swirl and fly around a man's face until he can't even see his horse's ears. Flakes pile up on the horn, on his hat brim, on his shoulders; the snow sticks to anything, horizontal and upright, until man and horse look like a statue carved from ice. The statue plods on through the blizzard, the man's head down and the horse's head down, a portrait of resignation and discouragement.

Another day, and a chinook comes warm from the mountains and drinks up two feet of snow in half a day. Or the drizzle follows the wet snowstorm, so that a horse's hoofs find hard-frozen crust and knee-deep snow on the shaded, windless sides of the hills, glazed drifts in the gullies, and half-thawed mud in places where the sun hits the ground.

After reaching the west fence line of the Robbins place, Pasque rode through a day of dripping, endless, vertical rain, and then a day of reluctant sunshine. On the third day, April decided to open up the blue skies and let the warm sun draw the steam from the earth. Pasque was up early, glad to be out of his wet bedroll. He was glad to stomp out the smudgy fire made of wet wood, swallow the last of the coffee, and pack up.

The sun was just starting to get nice and warm, when he struck a trail of sorts — the kind of tracks that cattle make when they move back and forth between a windmill tank and open range, or when a salt block has been left on the range. It went in his direction, roughly, and so he decided to follow it a way.

Predictably, the rut dipped into a gulch that was still drifted with crusty snow. Then it went up a slippery slope of thawing clay that was slick as grease. It was good clay for making adobe bricks, Pasque thought to himself, but it was hell on horses.

His saddle horse slipped and slid in the wet clay and stumbled and slipped again. Leaning over the near shoulder, Pasque could see yellow adobe packed solid under one hoof, and he could feel the jolt when the horse tried to balance his weight on that mud ball.

Pasque pulled up, although the ground still had a steep slope to it, and swung off to take care of the packed-up hoof. He should have given some thought to his own two feet, though, because, before he knew it, his old, slick-bottom, high-heeled boots were sliding on that slithery clay like two greased pigs going down a cellar door. He threw out his arms for balance and spooked the horse into jerking the reins loose. The horse moved away, and the pack horse followed. Before he hit the ground, he had just time enough to wonder if he was coming down on a rock or a cactus — it turned out to be a rock — and he landed hard on his butt and went sliding on his back pockets farther down the hill and finally stopped himself by digging in his heels and grabbing for handfuls of yucca, bunchgrass, and mud. Mostly it was mud. Mud had also gone up his pants leg, and down inside his boot.

He was sitting there, picking sticky globs of adobe off the palms of his hands, when he heard laughter. It sounded like a little kid laughing.

It *was* a kid. Ten, eleven years old, maybe. In a hat that was too big and had lost its shape somewhere in the previous century, coveralls, and a gingham shirt, this kid stood laughing like hell at the sight of Pasque, sitting in the mud. But before Pasque could yell out to him, or find his wits to say anything at all, the kid had turned and vanished behind the hill.

The kid's tracks weren't hard to follow, once Pasque got the clay scraped off of his clothes and caught up both his mount and the pack horse. After following the kid's footprints for a half mile or so, Pasque heard the ringing of a heavy hammer on an anvil. The sound led him to a clearing in the scrub, and the blacksmith's camp. The whole lash-up consisted of a big wagon, one of the old-fashioned prairie schooner kind, a four-post *ramada* with a tarp and some deer-skins thrown over it to make a shed, and another open-faced shed built out of crooked cottonwood logs.

The kid was up on the wagon seat, looking at him. A woman sat on a stool nearby, patching a pair of pants, and a man was tending the forge. Pasque could smell the sharp odor of burning coal.

The man was something to look at. He could have been half-brother to Old Buffalo Coat, the giant Christmas stranger. He was big enough. He wore a patchwork shirt of all kinds of bright colors and patterns. Over the shirt he wore a thick leather apron. On his head was a tight leather cap, like a helmet. His beard looked like a thick, red tumbleweed glued to his face, and it went down all the way to his waist. The smith stopped hammering and looked up, when Pasque rode in.

"Welcome!" His voice was as big as he was. It boomed across the clearing. "Why don't you step down and stay a while?"

His voice seemed to echo, and had a thickness as if the man had pebbles in his cheeks and was trying to talk without losing them. "It's a beautiful day, is it not?"

Pasque dismounted and tied his horses to a sagebrush at the edge of the clearing. And when he turned, the smith had two pewter mugs in his giant hands. He held one out to Pasque.

"It's wine we warm by the fire." The big man sipped his. "Just the thing after a long ride."

"I'm from the Keystone Ranch . . . ," Pasque began.

"Yes, I know. Arthur Pendragon's place. And this land belongs to Mister Robbins. Well, I'm Evan Thompson, blacksmith and farrier."

"Thompson?" Pasque echoed. There were lots of Thompsons around, but the name still seemed to stir some vague memory just the same.

"You're thinking we came from Kansas, no doubt." Thompson said. "Ben Thompson? And Billy, his brother? They are only cousins" — he laughed — "and rest assured that my family and I are not on the run from the law. How's your wine? Warmed enough?"

That was it. Ever since the murder of Jim and Chris, Pasque had made it his business to talk to anyone he ran into who had been in Kansas. Two men, first an Army horse buyer and then a grub line rider, had told him about the only outlaws they knew of — Ben Thompson was a gambler in Abilene, before Hickok killed his partner, and Billy Thompson was wanted for killing somebody in Wichita, or maybe it was Dodge. More Kansas murderers.

Pasque shifted the mug of wine to his left hand, and kept his eyes on Thompson.

"Now" — Thompson smiled, putting down his mug and reaching up to pump the handle of the bellows — "you'll be wanting to tell us to pack up and move on. And move on we shall. But you'll stay to supper, and you and I will swap a few tales around the fire, have a good night's sleep, and our business with each other will be concluded."

He blew air into the fire and reached for his tongs. The conversation was apparently over. He had finished his wine and was going back to work.

Pasque set down his saddles and pack and arranged his blankets at the edge of the clearing, up against the thick underbrush and as far from the wagon as he could put them. He hobbled the horses so they could graze. He still had time for a smoke before supper.

He sat with his back against the pack saddle, watching the blacksmith work. With a rhythm like a machine, Thompson would seize one of the glowing rods of red-hot steel in his tongs and lay it across the horn of the anvil, then hammer it into an oval. Then he thrust it back into the coals and blew with the big bellows until fountains of fire flew into the air. Then again the iron went to the anvil under the hammer. Thompson plunged his hand into a sack and lifted out a handful of white powder that he threw onto the red iron. With a few blows of the hammer it was welded to another iron oval and another. Link by link, a heavy chain was taking shape at the anvil. The *whoosh* of the bellows and the sizzle of the quenching water, together with the ringing of the hammer, were hypnotic.

When the smith seemed satisfied at last with his chain, it looked too massive for a single man to lift. With his largest tongs, Evan Thompson picked up the whole chain and dropped it into the coals again, then plunged it into the barrel of water.

The sun was low; the evening glare was in Pasque's eyes. Steam rose in clouds, blotting out the dying sunset behind. The enormous shape of Evan Thompson became a dark shadow against the vapor. It was the outline of a floating human figure dozens of feet tall, and for an instant it looked like a giant wearing a buffalo coat and dark hat. It was a trick of shadow and light. When the cloud had vanished, the blacksmith was looking at Pasque just the way the Christmas stranger had looked at him.

After supper the two of them stood next to the warm forge, smoking. Pasque took a bit of charred wood and drew the crossed oval brand on the side of a water barrel. "You ever see a branding iron like that in Kansas?" he asked the blacksmith.

Evans smiled broadly, but did not laugh. "Of course," he said, "but that's not the one you're to be looking for."

"What do you mean?"

"You're young, Pasque." He had not told the blacksmith his name. "Like this country around here is still young. There was a time when a man made his reputation with his fists, or his gun. Restless men they were, driving the herds northward, slaughtering the Cheyenne, killing the buffalo. And each other."

Evans lifted a coal from the forge to re-light his pipe. "How many times did your family move, Pasque?"

"Move? Oh, every couple of years, I guess."

"Every couple of years. Well, those days are coming to a close, to an end. My generation learned to fight the land, and lived for revenge when somebody tried to stop them. But your generation needs to learn a different kind of life."

"Is that right," Pasque said. He tossed the butt end of his smoke into the fire and watched it burn to an ash. "What about that Oval Cross brand?"

"You will find out that it means nothing. Except, perhaps, that you might kill innocent men because of it. The law will someday catch up with the murderers of your brothers, you know. Even in all this vast and empty prairie, the law is in motion. You do yourself no good, when you keep worrying about brands and strangers."

Pasque looked Thompson in the eye. "I ain't seen much law out here. On the Keystone we're still on our own when it comes to rustlers. And squatters," he added.

"You don't believe me," Thompson said. "Well, let me ask you this . . . what did you learn when you rode north this winter?"

Pasque stared into the fire. "Can't say I learned much."

"Oh? Nothing at all? Nothing unusual happened up there, while you were looking for these men you want to kill?"

"I shot a lion, if that's what you mean."

"And what about afterward? Feel pretty proud, pretty satisfied with yourself as a hunter, did you?" The smith talked as if he were smiling, but he wasn't smiling.

"No. Felt pretty bad about it, if you want to know."

"Killed the cat." The smith looked straight into Pasque's eyes. "But the spirit of that ol' mountain lion just wouldn't leave you, is that it? Maybe you felt responsible for its death?"

"Might say so."

"And, afterward, did you find yourself looking even harder for these Oval Cross men? Or did you stay around the ranch after that?"

Pasque was silent for a long time. Finally he spoke. "I guess I stuck close to the ranch. I just didn't think they'd gone north after that."

Evans laughed. "That's not it!" he boomed. "A little wisdom came when you killed that mountain lion. Something in your head told you that branding iron could have come from anywhere. Those men could have picked it up on the trail, or they might have salvaged it from some old pile of ranch scrap. They could be range detectives, looking for rustlers that dropped it. No, Pasque, something told you that a branding iron could mean nothing. At least not enough to kill someone like you killed that lion. You might not know it, but you had a visit from Old Man Wisdom, and he said . . . 'Pasque, why should anybody else die? Maybe you'll die yourself. Maybe some fella will die that didn't do anything.' Old Man Wisdom," Evans repeated. He stopped and smoked a while and had some of his wine.

"Do you know what the Cheyenne say?"

"Can't say as I speak Cheyenne," Pasque said.

"The Cheyenne would say that you had ridden northward through your medicine circle. Only your medicine circle is as big as the whole territory. Ever see a medicine circle? A sun dance, maybe?"

Pasque thought a minute. "Saw that wagon wheel thing once, up in the Bighorns. Big circle on the ground. Old trapper up there, he said somethin' about medicine, too."

Thompson looked serious. "He was right," he said. "You're talking about that big circle of stones with the lines through it that look like spokes, aren't you?"

"Sounds like it," Pasque replied. "Kinda high on a sort of flat top place."

"Medicine circle," Thompson said. "Probably a place where they took boys to teach them about life being a circle. Lakota do the same thing."

"Life is a circle, huh?" Pasque said. "I heard Gw . . . Missus Pendragon say that once."

"Take some more of the wine, there," Thompson said. "You see, Indians don't have clocks and calendars. No roads, no fences to keep reminding them that they need to keep going in straight lines. Ever think of that?"

"Guess not," Pasque answered.

"They see life in circles. Circles everywhere . . . the clouds taking the river water back to the mountains again, flesh turning to grass so the animals eat it and make it flesh again, the sunrise moving across the horizon and back again, spring turning into summer, winter into spring again. They follow the herds, moving from high country to the flat prairie, from the cold north to the warm south.

"Look around. Out here you can see the horizon in every direction, can't you? It makes a big circle around you. Every direction has a different power to it. That's the medicine. Knowing where your place is in the world-circle. If you know that, you know where you have been and where you might go. Great are the ones who can put the medicine of all four directions into balance with each other. The *wakan*, the spirits, they treat those men very well!"

Pasque sipped from his mug and stared into the glowing coals of the fire a moment before he spoke again. "So," he said, "these Indian kids learn all this stuff in that wagon wheel thing, like goin' to school?"

"No," the blacksmith smiled, his teeth shining in the darkening twilight. "They only learn *about* it. The real medicine school is right here" — he stamped his foot on the ground — "and out there" — he pointed eastward toward the Great Plains — "and there" — he pointed north — "and there, and there, and all around us. This whole country is your medicine circle."

"The whole country?"

"Yes. Out by the Missouri there's a high bluff where yellow rocks are found, rocks you can't find anywhere else for miles. Far to the south, past the Arkansas River, there's a certain mountain that is always green. Far north, beyond the Tetons, but not that far, there is a mountain that looks like a mesa and is white stone. Many travelers have mistaken it for snow. And west of here, where I am going now, there is a cañon so deep, they say, that the sun never reaches the bottom. It is always black down there.

"And those, my friend, are the boundaries of the Indian medicine circle. As I said . . . only the wisest of their men have seen it. But you're luckier than most white men, Pasque. Few white men have ever stepped into the medicine wheel."

"I guess you don't mean that stone thing up in Wyoming, then," Pasque said seriously. Whether he wanted to or not, whether he liked it or not, he found himself getting serious about all this stuff that Thompson was saying.

"You went north and found a little wisdom, didn't you? Something about darkness and death? And it was white all around you?" Thompson asked him. "Well, now you're in the east, and you're thinking you have learned something here by my fire. East is toward the sun, the eagle direction. Illumination. Seeing the light, some call it."

"I guess I don't follow you," Pasque said, but inside he knew that he understood. He wanted the blacksmith to tell him more, but he didn't want it to look like he was being taken in by all this Cheyenne and Lakota superstition.

In the dark, with the glow of the fire fading, the figure of Evans looked even larger than before. In that fireglow, his face looked brown and weathered like old leather.

"I'll be straight with you, then," the blacksmith said. "Your next ride will be south, because the man you're looking for lives beyond the mining camps, past the river. Not the Oval Cross men. The other man. But before you can learn anything from him, you'll also have to ride west."

"I still want those two fellas with the branding iron."

Evans laughed. "*You* know the man I mean. Before you find the other two, you have to find him. If you don't find him before spring, you may never find him at all."

"So you say I need to go ridin' off in all directions? Don't sound too sensible to me."

"If you were a Cheyenne boy, you would learn that the west is the direction of the bear, the dark place for looking within. You need to look within. As for south, that's the green direction. You went north, and you ended up thinking a lot about that dead lion. Did you ever watch the way a buffalo seems to think, slow and thoughtful?"

"Yeah, but I never thought much of it before."

"You came east, and you are beginning to see a very big medicine picture. Like you were high over it, looking down. It's just beginning, but it is beginning. The eagle can see where things are."

"I can see like an eagle? That what you want to say?"

"You see more than you want to say, Pasque. Much more. You aren't about to admit it, but most of what I'm saying is sinking in. Now, when you go south, go like the mouse. Go quiet and look all around. Stop and do small things. Touch things. Trust yourself. Trust everything. Trust everybody you meet."

At this, Pasque glared at Thompson in disbelief. "Trust everybody? Like the men who murdered my brothers? Oh, sure, I'll trust 'em, all right . . . right up until I cut 'em down."

"Pasque," Thompson's voice was firm and soothing, "do you think I don't know how it feels to want justice? With two of my own family maybe dead or jailed right now, maybe needing me? But I'm telling you, we've got to change. Justice isn't in the six-gun any more, or in the rope tossed over a cottonwood branch."

"Then just forget it, you're sayin'?" Pasque said.

"No such thing. Remember it as long as you can. But before you go in search of these two men, you'd better go look to find yourself. And you start by finding that other man first."

Evans's wife came up to the darkening fire with another bottle of wine to replenish their mugs, and Evans insisted that they make a toast to each of the stars. But they ran out of wine long before they ran out of stars, and Pasque noticed that some of those stars were starting to jump around, when he tried to point his mug at them.

Pasque and Thompson went their separate ways to their separate bedrolls.

Go look to find yourself, the blacksmith had told him. What kind of sense did that make? As much sense as looking for a man seven foot tall who could get shot through the chest and ride away, laughing.

Pasque's sleep was deep with dreams. In the first dream he was in a blinding blizzard. In the next dream he was somehow soaring above the summer prairie. Then he dreamed about stumbling into the blackest corner of a pitch-black cave. He woke up in a sweat and struggled up into a kneeling position, looking around and unable to remember where he was. It was getting light, and he was in a clearing in the sagebrush.

Pasque rolled his head, which hurt like hell, and looked over at the horses tied nearby. His riding saddle was there by the head of his bedroll. He felt under it and found his Colt in its holster there, tucked underneath out of the night dew. As his head cleared, he remembered what had happened the night before. The dreams stopped whirling around in his head, and he began to remember where he was.

He got to his feet, even though each move of his head made that pain slosh around inside. He stared at the empty clearing. Evan Thompson, the smoking forge, the old-fashioned wagon, the quiet woman, and the little boy were gone.

The fire pit where the woman had cooked was still there by the frame of the *ramada*. Pasque walked over and knelt down to touch the coals. They were as cold as if there had been no fire there for many days. He saw his own tracks and those of a much larger boot. He saw a woman's footprints, and some that were probably the boy's. But the edges of the tracks were crumbly and eroded and sage leaves had blown into some of them, and they were as dry as the sand around them. They were old. Many days old.

Pasque stood up straight again, and the blinding yellow rays of the rising sun struck him full in the face. He blinked, rubbed his forehead, looked straight into the sun for a second, and then looked south. He was never much of a believer in such things. Until now, he had never even thought much about it.

If there was such a thing as fate or medicine or whatever, and if he *did* believe in it, he seemed somehow to know that his own would lie somewhere in that direction. The green direction. South.

Or Thompson was just an old blacksmith who drank too much and needed a shave. Either way, Old Buffalo Coat had said he lived somewhere south of the Arkansas and that's where he was going to go.

CHAPTER
SEVEN

The Price of Gold

Gwen gradually pried the story out of him during supper one night. He told them how the blacksmith had disappeared. He did his best to describe all the talk about the bear wisdom and buffalo and eagles and mice and medicine circles. But he soon found that he couldn't get it all straight. He seemed to know what it was all about in his mind, but he couldn't put it into words. There was one thing he could tell them clearly, though: he knew that he would have to leave the Keystone and go looking for the home of Old Buffalo Coat, the Christmas stranger.

He spent the next few days getting ready. He picked out a good pack horse and put his food and gear together, repaired his saddle and checked his bridle, and cleaned and oiled his guns. Mary fixed a particularly large supper on the night before he was to leave.

"I'd like you promise me somethin', Uncle Art," Pasque said as they were eating.

"Sure," Art said. "What is it?"

"If Link or Moore come back here while I'm gone, I want you to keep 'em here till I get back."

"I'll do my best," Art said. And then as if to change the subject: "You think you'll catch up to our buffalo coat stranger somewhere around Denver City? Or south of there?"

"I don't know," Pasque said. "Didn't he say his place was at the minin' camps on the river, or somewhere south of the camps?"

"I don't recall which it was," Art said. "Either way, it sounded like he said it was south of the mining district. A man might pick up the Platte River around Cherry Creek and follow it upstream into the mountains, see what he finds."

Art went into the office and came back with an old map. He unrolled it and spread it on the table.

"I was down that way once, but it was quite a few years ago." He pointed to a long black line on the map. "The Arkansas starts up here in the mountains at a place called Leadville. Then it gets out onto the plains and goes through this place marked Bent's Fort. But Bent's Fort isn't there any more. They say Bent himself blew it up. Didn't want the Army to have it. If you get that far east, you might get to Fort Lyon. Somebody probably heard of him there, if you ask around."

"What if I don't get that far east?" Pasque said.

"There's lots more rivers south of there. This one here," Art said, pointing to the map, "we called that one the Picketwire. That could be the river Old Buffalo Coat was talking about. But by that time, you'll be in Spanish country. Superstitious bunch of people. And watch out for those damn' chiles they eat." Gwen raised an eyebrow at Art's choice of words, but he went on as if he didn't see it. "Next you come to the Cimarron River, and then the Canadian. Then you'll be darn' near in Mexico."

"Tell you what," Pasque said. "If I get clear to Mexico and don't find hide nor hair of him, I'm gonna turn back."

"I'm sure that nobody would blame you," Gwen smiled. "We hope you'll be back before summer is over."

Art frowned at his map. He hadn't thought about that long trip he had taken so many years ago, when he was younger than Pasque. That country down there wasn't anything like the Wyoming Territory. It was a dry, strange country, where the Mexicans believed in witches and the Apaches believed in mountain gods.

By June, Pasque was well into the mining district. He had been traveling slow and easy, saving the horses, stopping at ranches and farms. He was never a man who talked to people easily, but he gradually got into a kind of pattern of doing it. Usually he would stop at a livery stable in some small, crossroads town, or at a ranch or settler's cabin, ask to water his horses, then start to talk about the weather and talk about all the new people who seemed to be moving into the territory. Eventually he would get around to asking about the big stranger on the big horse.

He asked about the blacksmith named Evan Thompson, too, because Pasque had a feeling that, if he could find Thompson, he would find Old Buffalo Coat. Between stops, he sat straight in the saddle, his light blue eyes always on the move, always watching for some sign of the man he sought. Going through a town, Pasque rode slow past barber shops and saloons, leaning over to get a good look in the windows for a giant figure of a man. He studied the horses at every hitching rail and in every livery corral, hoping to find that one particularly massive saddle horse.

But everywhere he went, all he saw was ordinary men and ordinary horses. People he talked to had never seen such a thing or had just arrived in town; none had seen the man Pasque described, although most of them had seen some unusual character of one sort or another.

"Now, if it was a short, one-legged man you'd be after . . ."

"Well, I *did* see a skinny kid last week, must have been six and a half feet tall, walkin' and carryin' a pack with a shovel in it, headin' for the mines . . ."

"Ol' Eli, now, he's big and has a beard down to his belly. 'Course, he's so near-sighted, he can't tell mule from elk . . ."

Pasque crossed a hill one morning and found himself looking down into a miserable little collection of tar-paper shacks at the mouth of a cañon. All the trees had been cut for firewood and mine props. Stock had eaten both hillsides bare so that it was nothing but dirt and gullies and clumps of mostly dead brush.

Pasque heard cussing and shouting. A lot of cussing and shouting. He rode down the hill carefully and easily until he could look between the shacks. He saw two men with clubs beating a third man who lay huddled upon the ground, trying to protect his head from the blows and kicks.

"That doesn't seem fair," Pasque said. He unwrapped the pack horse's lead rope from his saddle horn, hoping the animal had the sense to stay put. He pulled out his Colt.

The two men heard his horse running at them, and they spread out fast. But they didn't run away. Pasque saw that they were ragged and thin and filthy. Such men were all over the mining country, out of luck and half crazy because of it. These two, with hunger in their hollow faces and their torn clothes hanging from their starved bodies, had been hijacking the third man's pack string.

Pasque galloped on, leveling his Colt at the man on his right. But the one on the left let out a howl and came at him, swinging a busted pick handle. Pasque didn't want to shoot, but, even with the muzzle looking straight at him, the man kept coming, lunging for the bridle and swinging the pick handle. Pasque swung his Colt back to the other one, the one on the right. That one was coming at him, too, and now the horse was beginning to rear up and dance around, making it hard to aim.

When the shot finally came, everything seemed to stop dead for a second. Even the horse stood still, eyes rolling wild, muscles tense. Now the one man was running away down the gully, holding his arm where the bullet had ripped through. But the other one lashed out with his pick handle and caught Pasque full on the thigh with a bruising blow. Pasque brought the .45 around and fired.

109

Through the gunsmoke Pasque saw the second figure running for his life down the trail. And suddenly he was alone with the third man.

Pasque got down and helped the muleskinner to his feet.

"Hurt bad?" he asked.

"Not bad," the man answered. "Could be worse. They was just startin' in on me when you showed up. Grateful to ya."

At first, Pasque had taken the muleskinner for an old-timer. But up close, he could see that the man wasn't much older than himself. From any distance at all, the baggy overalls and oversize boots and the dirty shirt and beard made him look like an antique.

"They call me . . . ," the 'skinner began, but suddenly pointed down the trail where Pasque had left his pack horse. "Hey! The thievin' bastards are after your gear now!"

Pasque was back in the saddle and had the horse wheeled around almost before the muleskinner had finished his sentence. The two skeletal bandits were frantically trying to get the pack horse calmed down so they could run it off. One had the lead rope, the other had a hand in the halter, and men and horse were slipping and twisting around in a wild little rodeo.

This time they didn't wait around to face that .45 again. Pasque cut two more shots toward the running figures, and then grabbed up the lead rope and dallied it around his saddle horn. He didn't aim to hit the thieves. He just wanted to make them a little more interested in speed.

★ ★ ★

"Name's Thomas Thorson," the muleskinner said.

"Pasque."

"Sounds like a French name," the 'skinner said. "I'm Finnish myself, at least my folks was Finns a few generations back."

Thorson started to boil up some coffee, and, when he went to dig his pot and can out of his panniers, he also came across some biscuits left over from breakfast. Pasque took one, and wondered which breakfast it might have been — it sure hadn't been within the past week or so.

"You live here?" Pasque asked, while they waited for the sooty tin pot to come to a boil. The place looked like a ghost town. Thorson squatted by the twig fire. Pasque stayed on his feet, still watching his back trail in case the other two came back.

"Sometimes. Mostly I camp here on my way up to the mines, like today, an' generally it's pretty safe 'cause this town ain't had anybody in it for more'n a year since they all moved on after the gold, you know. They say there's silver farther on up, over the divide."

"That where those two were headed?" Pasque nodded in the direction the thieves had gone.

"I s'pose." Thorson dumped a handful of coffee into the pot and smiled with satisfaction at the froth that boiled over into the fire. "Prob'ly figured to take my gear and grub and mules and go hunt themselves up a rich strike, but these here hills are full of busted-out miners like that, doin' anythin' for one more chance, one more dang hole in the ground."

Pasque drank the thick coffee and chewed on the tough biscuit. *Silver,* he thought. *And gold. Well, my giant friend, Old Mr. Buffalo Coat, might just be a mining man. Could be worth a look.*

"Mind if I ride along with you a while?" Pasque asked.

"Mind? Hell, I'd pay you to. Two of us, we'd stand a whole lot better chance of gettin' this string of jacks up to the mines, 'cause there's no tellin' how desperate them boys along the way has got. Tell you what, when we get there, an' I get paid my freight, you and me, we'll figure you out a share o' the profits."

Thorson said he'd never seen or heard of a huge man with a curly beard who rode a monstrous horse, but the idea of it set him off on a long, garbled account of an old Finnish legend he remembered. As far as Pasque could make out, it concerned some kind of hammer-swinging hero who went around Finland scaring people to death.

The story and the coffee ran out at about the same time. Thorson dumped the grounds on the twig fire, shoved the dirty pot and his battered cup back into the pannier, and announced that it was time to start the mule train — all six of them — for the mines.

"Upcañon?" Pasque said, riding to the front with his pack horse in tow. "That the way to this mine you're goin' to?"

"That's right." Thorson's hand made a chopping movement in that direction. "She's practically due west of here."

*   *   *

Around every bend, on every hillside, Pasque saw the dark mine mouths — holes too low to allow a man to walk without making himself into a hunchback. From every hole there poured a yellow landslide of broken rock, and the mountains that used to be covered with forests were now covered with nothing but stumps. Twice they rode past stamping mills where monotonous hammers rose and fell against ore being fed to them from high-sided wagons. The river turning the water wheel was nothing but thin, yellow mud. Yellow mud made silt dams in the river. Yellow mud stained the rocks as high as the spring flood mark.

As he rode farther and farther west, Pasque felt a thirst for the clear-running creeks of the Keystone range. He remembered the tiny stream running through the chokecherry thicket where he had met Gwen and how clean and fresh it felt there. Thinking of her and the way her eyes had smiled into his, he started to feel trapped here in the cañon — it was steadily closing in on him.

He looked at the stumps and thought of pine forest foothills where cattle could graze and where a man could build his cabin and corrals from the woods and still see trees everywhere he looked. He saw miserable pale shoots of grass struggling to grow in the yellow silt next to the yellow mudflow river, and remembered one stretch of prairie range where the bluestem brushed his stirrups and grew so thick that he could look back and not see his own trail.

As for the men he saw in the cañon. There were silent, brooding men hunched on wagon seats, listlessly whipping the lines on the backs of tired-looking mules,

113

hauling rock to be crushed. Others crouched beside the water, trying to pan nuggets, staring into the pans without hope. Still other men were going downstream, busted and heading back to beg or steal another grubstake, or starting home to St. Louis or St. Joseph, or to find gold-rush widows back East.

These were the ones he watched closely. Their eyes were red from months in the tunnels, hammering the granite walls into dust. If they were riding, they slouched as if they were still bent over in those low holes; if they walked, they slouched and shuffled.

All for the gold.

For three days, Pasque and Thorson urged the loaded mules up the cañon. Three nights, each one colder and higher. They seemed to be going back into winter. Sometimes Pasque would catch a glimpse of a snow-topped peak and would wish Gwen could see it, it was so beautiful. Far away, and beautiful.

On the last night before they reached the Glory Hole, they camped in the shelter of a cliff, a small trickle of a stream that miraculously still ran clear, and wood for a good fire. Supper was beans, but at that altitude no amount of boiling could soften them. They had coffee that would float a lead bullet and Thorson's biscuits. The man had a knack for taking fresh biscuits and making them taste like they had ridden in a rawhide pannier. Pasque took a bite of biscuit. Make that a green rawhide pannier.

"It ain't right," Pasque found himself saying, after supper. The two men were having their smoke before turning in.

"What's that?" Thorson asked.

"Aw, all this." Pasque waved his hand toward the yellow river and the gullied hills. "All these men. Gettin' sick, killin' each other, stealin' . . . for what? Suppose they did get rich, get their big houses and buggies and servants and such. Why, there's nothin' to a life like that."

"I s'pose you'd rather be ridin' through steer shit at forty bucks a month and beans."

"Well, my cowboy *frijoles* are a damn' sight better than these elk turds that you miners and jack-whackers call beans," Pasque replied. "But I'm talkin' about bein' in the open country, where a man has some self-respect.

"Tell you another thing, too," he went on, "the ranch I work on, we treat the land right, or we draw our pay and move on. You graze it, you make your living from it, you watch out that it doesn't get overgrazed into gullies. You take care of your running water, because you need it. Take care of you neighbors, too. Hell, it's every man for what he can get up here, but out in ranch territory you look after other people."

Thorson rolled himself another cigarette and looked into Pasque's eyes. "So," he said, "if it's so good, how come you're chasin' around in this country?"

"Told you. I'm lookin' for a man. But you know what? Comin' up here sorta cleared my head. I got some honor at stake, you see, but, when I see this torn-up country and these miners that aren't anythin' but a bunch of human gophers . . . except that gophers don't murder each other over a bunch of rocks . . . I see where I belong. Get this hunt over with, and that's where I'm goin' back to.

"I'll tell you somethin' else, just for the sake of talking about it. I'm not gonna be a forty-dollar buckaroo all my life. Might not live through the year anyways, but, if I do, I'm gonna find my piece of range and live with it. And every time I feel like cussin' the weather, or the price of steers, or don't feel like helpin' my neighbors, I'm gonna remember this damn' bald cañon. Hell, Thorson, look at those mine holes over on that slope there. Those gold mines are nothin' but graves. Graves with living men in 'em."

Thorson stretched and flipped his cigarette end into the fire, then reached inside his patched coat to scratch at something infesting his long underwear.

"Well," he said, "maybe you're right, and I'm just a dumb jack-whacker, I guess, an' never had much learnin', but, sittin' here listenin' to you, I sure have found out one thing I never knew was true."

"What's that?"

"That whoever says cowboys don't have much to say is a damn' liar."

Pasque grinned and rolled down into his blankets, listening to the wind play tag across the peak tops and the little creek clucking and bumping down over the rocks nearby. Tomorrow they would be at the Glory Hole camp, and the day after that he would be heading out again, maybe to find the mountain source of that one big river Thorson had told him about, the river that lay to the south.

116

*   *   *

The sound of hoofbeats came at dawn. Pasque was finally in a deep sleep after spending most of the night curled up with his teeth chattering. He was dreaming of a certain winter day, back before the big man had paid his Christmas visit, a day when Gwen came in from the cold with her cheeks all glowing and a bright twinkle to her eyes. It was starting out to be a dream with some interesting possibilities to it.

The hoofs stopped. As he came awake, he was aware of someone talking in low tones, and a lot of shuffling noises down where the mules were tied. Thorson struggled to get out of his bedroll, waving his Navy revolver.

"Hey! Damn your eyes, get away from them mules! You're dead meat, friend! I'll perferate your gizzards an' leave y' for the buzzards t' skin!"

Pasque got his own blankets and ground tarp unwrapped and grabbed up his Winchester. Two ugly-looking *hombres* on horseback were in among the mules, cutting them loose from the picket and spooking them off.

The two rustlers turned and saw two lanky men standing there in their long johns, one of them pointing a pistol and the other shucking a shell into a Winchester. They suddenly decided that the mules would slow them down.

Thorson let fly with his old cap-and-ball revolver. The first chamber went off with an echoing *Phlow!*, the second one misfired, as did the third, and the fourth sounded more like a slamming door than a pistol shot. Wet powder.

117

"Well, shoot!" he yelled at Pasque. "Let 'em have it! Shoot!"

Pasque was shivering in the cold mountain air, but he took steady aim and splattered a rock off to the right of the galloping horses. His second shot kicked up dirt to the left of the lead rider, and then the two mule thieves were over the edge of the valley shelf and gone. Three mules walked to the edge, looked over, looked back at camp, and lowered their heads to crop the thin grass.

"Dammit!" Thorson exploded, pounding the top of his pistol with his fist, and glaring at Pasque. Pasque was working his way into his Levi's, while he looked to see if there were any hot coals left in the fire.

"You didn't even try to hit those thievin' snakes!" Thorson yelled.

"Nope," Pasque said. He piled twigs over the warm coals and fanned them with his hat until he got a fire going.

"Didn't even try to hit 'em," Thorson mumbled, setting the pot on to boil.

"No reason," Pasque said. "Why start killin', when they didn't get away with anything? The next thing you know, their *compañeros* will start killin' first, just to be on the safe side."

"You could've shot their horses. Maybe we could've caught them, then."

"I won't kill a horse, unless it's hurt bad, like a broken leg. I won't shoot a horse for you, and I won't shoot a man without havin' to. Of course," Pasque smiled, "they don't have to know that."

Thorson was still mumbling as he sliced bacon into the pan. "Now those sons-a-bitches will be back, you know, and, even when we get to the camp, they're gonna be layin' for me to get my mules. Should've shot 'em."

"Well," Pasque laughed, "then, I guess, I'll have to stick with you a few days longer than I'd planned. They'll get the idea and probably go look for easier pickin's."

He rolled his blankets into his ground tarp and set the roll next to the fire to make a seat. "Meanwhile, I'd better show you how to store your gunpowder and how to load that old cap-and-ball of yours. That was the most pathetic shootin' I ever did see."

CHAPTER
EIGHT

And the Third was a Priest

The foreman at the mine counted coins from a strongbox into a small pile on the battered desk. He wasn't angry or disappointed, just tired and bored. He counted the pile a second time and shoved it across the desk to Pasque.

"Hate to see you go," he said. "With you leavin' and McCarty goin' back to Saint Louis, I'm gonna be shorthanded for guards."

Pasque picked up the coins and shoved them into the pocket of his Levi's. "I appreciate the work," he said. "And the money's gonna come in handy. But I got a ways to go."

"Well, if that ain't enough of a stake, you can sure stay on another month. The old mine ain't played out yet."

"No. Thanks, but I'll just be goin'."

"If you want to hang around another week, your friend Thorson oughta be comin' in with a load of stuff. You'd probably like to see him before you go."

"I guess not. Trouble finds him like lightning finds a chimney." Pasque was headed out the door of the shed. "See you."

"Yeah," the foreman said. "See you."

It was only one of the dance-hall girls. The front of her green dress showed the bare curves of her breasts. Her lips were bright red, almost orange in the light of the oil lamps, and her heavy rouge made her face look feverish.

She smiled to find him staring at her, and made a little motion in his direction as if she were starting to walk toward him. But Pasque quickly turned his gaze to the dealer.

"Changed my mind," he said. "Deal me in."

The dealer, who had seen the woman and the smile, lifted a quizzical eyebrow, until he saw the way Pasque's cold eyes were looking at him. "Seven card," he said. "Joker wild."

That night, Pasque lay on his cot in the mine shack, unable to get to sleep. And when he finally dropped off, his restless dreams were full of women. Each one was a stranger, yet each one looked somewhat like his uncle's wife. Each one smiled and beckoned. Some seemed to be whores or dance-hall girls, and others seemed to be just everyday beautiful women. Toward dawn, as he twisted in his blankets, a dream came in which he saw Gwen rising up from her bath and sliding a long white gown down over her body. And then she was leaning over his bed, her breasts visible through the open neckline, her smile holding an offer and a promise.

That same morning he told the foreman that he was quitting his job as a mine guard. The next dawn saw

Pasque, with his pack horse in tow, riding south down the mule trail beside a roiling, yellowish creek that would lead, eventually, to the big river called the Arkansas.

He rode through a low range known as the Wet Mountains, and, when he was in the foothills once again, Pasque felt a sense of freedom and relief. The grim mines were behind him, and so were the logged-over mountains and cold, dark cañons. He was back in piñon pine and juniper country, country where a man atop a horse could see for miles, where the sunshine always seemed warm and clean, and where the sand was good underfoot. Everywhere along the upper Arkansas, where it ran crashing through its cañons, he had seen men who were out of work and out of hope, men who squatted in lean-to shacks or leaky tents, wishing they were some place where they could get a job. A job doing anything. He stopped and talked to them, asking about the giant man. None had seen him, or anyone like him. But then, as they usually pointed out, they were not from this territory originally. They were only stuck here a while, waiting for a grubstake. Then they would get rich and go back home.

As he rode, Pasque thought about how his months of wandering had started with Old Buffalo Coat at the Keystone. Then he had taken this detour into the mountains, probably because of that other giant of a man, the blacksmith.

Then a third large man showed up. And the third man was a priest.

123

Pasque slid out of his bedroll early that morning. The sky was light, but the sun was still below the horizon. He shivered in his long johns, while he got a small fire going, then picked up his scrap of towel and his soap and his Winchester and went to the edge of the river to get it over with. It always felt good afterward, to be washed and shaved, it was just that it was so damn' cold doing it.

He chose an opening in the willows on the riverbank where he could still keep an eye on his campfire and the horses. The robber must have been hiding in the piñons, watching and waiting for his chance, which came when Pasque knelt down to splash water on his face. But the sound of running feet and the whinnies of spooked horses made Pasque turn in time to see the man running out of his camp. He was running with the saddlebags that held most of Pasque's money, all of his extra ammunition, spare shirt, and socks — almost everything except the bedroll and cook kit.

Pasque broke out of the brush on the run, raising his Winchester and cocking it as he drew a bead at the fleeing thief. He swung the rifle to lead him like he would lead a deer running through the trees, figuring where the next opening was and aiming for it, and waiting for the first glimpse of him to come into the opening so he could squeeze off the shot.

That was when an oversize hand seemed to come out of nowhere and grip the barrel and force it down. "You don't want to do that," a deep voice said.

Pasque looked up. He was expecting to find himself staring down the barrel of another gun. But he was looking at a priest, instead. A priest in a plain, black hat, a plain black suit, black shirt with a white collar, and a long, leather riding coat. And while Pasque had a full six foot of height himself, the priest was head and shoulders taller than he. Slightly smaller than Evan Thompson and quite a bit smaller than Old Buffalo Coat, still he was a hell of a big man.

The priest let go of the gun. "He's gone now," he said.

Pasque only glared at him, his eyes reflecting the new morning sky to the east. His money and ammunition were gone, too. And that old Dragoon revolver, the one he would need when he finally found his giant. Pasque had only one hope that he would survive his meeting with the giant, and that hope was that the antique cap-and-ball pistol held the secret to the trick of getting shot without getting killed.

"Well" — Pasque drew out his words carefully, stepping away from the priest — "I guess now I'll have to saddle up and track him down."

They heard hoofbeats racing away. "Probably has a good start on you by now," the priest said. "We may as well have coffee first, and break some bread together." He walked over to the buckskin riding mule that had been left ground reined and led it into camp.

For years afterward, as often as Pasque told this story, he never could explain what kept him from riding after the thief and shooting him down. He still had his Winchester and the Colt, which he had stuck under his saddle for the night, and, even with the time it would have taken to saddle up and pack the camp gear,

125

he still could have tracked the man. It was not respect for the collar of a priest that kept him from his pursuit, because Pasque was not a particularly religious man. All he knew was that he was in the presence of a kind of calmness, a calmness from which he could not break free.

"We pray," the priest said. "We are always praying that the men of this new country . . . men such as yourself . . . will soon be able to value human life above human property. To kill for things that we can live without . . . it is not a custom upon which to build a society, do you think?"

So Pasque added water to the pot, built up the fire, and sliced some bacon to fry alongside of the *refritos* in the pan. The priest took a bag from his saddle horn and brought forth a thick loaf of Indian bread and a brick of cheese.

"That's a good-looking mule you've got there," Pasque said, after he had relaxed enough to start making conversation.

"Yes," the priest said. "She's carried me many a long mile, and without complaint."

"Traveling through, are you?"

"Yes." The priest brought out his tin plate and cup, and offered Pasque a hand the size of a Stetson. "The name is Nicholas," he said. "Father Nicholas, if you prefer."

"Pasque."

"Pasque. And you are also just traveling through this country, are you?"

"Might say that. Sort of lookin' for a man." Pasque fished the pan out of the fire and set it to cool, and poured a handful of coffee into the boiling water.

"Anyone I'd know? I do travel through here about once a year. A bit later than this, usually."

"Big man," Pasque said. "Bigger than you. Has a dark beard, rides the biggest saddle horse I've ever seen. Last time I saw him he had on a big old buffalo coat."

Father Nicholas cut bread and cheese into the plates and ladled himself some of the *frijoles*.

"I work at the cathedral in Santa Fé," he said, as if that information was somehow connected. "Once a year I carry special documents to Father . . . excuse me . . . to *Bishop* Machebeuf in Denver City. Would that coffee be ready yet, do you think?"

They ate, and they talked about riding mules and speculated about the thief. They had the usual travelers' discussion of weather and trails and accidents and hazards, and gradually the talk came back again to the big stranger Pasque was searching for.

"You say you never ran across this big rider that I was tellin' you about?" Pasque asked.

"Oh, yes. I have certainly encountered him," Father Nicholas said. "Of course, that was before . . . ," and with his fork he pointed to his clerical collar.

"Not around here, then?" Pasque continued.

"No, not around here. But it was here that I came in search of him afterward. Just as you have done. And I found sanctuary and the opportunity to begin a

127

vocation at the Cathedral Saint Francis in Santa Fé not long after that."

Pasque ate in silence and watched Father Nicholas. In his months of asking people whether they had seen the stranger, he had gotten an instinct that told him when to be quiet and let the talk dance around the subject. He usually found out more that way, than by asking more questions. The priest went on.

"Like many men, I came to chase gold strike rumors at Pike's Peak . . . a good many years ago. The work was hard, and the life was brutal. One day, dead broke, I went to town looking for some work so as to earn myself a stake. It was so I could go on with my pointless prospecting. And I found a job. I was hired by a saloon owner to keep the peace in his establishment.

"I'm larger than most men, as you can see, and working with pick and shovel had made my muscles hard. I was a very effective bouncer. Sometimes, when I picked up an obnoxious drunk to toss him out of the place, men would wager on how far out in the street he would land. Once or twice a week my employer would even promote a bare-knuckle boxing match, pitting me against all comers. At that, I was very good. Whenever some luckless bully managed to land a punch that really hurt me, I would become enraged. The more I was hurt, the more violent and vengeful I became, with no regard for rules or fair play or even human life. I think, had I gone on, that I would have eventually killed someone with my fists.

"And then one evening, rather late, your giant stranger rode into town on his enormous horse. Seeing the size of him, my employer turned down his wager. Clearly, it would be an unfair fight, and he would lose money. But Hochland persisted . . .''

"Hochland?" Pasque interrupted.

"That is his name. Tallak Hochland. He offered a bargain . . . a challenge to my pride. He said that we would stand face to face, bare knuckled, and he would allow me the first three blows. Should he still be conscious after that, he would deliver three of the same to me."

Father Nicholas set his coffee cup down near the pot to indicate that Pasque should refill it. He stood up in the stance of a prize fighter, his huge fists curled into sledgehammers. As he got into his story, his voice took on a slightly Irish flavor.

"My first punch," he went on, "went to his chin like a pile driver, straight from the shoulder, like this." He demonstrated — it had enough force to drive a fence post through a brick wall.

"And he never wavered. Just stood there, waiting for the next two. My only chance, I figured, was to hit that jaw with a left haymaker, hard, like this" — his left hand came whistling in a curve — "and, while his chin was still moving in that direction, run into it with my best right-hand haymaker, like this . . . uuhhh!" Father Nicholas unclenched his fists and sat down again next to the fire. He was quiet for a moment before continuing. "I broke his neck."

The statement was simple, and spoken with a tone of awe. "Others saw it. They heard it. His head flew to one side when my left hit him, and, when my right hand caught his chin, his head popped back the other way. There was a cracking noise, and I looked, and he was still standing there. But his head had fallen over toward one shoulder, like this." Father Nicholas cocked his head as far as it would go.

"Hochland only laughed. He just straightened his head with his two hands and went out of the saloon. He got on that big horse and challenged me to come to his house, where he would return my blows. It was nearly a year before I found him again."

Pasque sat dumbfounded. "How did he live through being hit like that?" he asked.

"Ah, Pasque. I don't know. To this day, I don't know. Some of the saloon regulars said it was the thick beard, that it cushioned my blows, that he concealed some kind of noise-maker to make the snapping sound of a man's neck breaking, that he was one of those circus freaks, a contortionist. But I was the one behind the fist, and I know that I hit solid flesh and bone, and I know it should have killed him.

"Shall we clean up these things, now, and be off?"

Without asking and without discussing it, Father Nicholas joined Pasque in his ride southward. Along wagon roads and wide trails they rode side by side all day. Twice Pasque asked about the priest's second encounter with Hochland, but the answer was evasive. All he learned was that the priest had found Hochland and had lived to tell about it. That, and the obvious fact that something had changed him from being a barroom fighter to being a priest.

As they rode, Father Nicholas pointed out birds and named them; he told Pasque the names of flowers and shrubs. He told him what the mountains were called and spoke as if the mountains, like the birds and plants, had living spirits of their own. The priest took great joy in each new glimpse of life, whether it was a rabbit running in the dirt track ahead of the horses or an antelope suddenly breaking out of the cedars and piñons.

At last they came to a place where water ran and the grass was rich for the animals, and they could have dinner and a noon rest in the shade of cottonwoods. Lying there, cooling off, and letting his back relax from riding all morning, Pasque again asked about Hochland.

"Think I'll find him?" he said.

"I think you will. And when you do, will you be afraid?"

No man had ever asked Pasque if he were afraid. Even when he was a kid and the older boys would pick on him, it only took one look at those clear, steady eyes to convince them that he was not scared. After their run-in with the bear, Gwen had asked him — "Weren't you afraid?" — and all he could do was look at her and shake his head and say: "I guess I didn't have time to think about it."

But this time, when Father Nicholas asked the question . . .

"I expect I will. Kinda hard to avoid it," Pasque said.

Father Nicholas brought out a pouch of piñon nuts and offered a handful to Pasque. They relaxed in the

131

shade, cracking the shells in their teeth and eating the sweet nutmeat. The priest held a particularly fat one between his fingers and studied it.

"How do the trees know where to scatter this seed, do you suppose?" he asked.

"Beats me," Pasque replied. "Probably don't know. They just let the wind and the squirrels do it for 'em."

"And they can't be sure of the outcome, can they? The trees, I mean."

"I guess not."

"Faith."

"What?"

"Faith. You see, Pasque, those piñons up there on the hills, they have to put their trust in the wind and the animals to carry their seed to the right places. It's like when you're traveling, and you have to trust strangers to tell you which direction to go. And the outcome . . . well, I think nature puts the seed in the ground and has faith that it will grow, faith that the same tree will be reborn out of its own seed."

Pasque looked at Father Nicholas. "You give most of the sermons, down at Santa Fé?" he asked.

Nicholas laughed. "No sermon intended. Shall we be on our way?"

By late afternoon they reached a high divide overlooking the Arkansas. They could see mile after mile of a thin green line of trees that marked the river's meandering course all the way out into the Kansas Territory. Behind them were the snow-tipped granite crags of the Spanish Peaks, which the Indians called the *Wah-to-Yah*. It looked as if the Rocky Mountain range had come to an end there in one final and monstrous jumble of stone. Ahead of them lay a long, flat valley, one that would take two or possibly three days of riding to get across. Dim and distant in the faraway haze was the low outline of another mountain range.

"Hochland's winter regions," Father Nicholas said. "When spring comes, he will be coming this way again."

After supper they turned in for the night. Lying there in his bedroll by the fire, Pasque said he was getting short on food. He would have to either find some game or find some work down in that valley. Not only was his store of food running low, his money had gone with the saddlebags.

"I'm sure that a courageous, polite man such as yourself will have no trouble finding work down there," the priest said. "On this very trail, in fact, there is a *hacienda*. You will see it. Don Diego will hire you, or at least let you work for some supplies, for as long as you wish."

"Can't be stayin' long. You know these people at this *hacienda*, do you?"

"Oh, yes. The Godinez family. You'll see their coat of arms on the gate."

"Coat of arms?"

"The family is descended from the *conquistadores*, and has been on the land here for . . . well, over a hundred and fifty years. And you will stay longer than you think . . . you have plenty of time."

"You sound pretty sure of yourself," Pasque said.

133

Father Nicholas laughed. "Our friend Hochland will not be home until the first snow flies. When it is time, the toll-taker will point the way for you. Into those distant mountains."

Pasque was quiet, leaning on one elbow to stare across the dying fire into the darkness toward the south.

"What toll-taker?" he asked.

But there was no answer. Father Nicholas was already asleep. Morning came, but Pasque slept late. And he slept soundly. The sun got high enough and hot enough finally to wake him up, and he discovered that Father Nicholas was gone. The mule tracks led west, straight toward the Spanish Peaks.

CHAPTER
NINE

Pasque Gets Caught

Pasque rode alone again, making his way along the piñon and cedar slopes of the Purgatory Valley. He crossed dozens of creeks and twice that many arroyos, some of them dry and some with a trickle of water in them. Pasque did not know their names, but descendants of Spanish pioneers, who were farming this valley when Lewis and Clark were still schoolboys, gave the watercourses such names as Huerfano, Oñote, Trampas, Culebra, and Cuchara.

Riding this piñon-forested country today, staying well up on the slope, he sometimes discovered a narrow trail or a ditch coming out of a rugged side cañon. Following one of them, he found the remains of an old stone dam that once blocked the creek and diverted the water down the ditch. It was the *acequia* of an early Mexican settler, perhaps the *acequia madre*, the mother ditch of an old settlement. A century and a half earlier, every spring the men of the valley had gathered to repair and clean the ditch and let the water flow to their fields.

The belief that built the *acequias* of New Mexico is not complicated: man is better off with clean water and

135

seed for the earth, than with the gold that comes from ripping the mountains apart and defiling the streams with yellow mud. Better to cut the piñon pine for your house rafters and the *vigas* that support the mud roof, than for mining props. Water for the seed and to make the adobe bricks; seed to save for the new plants and kernels to grind into bread; earth to carry the water and to be a womb for the seed and to become the adobes of the house. Water, seed, earth, these are the three sacred vessels of life.

The sun was high and hot, when Pasque came to a wide *acequia* running cool and clear. He filled his canteens and let the horses drink their fill. They buried their noses in the cool water and snorted when they came up for air. He sat nearby, enjoying the warm sand. Still hot. Just being in the sun, without doing anything, could make him sweat. He figured it was September, but this far south of his own range there was no telling what month it was. It looked different in ways hard to pin down. Back home on the Keystone they had trees and grass and cactus and sagebrush, too. Wyoming had mountains, except that they were higher and steeper. Maybe it was just the color of things, or the feel of that hot sunshine. It made a man want to move more slowly. It was a softer, easier kind of country.

He mounted up and followed the flow of the ditch that eventually led around the shoulder of a hill from which he could see buildings and corrals off in the distance. Maybe a mile, maybe more. He could see the deep, thick green of cottonwood groves and a glint of water from a pond and square patches of ground that had been cleared and fenced. He figured it was the *hacienda* that the priest had told him about, the ranch of — what was that name? He had forgotten.

The owner of the land didn't matter, since Pasque was already on it. He decided he might as well ride on in and ask his questions. The owner might let him at least have a place to throw down his bedroll for the night.

Pasque wiped sweat from his forehead with one of his sleeves, and caught a strong whiff of his shirt. "*Whoooh!*" he cried, sniffing at his underarms. "Maybe that's why that priest rode off without sayin' good bye. He was tryin' to get upwind of me. Better do somethin' about this."

He turned and retraced his steps along the ditch until he could no longer see the buildings, then he tethered the horses in the shade of a big juniper, and started stripping off his clothes. The Levi's just needed dusting; he had been wearing his chaps ever since getting out of the mountains and into this brushy country, so the Levi's were still relatively clean. When he had taken everything off, he looked around once more and then squatted there on the bank, buck naked, hat and pistol next to him, using his chunk of hard yellow soap to scrub the sweaty smell out of his socks and shirt and union suit.

Once they were spread out to dry — which wouldn't take long in this hot, dry country — Pasque looked at the flowing water in the *acequia*. Inviting. Cool. The ditch took a little turn here, making a kind of eddy in a corner. It was a good place to take a bath, which he

137

needed, and the day was so warm that it would feel good anyway, and so he waded in. The fresh water was cold, and the soap was rough on his white skin. Soon he was splashing and yelling and carrying on like a kid in a farm pond.

"*Whoop!*" he yelled to the piñons. "Biggest fish in these parts!" He dove to the bottom and shook his hair underwater. "*Phooey!*" he spit, coming back to the air. "This beats a tin horse tank for a bathtub! *Whooey!*"

Pasque got out of the ditch and danced and waved his arms to get rid of the goosebumps. Barefoot, bare butt, and full of himself, he sprinted over to the juniper to see if his shirt had dried. But in doing that, he also sprinted himself about twenty feet away from where his revolver lay — and he put himself about fifty feet from his horse and his Winchester.

All of which was a mistake. He knew it was a mistake as soon as he heard the soft, female laughter behind him.

Who's to say what he saw first. Maybe the twin barrels of the small-bore shotgun pointing down at him. Maybe the two beautiful dark eyes aiming it. She sat relaxed in the saddle, aiming the shotgun down at Pasque. She had both brown eyes open and her small chin held quite high, looking over the gun rather than along it. There was no question about whether she was actually aiming or not. She was.

She laughed at the look on his face, when he turned around. Poor naked Pasque was frozen in a half crouch, one hand still touching his damp shirt, his other hand covering himself, and every muscle tensing up to make a run for the Colt. But he did not move. He finally stopped staring and managed to narrow his eyes so that he could fix her with his steady blue-eyed stare. He found, however, that his cold blue eyes had met their match. Her own eyes, dark brown and lustrous and deep, did not blink and would not turn aside from his. He sensed that she was not seeing his nakedness, that all of her attention was fixed on his eyes. He had the feeling that, if he blinked or looked away, she would see the rest of him.

Careful to keep his eyes locked on hers, Pasque managed to get into his shirt. Then he pulled his union suit around in front of him.

She laughed that laugh again. It was more of a chuckle than a laugh, making the shotgun muzzle jiggle. But it jiggled only a very, very little. Pasque took his socks from the juniper, picked up his Levi's and boots, and ducked behind the tree to dress. But he made no move toward the Colt, or toward the horses. The Mexican girl was obviously amused at finding him stark naked. She might be thinking it would be funny to put a load of birdshot into his skinny butt.

When he sat down on the ground to tug his boots on over his wet socks, she rode to where his Colt was laying and leaned down out of the saddle to scoop up the belt, holster, and gun. She buckled the belt and looped it over her saddle horn. Pasque adjusted his Stetson over his wet hair. Then he casually knelt down to fasten his spurs. He was trying his best to look relaxed and comfortable, like he was pretty much in charge of the situation.

The Mexican girl began to question him in very clear English, and it was obvious that he was *not* in charge of the situation. Did he make a habit of dirtying the clean water of others? she asked. Did he have any idea where this water was to be used? Did he care whether it went into the fields or to the kitchen *cisterna?* What was he looking for, this high on the slope of the *cerro,* the hillside? Unbranded cattle to steal? How many other riders was he with, and where were they at this moment?

Pasque stammered out his answers. It was similar to when he had first met Gwen, trying to find things for his tongue to say while his eyes were talking to his brain about other things. That this woman was lovely, there was no doubt. The long, shining hair beneath the tan sombrero was the color of raven wings. Her lips, perfect in shape, had the deep red of dark, wild raspberries. She was dressed from head to foot in soft brown — a split riding skirt, an embroidered vest over a white shirt, high boots, sombrero. Her skin was golden and perfect.

He was well into his apology, and was working up the courage to ask who she was, when she lowered the hammers on the shotgun and rested it crosswise in front of her on the saddle. But at the same time she drew his Colt from the holster and cocked it. She fired twice, the shots making the horses dance wild-eyed for a second. She put the revolver back in the holster and then tossed the rig to Pasque.

The shots brought two men riding out of the trees. One was obviously a *vaquero,* a rider for the *hacienda.*

The other was apparently the owner himself; he was older and looked like the girl's father. He politely introduced himself as Don Godinez, and followed that information with a burst of Spanish. The girl translated.

"Our house is your house," she explained. "My father is Don Diego Godinez, and I am his daughter, Elena Victoria. Father invites you to our home and asks the privilege of being your host."

"I thought I was going to be target practice," Pasque said. He retrieved his soap and towel and stuffed them back into his pack, then untethered his horses, and swung into the saddle. He'd never realized how much more comfortable it was to be eye-to-eye with a woman — especially the *Señorita* Godinez — than to be looking up at her.

"Name's Pasque," he said, as the four of them started down through the trees together. Don Diego laughed. "*Si. Señor* Pasque." He seemed to find it amusing.

"We were expecting to find you farther out," Elena told him, "out to the east, on the *Ilano* . . . the flats."

"Expecting? You knew I was coming?"

"Oh, *sí!*" she laughed. "*padre* Nicholas told us, of course. The *padre* stays at this *hacienda* on his trips. The young man of the blue eyes, he told us, *ojos tan cielo*, will come from the north." Her eyes danced and sparkled; she was obviously very tickled with herself for making him stand there naked and stammering, when all along she knew who he was. It was a mean joke she had played on him, but the rippling caress of her laugh was enough to make Pasque want to forgive her.

141

Forgive her for that and for anything else she might choose to do to him.

"Oh," Pasque said, "well, when the *padre* left me the other day, I kinda thought his tracks was headin' west, up into those peaks. He didn't tell me he was on his way to your place."

She shrugged. "Perhaps that is where he went after he met you. Sometimes he goes behind the peaks to visit at the *pueblo* of Aguilar. We have not seen him since it was springtime. He was coming from Santa Fé on his way north."

During his two months at the *Hacienda* Godinez, during conversations that carried them from the formal relationship of hostess and guest into an easy, intimate friendship, Pasque asked Elena how Father Nicholas could have known about him months before meeting him. Each time, she shrugged and smiled. "*¿Quién sabe?*" she would repeat, as if it were no mystery of any importance. Why trouble the mind?

Elena and Pasque rode everywhere. As was proper, one of the trusted *vaqueros* or one of the *hacienda* servant women always went with them. Elena had her own personal maid, a rather chubby woman named María, and it would usually be her job to go everywhere with her mistress. But María did not like to ride horses, and so a *vaquero* or one of the other women went instead.

Their rides took them across the valley from east to west and north to south many times, sometimes on the pretext of looking for horses that had strayed from the ranch, sometimes to see if some watering pond had dried up. In her saddlebags Elena carried bread and cheese and a flask of wine that had been made on the *hacienda*. They would picnic on hilltops looking out over the sage flats, the *llano* of her father's ranch.

The first few times they spent together, sitting on the large *pueblo* blanket with the picnic between them, their "guard" sitting some distance away, Pasque found himself thinking of Gwen. Being around a woman as pretty as Elena brought memories of Gwen's face and her voice, and he would start wanting to see her again. But then, on one warm, sunny day, Pasque finally let go of all those vague emotions of longing. It felt like waking up. He let go of disturbing memories. They slid into the distant past, old and dim like memories of his family. It was like suddenly realizing where he was. In this new daze he studied Elena's face while she talked.

They were on the hillside above the ranch. Their horses were tethered among the trees. Pasque sat with his back comfortably against a big warm rock, whittling on a piece of juniper, while Elena stood looking out over the plains to the east. She seldom spoke without looking directly at him — a trait that he liked, now that he had gotten used to it — but on this particular afternoon she was gazing far away. He was able to study her, letting his eyes linger a long time on the slim arch of her throat, the fullness of her moving lips, the way her black hair flowed down her back.

That was when something inside him relaxed. Something let go of him, and for the first time in months he did not feel the need to get on with his search, or any need to return to the Keystone. A few days earlier he had been helping round up some stock and a Godinez *vaquero* had told him that he was working too hard — "This is the land of *mañana*," Ricardo had said. "*Poco tiempo.* The steer will still be there tomorrow. We have no need to hurry things." And this afternoon, Pasque began to feel that slow-time feeling throughout his mind and body.

"A man would do well here, with the new breeds of cattle of which we have heard, my father has said." Elena was looking into the distance, and into the future. "Already we have seen the railroad's men, those who have the instruments to plan where the tracks will run. Off there," she said, indicating the distant blue range of mountains to the south, "*rancheros* are selling right of ways. Men are being hired to build the rails over Raton Pass. It will not be this year, or next year, but it will be."

"And this is going to kill his cattle business, according to Don Diego?" Pasque said.

"No. You are not listening. The Spanish cattle, and the ones you *gringo* cowboys call the longhorns, they were good to walk to the market. But with the trains, with such land as this, the fat, small cattle will bring much more money."

Pasque saw the point. Down here, where winter is shorter and milder, a man with some irrigated land for raising hay would have a way to ship fat cattle by railroad to all kinds of markets. North to Denver City, then out to St. Louis and points east; south to Albuquerque, and maybe someday from there to

California. Buying land would be the problem. Part of it was still a reservation for the Cheyennes and Arapahoes. Kiowas claimed part of it. Most of it, though, like the Godinez' *hacienda* was tied up in old land grants that were kept in the family.

That evening, as Pasque lay in his bunk enjoying the new-found feeling of peace within himself, and also enjoying the way he could remember Elena's face as she spoke of the future, he decided that he should stay around the *Hacienda* Godinez a while longer. He could help out, earn his keep, and spend his extra time looking around the region at the ranching possibilities.

Don Diego did not like having his guests do manual labor to earn their keep. It was fitting to allow the guest to help his *vaqueros* chase down a few steers; this, after all, was more like sport to a true horseman, a *caballero*. But to perform actual labor with his two hands, that was something a true *caballero* would not do. However, Don Diego was a gentleman and born to the code of unquestioning hospitality, so he gave permission for Pasque to work at whatever he wanted to work at, and ordered his *obreros* — the workmen — to provide the *Señor* Pasque with any assistance that he might need.

Pasque quickly found himself working hard, in spite of the philosophy of *poco tiempo*. The *obreros* who were building a new stable gleefully introduced him to the fine art of laying adobe bricks and even allowed Pasque to be their guest at carrying baskets of mud up the shaky pole ladder to the top of the wall. They also trusted him to lug the heavy mud bricks up the ladder.

145

They took him into the hills to search out the flat rocks for capping the wall to deflect rain and to support the roof beams, and he loaded rocks onto the stone boat until he was sweating in the cool October air.

Stripped to the waist, Pasque smeared and smoothed plaster until he had more clay on himself than on the wall. On one end of a crosscut saw, he helped cut the heavy *vigas* for ceiling beams until his muscles cramped with pain.

Out in the field, he helped clear the *acequia* and helped bring in loads of firewood, enough to last in case of a heavy snowstorm. This wood had to be carried and stacked in many places, for each room in the big main house had its own corner adobe fireplace for heat, and each fireplace was kept constantly burning during the colder days.

Chasing cattle was a slightly different proposition here than it had been at the Keystone. Pasque had always worn chaps, but here he learned why the Mexican *vaqueros* had perfected that particular tool of the cattle trade. Cattle loved to hide in the piñon trees which had low, stiff branches that could rip a man's leg wide open. On foot, wrestling with a calf or unruly steer, a man would run into the Spanish bayonet plant called yucca. On horse or on foot, there was the cholla to consider, armed spines long enough to pick your teeth with and branches high as a horse's shoulder. Those Mexican chaps were definitely necessary down here.

The cañons into which the cattle ran were made up of broken, black rock with sharp edges everywhere.

They were steep, jagged little cañons, full of mesquite and cholla, paved with busted stones like big cinders. When October winds blew dry and whipped around in the trees, the sand flew into Pasque's eyes and mouth and at times seemed to be smothering him. When the wet half snow, half rain came drizzling down, the sand turned into gooey clay like the stuff he had slid on when the blacksmith's kid had laughed at him, or like the stuff with which he had plastered the wall. It packed underfoot, clumping on the soles of his boots and under his horse's hoofs, and, if he didn't scrape it when it was wet, he had to take a hammer to it when it dried.

And yet, there came a cold, blustering windy day when Pasque felt that he could not live anywhere else. He was on the low ridge, coming into view of the ranch buildings. He paused to look beyond the ranch, studying the faraway ridge. It was the ridge that the priest had pointed out to him. Across those mountains, some kind of showdown was still waiting for him. He knew it, and his soul had made the decision to accept whatever outcome there might be. But his mind wanted that outcome to be life. He wanted to go on living in this strangely peaceful Southwestern land.

The thought bothered him. He felt that he was somehow betraying Art and betraying the country back up north. But he could imagine the Keystone going on as before, without him. He could imagine himself never missing it. What he could not imagine now was not returning to *this* place. The warmth of this sunshine, the colors of these trees and this earth; the texture of adobe walls and Indian blankets; the odors of burning

147

piñon wood and of chiles roasting; the taste of an oven-warm *tortilla* heaped with *refritos* and salsa; the sound of a Spanish guitar and *canciones* being sung to the evening stars — never to know these things again, and still call himself alive, was something of which he could not conceive.

While at the *hacienda*, Pasque slept in a small room in one corner of the main house. Its single doorway opened into the central courtyard, rather than into one of the hallways, which meant that he could come and go without disturbing Elena or Don Diego or the household servants. It was a nice room, and private, but his favorite place to spend chilly winter days, other than in the happy company of Elena, was in the workshop attached to the stables. There he and the *vaqueros* would sit for hours, mending harness or polishing saddles or doing ironwork at the small forge, swapping stories. They taught Pasque many of their Spanish words; he tried to teach them English.

One afternoon Roderigo told Pasque about an incident. It had taken place several years ago, when Elena was just beginning to show the first signs of budding into a lovely young *señorita*. Her mother, the Doña Godinez, and her older brother had ridden with two of the servants into the mountains to make a visit to old friends in Taos.

"But somewhere, you know," Roderigo said, "on that road through the mountains, perhaps near Tres Ritos, *la* doña and the boy vanished. The worst of it, well, who knew at Taos when to expect them? And the don himself, he did not expect them to return for a month perhaps."

"So what happened to them?" Pasque said. He was lacing together a saddlebag, but was having trouble with it. It looked downright homemade. Which it was.

"*¿Quién sabe, señor?*" Roderigo's face grew sad. "All through the *otoño* . . . the autumn . . . we searched, all the *vaqueros*, all the *peónes*, all the friends. Some people who come and go in that pass over the mountain, they had seen *bandidos*. Some had seen the *indios*, Apaches, in those mountains. And . . ." — he looked at Pasque meaningfully — "those *gringo* trappers."

"No trace at all, then?"

"Finally, yes. In the next summer, a sheepherder went up into the mountains far over by Taos, and at his hut there he found the two graves. Not deep, not good. We brought them back to lie in our own *campo santo*" — he pointed off toward the southeast corner of the main ranch grounds — "there."

"So Elena and her father are all the family?"

"*Sí*. All. But who knows? One day, perhaps Don Diego will marry again."

More death. Pasque stood and stretched his arms and walked out into the open air. The sun was bright, the sky was blue, and the air only a little chilly. More death. And a beautiful girl, just when she would need a mother to teach her those things that women must know when they become women, left to be raised by her father. And priests. Elena was sent to school, where she learned English along with her literature and

149

history and arithmetic. She learned to ride and to
shoot, presumably, from the *vaqueros* who treated her
like a spoiled niece.

He came around the corner of the building in time to
see Elena ride up. And she was riding fast, excited. As
soon as she reached the stable, she jumped down to tie
the horse on the corral rail.

"Pasque!" she panted, out of breath. "Quick, get
your horse! Get your rifle!" She took off toward the
house at a run, black hair streaming out behind from
under her hat, that proud little chin leading the way.

"What is it?" he called to her. "Where are you going?"

"For father's rifle," she yelled back.

Pasque saddled up, and was ready by the time she
came back with the rifle. He could see Don Diego in
the doorway of the house, watching her go. They mounted
and headed off in the general direction of a foothills
pasture in which the sheep were being held for the
winter. No servant or *vaquero* followed as their chaperón.

"Rustlers?" he inquired.

"*¡Pantera!*" she said, turning to him, her eyes bright
with excitement, her cheeks flushed from riding fast in
the cold air. "The mountain lion. Among the sheep. I
was hunting for birds this morning, the quail or grouse,
to surprise you and Father with a nice supper. And up
at the pasture, a lion was eating his kill, one of our
ewes."

"Probably long gone, now," Pasque said. "Anything
with legs would have sense enough to get out of range
of you and that shotgun!"

"I shot at him," she said, eyes still bright. "Both of the barrels. But not close enough."

It was easy to find the spot where the big cat had made its kill. From the claw marks on the bark, it looked as if it had climbed the tree and then crawled out along a limb over the grass where it had waited for a sheep to get close. Underneath, the ground was torn up with hoof marks and claw marks, signs of a quick but violent struggle. The sheep carcass lay there, neck broken, fleece and skin ripped open. But no sign of a cat.

Pasque and Elena dismounted to search the ground for tracks of some kind, but the earth was frozen. Here and there they found what looked like freshly broken grass stems, but the grass was old and dry and could have been broken by anything from a hopping crow to a steer.

She pointed up into a cañon where she was sure she would go, if she were a mountain lion who had heard two barrels of a shotgun going off. Pasque followed her.

After walking perhaps a half mile into the cañon, they came to a place where old snow would have shown tracks, but there was none.

"Over the ridge," she said, exasperated. "He must have gone there and into the next valley. We will have to climb up there."

"*Whoa!*" Pasque said, taking her arm and turning her so that he could look down into her face. It was still beautifully alive with excitement. "Let's think this thing through first. We haven't found tracks. We didn't see a sign of blood or hair back there anywhere. I don't think that cat's wounded. Probably just holed up somewhere, laughin' at us."

She pretended to pout, but her eyes were still sparkling. He held her arm to keep her from starting off on her own.

"Besides," he went on, "I'm not gonna help you kill that critter, even if we do find it."

She looked outraged. That a gentleman would refuse to do this one simple thing for the good of the whole *rancho* where he had been welcomed as a guest!

"Ah, that cat isn't any threat to your *rancho*. Maybe it takes a sickly, old ewe, now and then. But more'n likely it keeps the coyotes, maybe even the bears off this part of the range. Might have babies to feed, too. Now, if that big old kitty climbed into your window one night and went to chewin' on your leg or something, why I sure would shoot it."

Her eyes narrowed into mock seriousness. The little chin tilted up at him as if her honor had been violated. "And tell me, *Señor gringo* cowboy Pasque, *what* would you be doing in my room at night?"

She had never looked so lovely to him as she did in that moment. For reply, he did exactly five things. First, he took both rifles and set them against a boulder. Second, he placed his hands on her shoulders. Third, he pulled her to him and bent his head until his lips were an inch from hers, until he could feel her warm breath. Fourth, he said one word: "This." And fifth, he kissed her.

It was not the only kiss that afternoon. It was followed by the sound of two persons sighing, deeply.

152

The sighs were interrupted when their lips again searched and found each other and locked, more tightly this time, warm and moving. The kiss that came after that one made their lips want even more, and during that kiss, or the one after that, Pasque realized he could feel the full firmness of her breasts pressing him. A few kisses later, he was sure he felt her hot thighs warming his.

The sun moved in the sky. Somewhere a hawk called out to the mountains. Tree shadows grew longer, and the late afternoon breeze came, chilling, down the cañon. Pasque hardly knew that his feet were cold or that the muscles of his calves were locked and stiff and trembling. But he knew the push of her breasts and the nearness of her thighs. His cheek knew the warmth and texture of her face, his ears heard her breathing his name as a light whisper, and his lips — his lips had never been so thoroughly crushed and then teased with feathery brushing movements.

On the ride back to the house they held hands, each reaching out to the other. Sometimes they stopped to kiss again, as if afraid that if they did not, they would forget the ecstasy of it. He told her about a younger Pasque, one who would track and kill mountain lions, any animal, even a man. Any reason would do — for his honor, for pride, for justice, for a job — or for no reason at all.

He told her the story of the other mountain lion. He got so far into the story that he had to explain how it felt to find the animal, wounded, afraid, in that crack in

153

the rock, and because he had gone that far into the story and had to lay bare all of those feelings, he rode with his gaze fixed straight ahead and did not look at her and did not stop to kiss her again.

"And so," she said, "if you found the murderers of your two brothers, those whom your uncle told you not to chase after, could you drive them into a corner and kill them?"

"I don't know. For a long time, that's all I wanted to do. But I didn't like killing that lion. And I didn't like the feeling I got when I shot that buffalo coat *hombre*, either. But I still think I'll have to get those two in front of my gun before I'll know."

"Who did you shoot, did you say?" Elena asked.

"Never mind. I'll tell you sometime, maybe."

She studied him, this cowboy strong and hard as a *pantera*. She wished he would rein his horse around and suddenly sweep her from her saddle and make her sit in front of him and kiss her all the way into the house.

She said nothing, however. She went on listening to her *caballero* who rode with his eyes looking steadily forward. No man had every shared such thoughts with her before. And yet she felt that there was much, much more troubling him. Perhaps it was something that he would never share.

CHAPTER
TEN

A Private Cigar, a Public Bath

Elena came back from the mountain lion hunt with a glow in her face and a bright sparkle in her eyes. The women who worked in the house thought it was because the *señorita* had never really done such a thing before, and it made her feel grownup and independent. They were partly right. But her new smile had little to do with hunting a lion.

Elena began to spend more of her evenings with her father. Instead of reading or sewing in her room, she sat with him in the main *sala*. She brought him frothing hot chocolate or, if he preferred, fine Spanish brandy in a glass warmed between her hands. She fussed over him in soft Spanish, gently manipulating the conversation. Finally, one evening, Don Diego happened to come up with an idea. It was an idea that he thought was his own.

Next morning Don Diego went to look for Pasque and found him with Fidel, stripping bark from aspen saplings for the ceiling of the new building. Don Diego announced that he wished Elena to learn to shoot a rifle. He would be honored if Pasque would teach her.

"I would, of course, prefer that she learn to shoot my own rifle, the flintlock that came from Spain. But I know that the times are changing. She must learn to shoot modern weapons," the don said, speaking through Fidel, who was fluent in both languages. "With her small shotgun, she shoots very well. But for the mountain lions and bears that also come down from the hills, she must know how to fire a proper rifle."

"Tell Don Diego . . . please . . . ," Pasque said, "that I'm no expert, but I'll be glad to give it a try. But tell him that we'd have to get out of range of the house. Quite a ways."

Fidel translated. Don Diego agreed that it would be best. Some of the horses might be frightened. Property might be damaged.

"We'll take along the woman, what's her name . . . Elena's maid?" Pasque added. Wherever Elena went, her watchdog must also go. Fidel repeated this to Don Diego, who laughed and dismissed the idea with a wave of his hand. He looked away, somewhere into the distance, and made a little speech. Fidel translated.

"The don wishes *Señor* Pasque to know that he is trusted with the *señorita*. There is no cause for a servant to leave her duties to attend a shooting lesson. Besides," — Fidel laughed — "María . . . the maid . . . she hates to ride horses and does not like to be outside in the cold weather."

"OK, then. We'll get at it. But the next time the wagon goes to town, I'll have to have some cartridges brought back for my rifle. My supply got stolen back on the Arkansas."

Don Diego laughed when Fidel told him this.

"I am old-fashioned" — he grinned, and Fidel translated — "but not too old. I have many repeating rifles and all the ammunition you would need for your lessons, even if I had . . . God forbid . . . a dozen such daughters. Come, my *amigo*. We will find the right guns for this job. And we will also find my daughter in the house, I think."

Pasque came out of Don Diego's house with a whole new respect for the man. A room next to the don's study contained an arsenal of weapons, ranging from antique muskets to modern revolvers and rifles. The don proudly described how he had acquired each gun, then made his selection. He handed Pasque a perfectly matched pair of 1866 Winchesters. They appeared to be in brand new condition. He also gave Pasque a shooting bag containing four boxes of .44 rim-fire cartridges.

Pasque left the house with Elena behind him, skipping to keep up with his long stride, while tying the chin string of her riding sombrero. Pasque didn't say anything about it, but he wondered how often she wore her riding skirt and heavy leather jacket in the house.

"Those rifles . . . ," she said, "they are Papa's pride!"

"Those are them," Pasque replied. He patted the leather bag. "And enough ammunition to start a war. Oh, and look at this." Pasque took a small brass telescope from the bag. "Your papa thought I oughta have this. Said for me to keep it. He thinks we'll need it to see what we hit, he said."

"And with these rifles we can shoot something so far away as that?" Elena asked.

"I doubt it," Pasque said.

The two rode toward the foothills until they found an arroyo out of sight of the ranch buildings. Pasque built a fire against one bank of the arroyo to give them some warmth. Then he loaded one of the rim-fire Winchesters and showed Elena how to hold it tightly to her shoulder. It helped, she said, when he stood close behind her, bracing her body with his and using his arms, wrapped around her, to help hold the gun. After she got used to the loud *whang!* of the heavy weapon, Elena did a fair job of massacring a cedar stump up the gully. But the Winchester was too long and too heavy for her. Her left arm began to tremble from the exertion, giving her a shaky aim. The recoil hurt her shoulder, even through her thick jacket. Pasque took a turn at it. *Whang! Whang!* The noise echoed up and down the valley.

Their muscles trembled, and their ears rang. Pasque and Elena decided to suspend the target shooting and practice kissing, instead, an activity which she found ever so much more enjoyable. Every few minutes, either she or Pasque would shoot off a few .44 rounds — from the hip — just to let her father hear that they were still at it. But while the last echoes of those shots were rolling off through the hills, he would take her in his arms, marveling at the cold touch of her cheeks, feeling the cold tip of her little nose on his cheek, thrilling to the warmth in her lips.

Nearly every morning, unless the weather was terrible or Elena was busy greeting her father's guests or supervising special meals, she and Pasque would

158

bundle up and ride off to their arroyo and their warm fire and their long, breathless embraces. They whispered to each other — words of wonder at it all, happy, laughing words, serious words, words of a longing that they both felt.

"My love," she whispered, her arms encircling his waist underneath his long coat, her head resting affectionately on his chest. "I used to hate these cold days of winter! I was always asking Papa to send me to Mexico in December to get away from the cold. But now! Oh, they are our joy! No one else will come out in the cold . . . we are alone out here, with no one to see our love."

"Just us and the mountain lions," he laughed. He loved having her wrapped in his coat, where she felt so small and so firm and so warm. Sometimes the firmness and the warmth would make certain thoughts begin in his mind, and his hips would become restless and hot. She sensed it.

"If only the summer would come," she said once. "I truly think," she said, whispering in his ear, "that, if this were a warm summer day rather than a cold one in winter, you would have my clothes off. And yours."

Pasque held her out at arm's length and tried to give her a stern look of reproach. It was probably the most insincere and ineffective frown that a man in love ever made. So he grinned, instead, and gathered her back into his coat. "I suppose so," he said. "Except that your papa trusts me. And maybe I'm just a ordinary cow-driver, but I'm not one to make love to a girl and then leave her."

She did not want to hear about that possibility. And when he hinted that a day would come when he would

★   ★   ★

It wasn't unusual for a man to leave a job on sudden notice and ride out to find the next mining strike or to follow some money-making get-rich-quick scheme. Pasque had had different motives, but he hadn't volunteered what they were. He had had his own reasons for moving on, and that had been enough. What triggered it had been something that he had thought he had seen one night in the Golden Tail Saloon and Gambling Emporium.

He had a chair at the poker game, a fresh beer at his elbow. His draw hand was showing three of a kind. The game was quiet enough to be relaxing, and the other players were good enough to keep it interesting. Pasque's three of a kind got him a small pot, but it didn't mean he was in for a run of luck — he had to fold the next hand. He took a swallow of beer, leaned back and stretched his arms, and looked around the place.

And then he thought he saw Gwen. The hair, all shining and brushed into waves and curls, hung halfway down the back of a green dress. The slender back straight as a gunbarrel. The shawl draped across her back, resting on her bare arms, was identical to the one Gwen sometimes wore. Pasque started to say — "Deal me out of the next hand." — but didn't finish the sentence. He started to get up out of his chair, but he sat down again when the woman turned around.

121

have to ride south again, she put her two slim fingers against his lips to silence him, while her dark eyes searched his for answers. In that mood they sometimes rode back to the house in silence. He could not find it in his heart to tell her about the sort of death that might be waiting for him at the end of his search, and she did not have the courage to ask him why he must go.

Sometimes Pasque would pick up a tin can they had used for target. A .44 slug left a half-inch hole, collapsed on the front side and blown out like a funnel on the back.

After each lesson they would ride back to the house where Elena would go to her room and change clothes. Indoors, she wore the shorter skirts that most Mexican women of the time wore; her blouse was ordinary, just simple and white with a tiny bit of embroidery, cut rather low so that it would show the golden glory of her neck and shoulders; the rest of her indoor costume consisted of light slippers and a shawl. The shawl was part of a woman's everyday clothing in her culture, and, unless she was riding her horse, she was almost never without it.

As for Pasque, he still looked like a cowboy of the Wyoming Territory. He had only made two changes. Elena and Don Diego had presented him with a large Mexican silver buckle. Felipe had given him some silver *conchos* to decorate his belt and holster. He helped one of the young boys break a colt, and the child had given him a tiny jingle-bob bell. *Vaqueros* put them on their spurs to make them jingle when they walked.

Elena spent most winter days indoors, but Pasque liked to be outside. In the evening he would relax in his room off of the courtyard, or he would sit and talk with Don Diego — through Fidel or Elena — in the *sala* or in the don's study. Once in a while he would visit the kitchen, where the cook would spoil him with little treats of pastry. More than once he wondered about Elena's room and what it looked like, but she had made it clear to him that there were certain areas of the house into which a gentleman should never go.

One afternoon, Elena suggested to her father that Pasque would enjoy a nice smoke. The don nodded his permission. She led Pasque into the dining room where a humidor of long, slim cigars stood on the fireplace mantle.

As quickly as they had turned the corner and were alone, she whirled into his arms and kissed him quickly, breathlessly.

"I need to see you more," Pasque said, "alone. You don't know how much it hurts to watch you and not be able to hold you like this!"

"We cannot be alone together in the house, my love," she whispered, trembling in his arms, afraid and savoring the danger.

"Don Diego doesn't know that we're . . . well, that we have been . . . mean, he doesn't know about us, does he?"

"Of course, he does!" she laughed. "But it is not proper, you know. Around anyone else, you and I are only friends. But because of what is proper, you must not touch my hand or gaze on me that way, in front of

161

Father or the servants. Of course," she said, glancing away with a demure look and covering her shoulder with the shawl, "they are not always awake."

Pasque cupped her chin in his hand and kissed her. "So," he said, "then after your father goes to bed, I can come callin' on you, is that it?"

"Oh, no! No! You must not call for me. Even when we are to go out for our shooting. That is why I always send someone to find you and tell you that I am ready to go out and shoot the rifles. But . . ." — she beamed at him — "when the house is quiet and dark, if you let me know where you are, it is possible that I will be taking a walk because I cannot sleep. I might walk in the courtyard. Or in the *emparrado* behind the house . . . the arbor that is still hidden by grape vines even though the leaves have fallen."

He had to grin at her. Devious little devil.

"So how are you gonna know when I'm out there? Want me to whistle a little tune or somethin'?"

She took a half dozen of the long *cigarillos* from the humidor and tucked them into his shirt pocket under his vest.

"Someone might hear your whistling, my love. But my maid now sleeps with her window shut," Elena smiled, "against the cold air. I like my window open, a little. And the smell of those cigars, *mi querido*, they are enough to wake one up. Do you think?"

During the following days no one noticed that Pasque had developed a habit of strolling and smoking a cigar in the *emparrado* or in the courtyard before he went to bed. Sometimes he sat in the deep shadows behind the tall fountain. If someone happened to peer into the courtyard, they would see only his Stetson, lying on the stone bench. Next to it they might see a slender thread of smoke rising from a cigar that had been left there unheeded by its owner. When it was very late at night, there would be only a bit of ash on the stone bench, and soft breathless whispers would be coming from the deep shadows.

"It is for the cholla and yucca!" Fidel laughed. From the amazement in the face of *Señor* Pasque, one would think he had never before seen a heavy chain.

"The idea was the don's," Fidel went on, "to clear some of that *Ilano* for better grass. In the spring, when the sand is wet and loose, we will drag it . . . with a team of the oxen on each end of the long chain . . . and rip out the cholla, the yucca. Then we plant the grass. The *heno*."

Fidel and Pasque had gone to the wagon barn to hitch up a heavy coach. And there, hanging on the wall, was a new logging chain, a chain with long oval links forged by hand. Pasque could only stand there for a moment, studying it, until his mind was upright again. This was the chain he had seen the blacksmith, Evan Thompson, forging.

It was his reminder. It was there to tell him he had an appointment with Old Buffalo Coat, the man called Hochland. He had let it become less and less urgent while he spent more and more time with Elena. Now, however, the sight of the chain weighed on him as

163

heavily as if it had been twisted around his heart. It was there to let him know that the day was fast approaching when he must cross the last river and the last ridge and finish what he had started almost a year earlier. He shook off the dazed feeling as he bent to raise the wagon tongue between the teams and Fidel hooked the harness to the singletrees.

The coach party consisted of Don Diego, his sister who was visiting from Santa Fé for the Christmas season, two of Elena's female cousins who tended to giggle a great deal, Fidel driving the team, and María. Elena stood by her saddle horse dressed in riding skirt and short jacket, sombrero, gloves, and boots. She did not intend to ride with the rest of the women.

María and Don Diego begged Pasque to go along. The don was in a fine mood, spreading his white-toothed grin all over the ranch, wishing all the *vaqueros* the happiness of the season, giving them a half day off from their chores, giving them the freedom of the kitchen — "Ah, but not of the cook or the cook's pretty helper!" he exclaimed.

"Come with us!" Elena pleaded. "It is Papa's birthday, and you cannot refuse! Besides, it will be such fun with you. And on the way back, you will help me gather some green boughs for decorating the *sala*." She swung into her saddle and sat there, smiling. It was hard to tell what the smile meant.

Pasque had his horse ready, but he wasn't comfortable about it. He still had a vivid memory of the time Elena caught him swimming in the *acequia*, and the only thing covering him was her double-barreled sixteen gauge. This idea of taking a bath in some hot springs, with women, made him uneasy.

Pasque looked up into Elena's face. He scuffed the toe of his boot in the dirt a few times. That smile was full of delight and challenge, and, because he couldn't think of a good reason not to, he went ahead and climbed onto his horse. The things a man would do for love.

Elena had explained it to him the evening before, smiling that sweet little smile that a woman wears when she knows damned well that she is teasing a man out of his mind. The bathing was a ritual each winter. When the days finally stopped getting shorter and began to lengthen again, Don Diego celebrated his birthday with a December picnic and a long soak in the nearby hot springs.

As they road, Elena explained that the springs were up in one of the cañons, perhaps two hours from the ranch. They bubbled hot from the mountainside and ran through three very large pools, each one a bit cooler than the one above. They had the picnic hamper filled with red wine, some good beef to cook over a fire, roasted chiles, hot chocolate, many kinds of desserts, everything. And since he was their guest at the *hacienda*, she said, giving him a secret wink, she could not imagine bathing in the hot springs without him.

Well, *he* could imagine it. As they rode along, side by side behind the coach, he heard the women in the coach giggling — sometimes braying with loud laughs as Don Diego told his funny stories. Pasque pondered

165

how they might bray and howl and giggle, when they saw him without his clothes. He had a mental picture of it. Don Diego, his chubby sister, and the cousins, too, and all of them in their birthday suits. When the big ladies got down to the skin, he'd look like a pink weasel surrounded by stuffed woodchucks.

And when he imagined Elena without her clothes, each jounce of the horse got painful, and he wished he had a Spanish saddle with more of an undercut fork. It would be more comfortable with another inch or two between the fork and his Levi's buttons.

They rode higher and higher into the foothills. Pasque and Elena pulled up to watch how the mid-morning sun was glancing off a big river far away to the south. "It shines so far," Elena said, "with the sun upon it. Like I feel, when you are looking at me! Sometimes I think everyone can see my love for you in my face, like a reflection."

She was whispering, and, as usual, she was enjoying the way he fidgeted when she spoke love to him with others almost in earshot. Between the giggling of the cousins and the rattling of the iron wheels on the rocky wagon track, and the jingling of harness and clatter of hoofs, they would never hear. But still.

"Does Don Diego's land end there at the river?" he asked to change the subject. "Or does it even go that far?"

"To the Purgatorio?" Elena found the idea funny. The river was much farther away than it looked. "No. Before that."

"What did you call it? The Purgatorio?"

"*Sí, mi alma.*" She leaned closer to him while her beautiful lips deliberately whispered the name of the river in Spanish. She enjoyed the way the syllables made her lips pout. Pasque enjoyed it even more than she did.

"*Las Animas Perdidas en Purgatorio,*" she said softly. Her way of purring Spanish made Pasque's saddle uncomfortable again. "The River of the Lost Souls in Purgatory."

Pasque could not resist her lips. He shot a look at the coach to make certain no one was peeking through the back curtain, then stole a quick kiss. They rode on smiling and exchanging sly glances under the cover of their wide hat brims, but did not speak for a while.

Pasque abruptly straightened up in his saddle. *The Picketwire.* "The Picketwire!" he said out loud.

"What is it . . . ?" Elena asked.

"That river. My uncle called it the Picketwire. That's the last river I have to cross, I think." Pasque fell into a sudden sadness, all but forgetting the woman next to him, and altogether forgetting the dreaded hot springs bathing ritual, forgetting everything, except the words that came back to him. He had said them nearly a year ago. It was a year ago, north of here in a place that didn't even seem real any more, on a black, cold night, the light from the lanterns throwing weird shadows on the wall of the Keystone ranch house. Pasque's words haunted him.

"If he walks away, I'll follow him all the way to hell for the showdown."

"*Mi querido,*" Elena's urgent half whisper broke into the echoing gloom of his mind. "My love, what is it?"

For the next hour, the two of them rode far enough back so that the laughing people in the coach couldn't hear their conversation. Pasque told her the part of the story he had never told her about before.

"And now it's even worse, honey," he said. Elena furrowed her forehead at the word "honey," so he changed it to "sweetheart," an English word she understood. "Now I've gone and found *you*, and like I said the other night . . ."

"Ah, in that night of the full moon! So bright and so cold out there in the courtyard, too." She pouted a little bit — more to cheer him up than to tease him, this time. "And with your room so warm and so nearby, but you would not mention going there. Such a *caballero!*"

"Well, I *do* love you. And I've gotta ride off and leave you now. You can see that we just *can't* . . . I mean, I'm likely not to come back, and there you'd be."

"Oh, my soul. *Mi alma.* You will come back again. Our dreams will bring you back. This land, this country will bring you back. I do not understand this thing that you must do, but I know that you would not have been chosen to do it, if you were not worthy. And the revenge for your brothers . . . I understand that, also. It must be done. When it is all done, and you have finished your business with this strange man . . . Hochland? . . . you will return. I will wait. No matter if it takes years, I will wait, and you will return."

Sitting in the hot water, steam rising all around like a fog, Pasque felt pretty stupid. He should have known that his host, the *ranchero*, would never embarrass a guest. Don Diego's workmen had taken care of the privacy problem several years earlier by building a screen of peeled saplings down the middle of the largest pool. The barrier was too high to see over, and was anchored to the bottom. The poles had been well matched and trimmed to fit together without gaps, but there were still a few small cracks. Once in a while Pasque caught a glimpse of movement on the other side, but he'd have to put his eye right up to the little opening, if he wanted to look at something in particular.

Pasque had helped build a roaring fire so that Maria could heat the chili and the water for the hot chocolate. Fidel had hung a long tarp from the back of the wagon to the pole screen; the men undressed on one side and the women on the other, and both could come and go from the pool without being seen. And to ensure that there was no embarrassment, anyone who went into the pool had a long, heavy cotton poncho to wear. Pasque had followed Don Diego's example: first he sat down on one of the folding stools to remove his spurs and boots and socks, then Fidel helped him pull the tent-like poncho over his head so that he could take off his shirt and pants under its protection. He and Don Diego had gotten into the water, still wearing the robes.

Fidel sat next to the edge of the water, seeing that the brandy glasses never went dry and translating the conversation. Don Diego chatted on about this and that, nothing in particular. He told Pasque about his family history as well as the latest gossip about friends and neighbors. They talked about the way the gold

169

boom seemed to be about over and the coming of the new railroads. They discussed the merits of different guns. Don Diego understood the reliability of the Colt and Winchester, with their cartridges that would work in any weather. But still he liked the idea of the old flintlock rifle.

"When you have fired all of your cartridges, *amigo*," he said, "then you are finished. But with the old flintlock, you could save back a little powder, enough to get perhaps eight shots, instead of six. And the same powder, it worked in any gun. When you had shot all your bullets, you might still kill some meat by shooting the ramrod like an arrow, or use a round stone for a bullet. I have heard of men doing such things."

"Sure," Pasque said, "but, when the wind blows your powder out of your pan or you're standin' there in the rain, that old flintlock's likely not to work at all."

Don Diego smiled in agreement. "Ah, but you can again fill the pan, pick up a new flint from the ground. What if you find you have no more percussion caps, or no more cartridges? Can you pick them up from the ground?" He laughed merrily at his joke.

It was a pleasant argument. They went on to discuss the merits of different breeds of horses and cattle, of dogs, and even chickens. Here in the warm water and steam, deep in a cañon where patches of snow lay under the pines, they were no longer the host and the guest, no longer the Spanish don and the *gringo* cowboy. Here they became two stockmen who spoke the same language of ranching.

170

Gradually, as the warm water and the brandy relaxed him, Pasque lay back and floated lazily. Don Diego laughed at something one of the women said on the other side of the screen, which caused Pasque to look at him. And in that look, Pasque realized something. Nobody at the *hacienda*, except for Elena, had ever taken notice of his eyes. Usually when somebody got used to talking to him, they were likely to mention that his eyes were an unusual color. Some people looked away when they talked to him, as if his eyes made them uncomfortable. But not here, which was kind of strange. These dark-eyed people treated him as if his blue eyes were perfectly natural and not worth mentioning.

When he thought on it, nothing about him made him feel out of place here. When he spoke with Don Diego, Fidel, or one of the serving women who spoke English, and, of course, with Elena, not once did they treat him like a *gringo* or an outsider. In fact, the don treated him as though he were a neighboring ranch owner, instead of a common cowpuncher. No one asked about his background. He had the run of the *rancho*, could take any horse he wanted, ride anywhere, without question.

Yes, he thought, floating lazily in the warm water and hearing Don Diego making jokes with the unseen women across the screen, he felt like one of the family. He had never fit in so well anywhere, since he was a little boy at home. He had never felt so relaxed and happy. Elena had been right: this country and these people would draw him back from wherever he went.

Something hard bounced off his head and into the water. There was a giggle from the other side of the screen. Pasque looked around and found a pine cone floating in the water, soaked solid and heavy. The giggles told him that it had not dropped onto his head from a tree. He tossed it back over the screen. There was a shriek, then more giggles. Two more pine cones came sailing over, then two more.

The fight was on. Don Diego and Pasque threw cones as fast as they could, with their arms hampered by the water-logged cotton ponchos, but for every cone they could fire into the air, four or five came back at them. Pasque yelled in English. Don Diego yelled in Spanish. Yelling even came from Fidel, who by this time had been hit several times and was returning fire as fast as he could find pine cones. His yells were a mixture of Spanish and English. Above the yelling and the shrieking and the splashing, Pasque could hear the delightful laughter of Elena. She was probably the one who had started it.

Finally, everyone on both sides was overheated and exhausted from the great battle, and so they climbed out of the pool and into fresh, dry robes that covered them from the chilly air while they dried themselves with towels. As he was getting back into his shirt and pants, Pasque felt the tingling in his skin, the life in his blood, the blood surging and hot, running through every vein. He was more alive, at this moment, than he had ever felt before. Everything around him seemed fascinating — not just Elena, either, but everything.

He was trying to remember what Evan Thompson had said about the south direction on the medicine wheel. Gather things, he had said. Forget about thinking on death and revenge and honor and all; just touch what you can reach, and let the rest go.

Not only was there an awareness of himself, Pasque seemed in touch with everything. The aroma of piñon smoke, of beef slices stuck with whole green chiles between them, roasting on a spit over the fire, of chocolate steaming in a big coffee pot next to the flames. The sound of women's voices speaking in liquid Spanish, of horses stamping the ground where they were tied, of the water running down through the pools. The taste of the brandy on his tongue and a slight taste of salt from the perspiration that had run down his face and a little taste of the mineral water.

And colors. The women's dresses, all circled with broad bands of color; their shining jet black hair; their silver jewelry. The pine trees around the pools, a different shade of green than the spruce trees, different again than the cedar. One bush had silver bark, another had red bark, another was the deep mahogany shade of Elena's fathomless eyes. Even though it was winter, there were shades of color everywhere he looked. It made him think of the way he had felt about pasque flowers, back before all of this had begun. He liked them because they were the first touch of color on the winter-brown hills.

He looked around and wished there were pasque flowers here. It would make everything perfect. Elena brought him a plate on which slices of hot beef and whole roasted chiles lay on a warm *tortilla* next to a little bowl of red chili. Her smile and her dancing dark eyes made him realize that he did not need flowers to make life perfect. It was all here.

CHAPTER
ELEVEN

A Dangerous Detour

Old people like to talk about the old days. They tell how they miss the long wagon rides, now that the railroad makes traveling so fast. They say that they miss the seclusion they used to have in the winters before there were so many neighboring ranches. If, for instance, someone went on a trip from the Platte River ranch country down to Santa Fé, they might be gone for six months before anyone began to wonder when they would be back. If a man took the stage from Abilene or Ogallala to go to California on business, his family might get a letter from him after a month. They might bid him good bye in the autumn and not expect him back until the next spring. Back then, back when Pasque and Elena fell in love, time did have a different meaning.

Pasque's discovery of this unhurried existence that the New Mexicans called *poco tiempo*, or slow time, went with him that December as he left the *Hacienda Godinez* and rode south in search of the giant Hochland. He missed Elena. He thought about her across the lengthening distances. His mind went over every memory, recreating each word, each smile, each caress.

After he was gone, Elena sat by herself, often from the noon dinner until darkness came. She tried to keep busy at needlework, while sitting, but in her mind she was out riding with him. Often she thought of the last glimpse she had of him as he rode away down the trail leading south, slim and easy in the saddle, twisting around to look back at her, his hand resting on the cantle of his saddle. She pictured herself riding beside him, and day after day, when she was alone with her needlework or a book, she imagined over and over again that he was still riding like that, his face still turned and looking back, as if asking her to come riding with him.

There was no way for Elena to know when he would return. She could only keep her faith that he would return, someday. Perhaps it would be in the spring, when the flowers began to bloom up on the hill along the *acequia*. Perhaps it would be after the harvest, when the workers began bringing in wagonloads of firewood for the winter. Or during the Christmas season. Or perhaps, she sighed, sometime in the spring after that. She would be patient and supervise the house and take care of her father, and, when it was time for Pasque to return, he would return. But also in her thoughts was the knowledge that her mother and her brother had both ridden away from the *hacienda*, never to be seen alive again.

Pasque rode quietly, but he was anxious to find Hochland and get the showdown over with, one way or the other. He always took the most direct trail he could find between one landmark and another. If there was no trail, he took a bull-headed pleasure in making his own. On the bank of the Purgatory he could have ridden a few miles upriver to a bridge; instead, he swam the horses straight across, getting the pack soaking wet. He saw a winding road, snaking back and forth up the cañon toward distant Raton Pass, but Pasque thought it would be faster to go straight up the mountain. Pushing through the brush and searching for ways to get around the rimrock cliffs, he wasted hours. On the third day, he came out on a ridge. From there he saw down the other side and figured that it would have been faster just to follow the road.

The slope was dangerous. He would have to zigzag all the way down, and it looked like there were two rimrock ledges he'd have to find his way past. And all his hard work would only get him into another meadow. The main part of the range, including Raton Pass, was still in front of him.

For three hours Pasque stubbornly urged the horses down the loose gravel and sand. When he was finally past the first rimrock cliffs, he made camp. It was a dry camp with no water for the horses and not much for them to graze on. He spent the night cold, since he was in strange country. No telling who might see a fire on an open slope and come to investigate. Instead, he rounded up a pile of wood for a breakfast fire and covered it with his slicker to keep it dry.

Morning came bright and clear and so cold it was all Pasque could do to drag his shivering body out of the bedroll and get the fire going. The sagewood and pitchy piñon made a smudge that could be seen for miles, but he didn't much care, now that it was daylight. He kept the Winchester handy, while he cooked his coffee and beans and figured that, if anybody came along, he'd just make them wait until he was warmed up. Then he'd deal with them.

The sun helped, once it got high enough. Pasque had long since learned to camp on southeast slopes. There the sun would slide up out of the east and off to the south, clearing the horizon hills slowly at first, and before long it would be warm enough to coax the ache out of cold muscles.

Pasque finished his third cup of coffee and, feeling warmer, shrugged the saddle blanket off his shoulders. He stood up and set the rifle on the blanket and stretched his arms toward the crystal-blue sky. Then out of the corner of his eye he noticed something shining on the sand, a few feet away. He walked over. He hunkered down. It was a piece of a flint knife, a busted blade, just lying there. He picked it up, feeling the sharp edge with his thumb, admiring the jet black obsidian and the fine handiwork of it, all those tiny chips it had taken to change a chunk of dull black rock into this glistening blade.

He was so busy admiring it that he didn't notice the man who was sneaking up on him. Then some instinct, some feeling, made him slowly turn and look, and about fifty yards away he saw the man standing in plain view. Pasque rose, real easy-like, glanced over to where his Winchester was, and then looked back at the man.

Pasque's visitor looked as if he had stepped out of the past. A mountain man, an old one. Old didn't even seem like an adequate term. This one looked old enough to have hunted beaver for Noah. He wore the fringed leggings and knee-high moccasins of the desert Indians, and a short capote-style blanket overcoat. The thing on his head was supposed to be a hat and once had been an animal, but it was so worn out that it was hardly recognizable as either one.

He was holding his mountain rifle at hip level, aimed straight at Pasque's belly. It was a heavy old muzzleloader, the kind that would have a big bore to it. Probably .50 or .60 caliber. But what Pasque wanted to know about that mountain rifle, and what he couldn't see from there, was whether or not it was cocked. If it wasn't, he had maybe two seconds to get to the Winchester. If the old boy's rifle was cocked, then Pasque was going to spend the last two seconds of his life diving for his gun. But one thing was certain. If they were going to have a conversation, he was going to be holding a rifle, too. If the trapper shot at him and missed, it would take him a full minute to reload that old front-filler. That minute would give Pasque all the advantage he could ask for.

He decided his course of action. He casually dropped the flint blade and tensed his muscles for the dive for the rifle, at the same time trying to throw the mountain man off guard by raising one hand and smiling his biggest smile.

"Howdy!" he yelled across the distance between them. "Nice mornin' . . ." — and he whipped his raised

179

arm suddenly across his chest so the momentum would twist him, and he dove onto the Winchester and rolled with it, waiting for a roar from the other gun, expecting a big, solid, lead ball to come cracking into him, maybe in the hip, or the arm, and he did another roll with his rifle cradled in one arm, waiting for the shot that he knew was coming. He got himself hidden behind a redrock boulder and a sagebrush. At least he hoped he was hidden. As soon as he was hunkered down as good as he could be, Pasque cocked the Winchester's hammer and pushed the barrel out around the rock.

The old-timer still hadn't fired a shot.

Pasque peeked out. The old guy was no longer standing there. But there was a scraggly bush and a big rock off to the right that a man might use for cover. Pasque sighted the Winchester in that general direction, even though he couldn't see anyone.

Whoom! Splang! The shot came from somewhere off to Pasque's left and whapped into the sand next to the rock inches away from his face. Stinging sand hit his cheeks and eyes like birdshot, blinding him. With his left hand he rubbed at his eyes, while with his right hand he squeezed off a shot of his own. He heard the bullet ricochet a long way off, 'way high.

"Sure is a nice mornin'," the voice agreed. "Awful purty mornin'."

Pasque fired again, blindly, and knew that he was firing wild. He dug a finger into the corner of his right eye, trying to get the sand out. The old boy was probably reloaded by now. Pasque's vision started to come back; he looked out and thought he saw a blurry, watery outline of a man about fifty yards off to his left, so he squirmed backward to get better protection from the rock, and he kept squirming until he knew he was under the sagebrush. He poked the Winchester out from under the branches, aiming at what he hoped was the man's silhouette.

"Wonder if I might ask you some directions?" Pasque yelled.

Whoom! Splang! The boom of the old-timer's muzzle-loader hit Pasque's ears, and the sagebrush trunk exploded into slivers, and it felt like most of them embedded themselves in Pasque's cheek. He had to ignore the pain. His eyes were almost back to normal, and he had one minute or less to get the drop on that sociable old bastard while he was reloading his cannon. Pasque jumped up, sprinted in the direction of the shot, saw the only bush big enough to hide a man, ran to it, around it, leveled the rifle, and found nothing in his sights but thin air. The only thing he felt was the cold, hard, unmistakable sensation of a gun muzzle being shoved into the small of his back, about an inch above his belt.

"What directions did you have in mind?" the voice rasped.

"You got that gun reloaded that fast, did you?" Pasque replied. "Don't know as I believe you really loaded it. Probably empty, isn't it?"

"You believe in pistols?"

Pasque thought a minute. Many a man carried a sidearm. Some even carried two, maybe a little boot rifle and a pocket pistol, like a Derringer.

181

"Been known to," Pasque said. His face hurt.

The old man's gravelly voice was warm against his ear. Pasque could smell dirty buckskins and grease and sweat.

"That fire o' yourn," the old-timer said. "You makin' smoke signals for that god-damn uppity Paiute son-of-a-bitch? Or you just tryin' to make coffee?"

"Coffee," Pasque said.

"Let's go," the voice said. And Pasque led the way back to the camp, where the fire was nearly out. The mountain man hunkered down nearby, his rifle across his knees and his antique pistol dangling in one hand. He watched while Pasque gathered up the rest of the wood and piled it on the coals, then set the coffee pot on. Pasque gave up thinking he would out-shoot this ancient wreck. He just began pulling slivers out of his cheek instead, mopping the blood with a damp bandanna.

The old man had his coffee. Pasque went out in the brush to empty the earlier three cups out of his bladder — or what was left in him after that first shot hit the dirt four inches from his eyes. The mountain man was ready to talk.

"Kinda off the road, ain't ya?"

"Figured a short cut," Pasque said.

"Road's the best way. Mebbe nobody let ya know. Lot o' fellas, they try to take over the hill so's not to pay Uncle Dick his toll, see."

"Uncle Dick? That you, by chance?"

The mountain man spit on the ground. "No matter who I am. You'd knowed *my* name, back in the beaver

days. Yessir. You'd ast Bridger, ast Carson ... ol' Kit
... they'd tell ya. Young hoss like you, hell, your pappy
was still suckin' tit when I stretched my first beaver
plew. Tell ya th' way the stick floats 'round here, an' see
what ya say to it. Mebbe you 'n' me, we rides over t' the
road and yore on yore way. Or mebbe," he said, tucking
the pistol into his belt, and then starting to reload his
mountain rifle, "mebbe ya'd rather go back t' learnin'
how to be a pro-fessional movin' target."

Pasque said he'd rather hear about the road.

"This here pass," the mountain man said, waving his
arm to indicate that he was talking about the whole
Raton range from west to east, "she's got but one road
over her, an' Uncle Dick, he makes a little livin' with
collectin' tolls. Four bits for a horse, two bits for a
man."

"Pay you, do I?" Pasque said.

"Nope. Ya pay Dick. I might be nuthin' but a
pot-hunter, just gettin' venison to sell t' Wooton's place
an' t' the wagons and sech, but I ain't gotten low
'nough to be no toll-taker. Not yet."

After cleaning up his face, Pasque erased the signs of
his campfire and saddled up. His companion vanished
for a while, then came back astride a big gray mule.
Without much talk, just a couple of words, they set out,
Pasque following the mountain man off across the crest
of the ridge. They settled into a kind of quiet truce;
apparently the old fellow had decided that Pasque
really had missed the road out of innocent ignorance
and not because he meant to cheat anybody out of a
dollar.

183

Pasque decided not to push his luck by asking questions, at least not at this point. Maybe when they got to the toll station. If anybody would know the whereabouts of the giant rider named Hochland, it would be one of these old-timers.

The other thing Pasque had a curiosity about was that remark about an "uppity Paiute." A beaver trapper who had ridden with Kit Carson would surely know that the Indians in this area were Comanches, mostly. Some Arapahoes, maybe a few Utes. Paiutes were 'way off in the deserts, west of the Rockies. Never got this far, as far as his Uncle Art knew. Well, maybe he'd get a chance to ask, once they got to this toll station.

"Thar she be." The old buckskinner pointed to a neatly arranged set of log buildings at the summit of the pass. "Grub's good, an' so's the beds. No cot crickets."

"No what?" Pasque said.

"Lice. Seam squirrels. None of 'em in Dick's beds, less'n ya brung yore own."

"You comin' with me?"

"Nope. Thar's meat t' be got. Now I've had my practice target shootin', mebbe I kin hit a elk. Reckon?" he said, with a wink.

"I reckon you can," Pasque replied, fingering the fresh sliver wounds in his cheek. "See ya later, then."

"Doubt it," the mountain man said. "Took y' half a hour t' see me the first time." He turned his mule off the road and waved without looking back. "Mind yore ha'r!" he yelled. And was gone.

He was right. Wooton's toll station and overnight inn had comfortable bunks, and the place served up a first-class meal. His wife cooked plain food, but cooked it right and saw to it that there was plenty of it. There were six other guests that night, brave souls taking a chance on getting their wagon and a few head of oxen over the pass before a snowstorm caught them. At meals they chose to stay to themselves at one table while Pasque ate alone at another. That suited him fine.

He was just finishing breakfast, mopping up the last of the egg yolk and the gravy with a chunk of biscuit, when Wooton crossed the room, carrying the coffee pot and another tin cup. He poured Pasque's cup full, then helped himself to one, and sat down, hospitably placing the pot between them.

"Cold mornin'," he began. "Should warm up, though."

"Has a way of doin' that, down here," Pasque said. "But you go up north this time of year an' that sun never has any heat in 'er."

"I know that," Wooton said. "Spent some time trappin' up along the Green and clear t' the Yellowstone. Never been so cold as that. It's a dry kind o' cold, though. Not like that winter damp y' get down in Virginia, when it gets chilly. That kind o' cold goes right to the bone."

Pasque was not surprised to hear Wooton refer to Virginia. He had known several cowboys from down that way, mostly retired Confederate soldiers, and in their speech they all had that soft accent of the South. He and his tall, genial host discussed the weather and other matters such as the coming of the surveyors to lay out a railroad right-of-way over the pass and the

185

rumors of Indian unrest. When Wooton brought up the subject of Indians, Pasque saw his chance maybe to start asking some questions, questions that might point the way to Hochland's place.

"That old mountain man out there, he said somethin' about Paiutes . . . ," Pasque began.

"Old John? Met him, did you? Well, he an' I are both ol' Indian fighters, y' see. Killed a few Pawnee and Snake in my day. Him, too. But this Paiute thing . . . there's only the one of them. Local Indians say he's from out in the Nevada Territory somewhere, an' that he has powerful medicine. Magic, y' see."

"Magic. That right?"

"There's nuthin' to it, of course, but he thinks the ground is goin' to open up and swallow th' whites. All of us. But first the Indians have t' learn this dance of his, so he's been goin' around teachin' them to do it. Cheyennes, Arapahoes, some of the Pawnees, some of the Utes, all seem to be doin' this ghost dance thing."

"Is he around here now?" Pasque said.

"Just rumors, y'understand. Rumor is, he's supposed to be dying." Wooton offered to pour Pasque another cup of coffee, but Pasque waved it away. "They say he might already be dead. They say that Tallak Hochland took him in, at his ranch down by Fisher Peak. Hochland and his wife, y' understand, they have pretty big medicine themselves. She's half Paiute herself, so I've been told."

Pasque's heart seemed to be pounding so loud that he was surprised Wooton couldn't hear it. Might have been the coffee, or the surprise at hearing that name, but all the muscles from his chest down along his arms to his fingers seemed to be trembling. Hochland. Fisher Peak. He was suddenly on his guard, watching his words carefully and watching Wooton with equal care.

"So," he said at last, "do you think these ghost dancers'll take my scalp, if I ride on south?"

"They haven't bothered any travelers that I know of, not yet. Of course," the Southerner added with a laugh, "those that the Indians killed didn't make it this far t' tell me about it!"

Pasque didn't find Wooton's joke all that funny, but he smiled anyway. "Man maybe shouldn't camp alone, if he can help it," Pasque said. "I suppose he oughta find a ranch or stage station to stay at, nights."

"Well, there is a stage station once y' get down off the pass and quite a ways out. You'd have t' leave before sunrise to make it, though."

Pasque saw his chance. "This ranch you mentioned. It any closer to here?"

"Hochland's? Oh, I s'pose you could maybe make it by nightfall. Have to ride pretty hard, though. Y' understand, it's not on the road. Y' get off the pass, off the mountain, and the desert levels out. Off t' your left, you'll see Fisher Peak. Biggest mountain around there. It's sort of stair-step lookin', flat on top, with a big round mesa-like structure at one end. Looks like an old castle from England, as a matter of fact."

"Sounds like I won't make it tonight, though."

"I doubt it. Once you get to Fisher Peak, you still need to ride around it t' get t' th' east side. An' t' tell the truth, not many men . . . not even ol' John . . .

would want t' ride there, if it was startin' t' get dark. Spooky place, that."

"Well," Pasque said, rising from his chair and stretching, "guess I'll just take it easy and hide my camps."

Back in the bunkroom, where he had left his gear, Pasque dug around inside the torn lining of his left boot until he found some wrinkled bills — his holdout money. At least he had enough to pay the toll and to pay for his bed and meals.

He paid Wooton, told him that he'd be back, now that he knew how good the grub was, and set off with the pack horse in tow behind him. He looked back once, after he had ridden a while, and could see the thin line of smoke rising, marking Wooton's place. Chances were good, he wouldn't be coming back. That single, white streak of smoke, standing tall from the crest of the pass, seemed to mark the end of one world for him. On that far side of the pass was Elena, and the long trail back to the Keystone. On that far side of the pass, on the other side where that wisp of smoke was rising, there was a life, even more than one life, for him.

There was winter back there, it was true, but the kind of winter that always makes spring seem like a miracle. Everything seemed to die, gradually drying up and losing its color as October turned to November; by late December there would be no bright colors at all. But even as December came to a close, the sun was starting to stay longer. By March, by April, spring was a certainty once again.

188

On this side of the pass, the colors were a little more dull, more like sand and sagebrush. The air, once the sun cleared the horizon, was warmer and drier. He had heard an old Kiowa legend once, about how some Kiowa men had set out to find where the sun slept all winter. And they had found it, far to the south of their homes. But the sun's home was not for them; nothing seemed to die there, and so nothing new could be born. They went home, and they told their people that they had not found the home of the winter sun. There was no use in anybody else going to look for it.

CHAPTER
TWELVE

Apaches!

Pasque stopped to let the horses rest before going on. All below him was Southwest desert, rounded sand hills with patches of sage and piñon like a brocade in tan and pale green. It was a far cry from the ranges of Kansas and Wyoming. This country seemed older and wilder, more open, more vast. And primitive, even though, as Don Diego said, European civilization had been here longer than any place in America. The Spanish had followed the Rio Grande in the 1500s. Frenchmen had discovered the Arkansas River in the 1600s. Americans had started up the Santa Fé Trail in 1821.

Now, Pasque was looking down on the Cimarron River. Like the Purgatory, the Canadian, and the Washita, the Cimarron eventually flowed into the Arkansas River. He figured the way to find Tallak Hochland's house was to follow the Cimarron around to the east side of Fisher's Peak.

Trouble had begun on the Arkansas River two years earlier when a colony of white American farmers had started growing crops alongside that river. They had used irrigation — the first time it had been tried anywhere in the high plains. They had been the first irrigators on the Arkansas, but they weren't the first farmers. The Jicarilla Apaches had raised corn by the river long before whites had come along with their steel plows and oxen. They had hunted buffalo, too, but, as the whites had come closer, the herds had become smaller. Apache hunters had drifted west, following the animals. Apache women had moved the cornfields farther and farther away from the white men. American settlers finally had pushed the Jicarillas into the mountainous cañons of the Cimarron. There they had been kept from moving east by white farmers, had been hemmed in to the north by the gold camps, and had been obstructed by the Spanish *rancheros* to the south.

Desperate to feed their families, the clans of the Jicarilla Apaches had begun to drift apart in search of a means of life. Some had wanted to go live in the high mountains; some had sought peaceful trade with the whites; others had been in favor of making war. There was no longer a single voice, and many individuals — particularly young men of warrior age — had begun to make their own decisions.

Two years before Pasque had gotten there, at the same time the latest settlers were digging new irrigation ditches even on the Cimarron, the government had persuaded most of the Jicarillas to move onto a reservation far to the south. But some of the young men would not go. Raiding groups had ridden against the white settlements, stealing cattle from the Spanish ranches and ambushing travelers. Most people moving through any of the Arkansas River drainages, such as the Cimarron, had stayed in large groups and moved quickly.

Many whites had heard rumors of a Paiute named Tavibo. Tavibo had been going all over the West, preaching his ghost dance. He had convinced the Apache renegades that he could make them invulnerable to bullets. Not only would they be invulnerable, but their dead ancestors would come back and fight alongside them. If all the tribes would dance the ghost dance, wearing special shirts, the dead would return. Even the buffalo would return. With his painted shirts and magic ceremonies, Tavibo was turning Apache renegades into suicidal fanatics.

Pasque started his horses down toward the Cimarron. In spite of its being December, the day was almost warm. As the sun became warmer and warmer, he stuffed his gloves into his pocket and unbuttoned his sheepskin coat. He wished he had one of Don Diego's cigars to smoke while he ambled along down the ridge.

Somewhere behind him he thought he heard a horse's hoof striking rock. He stopped and looked back, but there was nothing. Still, he had an uneasy feeling that somebody was following him.

As he got down into the flat country along the river, Pasque didn't take much notice of the big rocks. He kept an eye on Fisher's Peak, with its sheer-walled top that looked like a castle. Huge rocks had split off from the cliffs above and rolled down onto the flats, where they were scattered around like petrified haystacks.

Farther on, Pasque did notice that the sagebrush was getting thicker. Once, he thought, he saw a flash of light high up on the mountain at the base of the castle cliffs. Then he saw a movement ahead of him, a running figure just vanishing into an arroyo to his right.

Pasque shortened the lead rope on the pack horse, drawing her up close to his leg where he could either lead her by the halter or unclip the lead rope and let her loose, if he had to make a run. He slid the Winchester out and levered a cartridge into the chamber, then held the rifle upright and ready with the butt resting on his thigh.

He rode on, watching the spot where he had seen the runner. That was what the Apaches wanted him to do. Pasque was still looking to the right, when a warrior on his left jumped from the cover of a juniper tree, raced across the few yards of ground, and made a grab at the pack horse. Pasque got the rifle on him and fired. The man whirled and screamed and fell. The horses jerked and started to run, but two more Apaches stood in the trail ahead, and there was no place else to go. Pasque kicked the spurs to his horse and brought the Winchester across to take a shot at the one on the left. He aimed the galloping horse at the man on the right, and prayed that the fourth Apache, the one he'd seen run into the arroyo, wasn't right behind him.

The Winchester spoke, and another Apache dropped. Pasque had no time to think about life and death and right and wrong. No choice, if he wanted to live.

While Pasque was levering in another cartridge and struggling to keep hold of his reins, the last warrior

193

made a leap at him and seized the rifle barrel and hung on, nearly ripping the Winchester out of Pasque's hands. Pasque got his foot loose from the stirrup and planted a kick to the chest that made the Apache drop.

Pasque spurred the horse hard and galloped along the edge of the arroyo. There was open country up ahead, if he could only make it. Pasque took a quick look back at the Apache who was running after him. Pasque was gaining on him, though, and he was getting into the clear. Then he saw two more Apaches running down the hill, running to cut him off. One of them stopped and aimed an old Sharps carbine at him.

The arroyo. Without thinking about it, Pasque headed both horses for the drop-off. It was the only cover he could see anywhere. The saddle horse made a clean jump off the edge and landed hard in the loose sand, spilling Pasque out of the saddle. Pasque hit the ground with a grunt and rolled, still holding onto his rifle like grim death. He got to his feet fast and saw that the pack horse had come down the drop-off sideways and was lying on her side now, kicking helplessly. Broken leg, Pasque figured. Damn it.

He ducked into the cover of the arroyo's overhang, catching hold of the saddle horse's reins to drag him along. In his possibles sack lashed on top of the saddlebags there was a box of ammunition. He had heard at least one gunshot go off almost at the exact moment that he made his jump into the draw. It had probably been the Indian with the old carbine; the other ones, those who had come running at him, didn't seem to have any weapons other than their knives.

Thwumk!

The arrow quivered in the sand a foot away from him. Well, Pasque thought, at least one of them has a bow.

He dragged the horse a few yards farther up the arroyo, where a small sagebrush would give better cover, and tied the reins to a driftwood log. Then he poked the Winchester over the edge and stuck his head up to get a shot.

Thwumk!

Blam!

Pasque heard a scream and saw something fall, a long way up the hill. Must have been an accident. He was shaking so hard, he probably couldn't hit anything more than ten yards away. That, and the fact that his target practice had consisted of kissing Elena and letting her pulverize stumps. He smiled at the thought. It would be rather useful to have her and that .44 rim-fire here now.

His ankle started to throb. Maybe landing in the sand hadn't been so soft, after all. Damn.

Thwumk! Thwumk!

Two more arrows, close by. One came from down the arroyo, one from up behind, maybe. He waited, watched, ignored the crawling fear in his spine that said another arrow would come from down the draw while he was aiming up the slope. Maybe the Indian with the bow is behind that big rock. That would be about right. If he'll just show a little more of his head, stand straight, and . . . ah! There he is, right behind that rock

195

just like Pasque figured, leaning out to send another arrow this way.

Blam!

Pasque whirled, levering another shell, while he turned on his injured ankle. It felt like fire. Was this his last shell, or was there still one in the magazine? He patted his holster to make sure that he hadn't lost his Colt during the tumble down the embankment.

There! *Blam!* The Winchester spoke again. The Apache down the arroyo either fell back or jumped back around the corner. Pasque backed up across the sand to the other bank. Better to change positions, even if it was more exposed. He could see farther up the hill, too. An Indian was moving there, maybe the same one who had been behind the rock. Pasque levered the Winchester. No more shells; the magazine was empty.

He dug out the spare cartridges from his sack and shoved them into the pocket of his chaps, while keeping an eye on the man up the hill, trying to see the one down the arroyo, too, and backing up to get a wider angle of fire. His foot caught a root, twisted. Pain shot through the ankle, and he stumbled and dropped two of the cartridges he was trying to load into the rifle. At that same instant he saw the Apache in the arroyo. The Indian stepped out into the open and let fly with another arrow. And this time it was on target. It sliced into Pasque's thigh, just above the knee, and stuck there, deep.

He hauled out the Colt and fired back, twice. Now he was starting to get mad. He was also getting reckless. Winchester in his left hand, Colt in his right, he stumbled toward the Apache, who was backing up and putting another arrow to his bow. Another shot from the Colt. This one caught the Indian in the arm. The Apache looked at him, then up at the edge of the draw, and Pasque saw the other two coming at him, running full tilt. The one in the lead was just jumping off the edge as Pasque brought the Colt around.

Blam! Might have got him. At least he ended up face down next to Pasque's feet and didn't move. The other was coming with a knife, running hard and screaming, and the one down the arroyo had started to run toward him, too, knife in hand. Did he have two shots left in the Colt? Let them get closer, then he'd find out, he told himself.

Boom!

The Apache who had been running toward the arroyo was suddenly flying sideways, blood spraying from him. Pasque took aim at the one coming up the draw. The warrior was still coming at him in spite of a busted arm and without appearing to give a damn that he was charging straight into the business end of a .44 Colt. It seemed like he was the only Apache left, and anybody with an ounce of common sense and healthy fear should turn and run. But he didn't. Not until he was a scant twenty feet away.

Maybe it was something in Pasque's face that made the Apache stop. Whatever it was, it wasn't fear. The Indian just stopped. He looked around at his dead companions, then looked at Pasque with a steady, level gaze. Then he turned, calm as you please, and spit on the ground and sheathed his knife and began to walk away. Pasque carefully aimed the Colt at the middle of his back. But standing there in the warm sun with cold sweat on his brow and blood running down his leg and into his boot, Pasque felt the anger and the pain and the desire to kill draining out of him. For the first time since the attack began, he stopped to think. He could think of lots of reasons to shoot this Apache in the back, but none of them seemed right. Pasque lowered the Colt, and he also turned and walked away. He also thought about turning and spitting on the ground like the Apache had done, but, unlike the Apache, Pasque was spitless.

All was quiet again, except for the weak whinnies of pain coming from the pack horse down the draw. Pasque hobbled toward it, picked up the cartridges he had dropped, shucked them into the rifle. He finished loading it with shells from his chaps pocket, then reloaded the Colt. He used the Colt to put the horse out of pain.

As the echo of his shot died away, Pasque looked down at his leg. The arrow was still there, with its broken shaft, and he had managed to give it a few good twists and hits in the course of all the action, so it had opened a fearsome wound. Warm blood ran in a stream inside his pant leg.

Well, damn, he thought. *I'm gettin' whoozy and weak, too. More Indians around, maybe. Gonna pass out. What was that other shot . . . big rifle? Who the hell?*

The last thing Pasque saw before everything went black was a figure in fringed buckskin standing on the

198

edge of the arroyo above him, ramming a lead ball down the barrel of an old mountain rifle. And the last thing he heard was old-timer John's voice.

"'Nother purty mornin'. I see yore still practicin' at bein' a movin' target. Gettin' better at it, too. All but one o' them arrers missed ya."

The next few hours were a blur. He remembered the jouncing of the makeshift travois and hanging onto the poles and a rope around his chest that held him. They had stopped a while. Somebody joined them, riding alongside the travois, looking down at him. A big man. He seemed to look like a giant against the sky.

The bouncing of the travois seemed to go on forever, then everything went dark again. And Pasque woke up in a bed that was bigger than any bed he had ever seen.

The wind eventually erased the signs of the fight that had taken place in that remote arroyo near the Cimarron River. Until it did, there were two dark bloodstains twenty feet apart in the sand. One was next to some boot tracks, and moccasin tracks marked the other one. Two men had stood there with weapons in their hands, while Death whetted the edge of his reaping scythe and laughed. The two men had made their choices. The young Jicarilla had cheated Death by choosing pride over anger. And Pasque had chosen to follow the oldest code of warriors, when he had lowered his pistol, rather than shooting his enemy in the back. The Apache could have shot him, anyway. Pasque had made a gamble with Death and had forced him to look for someone else to be his hired gun.

CHAPTER
THIRTEEN

"La Belle Dame Sans Merci
Thee Hath in Thrall!"

Pasque had been wounded just before noon, and it was early evening before he started to wake up and wonder where he was. He seemed to be in a room. Light came from an oil lamp turned down low. He could smell it. A little bit of light came through the open door. He could smell piñon burning. And food cooking.

His mind was floating in something thick and warm. His eyes drifted around the room, but the room kept waltzing in and out of focus. There was a hump in the bed covers, and he realized it was his leg, raised on a cushion or pillow under the covers. It was throbbing, and he wondered how it could throb so much without making the blanket heave up and down? His other ankle hurt like a hot poker had been run through it. He shifted his left foot, and the pain made him groan out loud. Someone moved out of the shadows. Pasque tried to see who it was, but his eyes weren't that steady. The doorway looked seven or eight feet high. The walls seemed to bend and bulge. The man's shadow was too tall for the room. It loomed over Pasque's bed like a fir tree about to fall. Then, apparently satisfied that the injured cowboy was awake, the man and his shadow turned and left. In the blur, it looked to Pasque as though the man had to bend over almost double to get through the door.

Through the buzzing in his head and the roaring in his ears, Pasque heard voices outside the room. One voice came nearer, and the silhouette of a woman appeared in the lighted doorway, a silhouette with long straight hair and a slim waist. She came closer to the bed.

"You are awake," she said. It was not a question, or even an observation. It sounded more like an order. Pasque tried to answer.

"Yehhhhaa . . ." — whatever he had started to say came out like the sound of a kid with his tongue frozen to a pump handle. His mouth felt like dry flannel.

The woman took a cup from the bed table and brought it to his lips. Gently she poured the liquid, little by little, into his mouth. It tasted of apricots and cinnamon.

"Thanks," he managed, after his tongue came unstuck from the back of his teeth.

"You are welcome," she said with a sort of foreign-sounding voice, but not Spanish. Why was he thinking about that? And beautiful. In the dim lamplight, her features were shadowy and soft, and she was truly beautiful. He tried squinting so he could see her better. She smiled and placed a cool hand on his forehead.

"Could you eat something?" she asked. "Some soup, perhaps?"

"Might be," Pasque said. That didn't sound quite right. "Thanks," he added. His head began to swim again, and now it was aching. By forcing himself to stare at a single spot on the wall, while moving his body a fraction of an inch at a time, he managed to drag himself into a slumped sitting position against the pile of pillows without passing out. He discovered that he was naked, except for the wide bandage around his leg. By the time the woman returned with the tray, he was sitting almost upright with the covers pulled up around his shoulders. He was also smiling, or hoped he was. At least, he could feel the corners of his mouth pulled back. *Probably look stupid*, he decided.

The woman turned up the lamp and sat on the edge of the bed, carefully feeding him the soup one spoonful at a time. It was salty and tasted like beef.

"John and my husband brought you here," she explained. "My husband heard shooting while he was out riding, and, by the time he located you, John was already building a drag. Do you remember? John believes that some renegade Apaches ambushed you."

"Remember bouncin' along behind a horse somehow. Some big fella ridin' next to me, I think." Pasque ran his hand down along his leg. "John wrap me up like this?" he asked. "Must've been a arrowhead in there."

"There was. A large one. I saved it for you," she replied. Pasque wondered if she was the one who had cut the arrow out of his thigh and then cleaned him up and put the bandages on.

She fed him the last of the soup and turned down the lamp before she left the room. He heard her in the hallway, speaking to another woman, telling her to let him rest. "We will need to keep the house quiet," she said.

"*Sí,* Ama," the other woman replied.

Ama, Pasque thought, as his mind began to drift down into the softness of the pillows and his eyes began to fall closed. *Ama. Lovely name. Ama.*

At some point in the night he had a dream. Everything about it was distorted and abrupt and leaped from place to place, but, when he came awake, he remembered Link's being in the dream, grinning at him, and Pasque had an old singleshot rifle, but a priest kept pushing the barrel aside, and he could see the Apache talking with the blacksmith and drawing circles in the sand. And then he followed Link, but he didn't have his gun any more, and they went into a courtyard where a fountain was splashing and a woman was coming to bathe, and she was only wearing a loose cotton shift.

Gwen. His eyes opened. A thick film covered them, and he couldn't blink it off. In a red, tight-fitting gown or robe, with bare shoulders and a low neckline, she was bending over him. Light from the window struck her hair and made the gown look even thinner. Gwen. Ah, Gwen. Pasque felt himself stirring, his naked body sensitive to the touch of the blanket, his wounds forgotten.

His arms reached for her, and she let his hands take her shoulders and pull her against him. Gwen was like that. She would let him draw her to him and would let him touch her and hold her that way, but she would not come into his arms unless he wanted her to. Her mouth was coming closer. The softness of her hair brushed his hand. His mouth felt her warm breath, warm like a feather stroking his lips before the kiss. He had wanted her for so long. He had dreamed of her so many nights.

No. No. He was better than this. She was Art's wife. No matter what he felt, what he wanted, this wasn't right. He pushed her away.

"Good morning," she said. It was the woman. He was in an adobe bedroom with bright winter sunlight streaming in the window.

The woman. She sat on the edge of the bed, wearing a red nightgown and a thin red robe. Her breasts were barely covered; her long dark hair curled all over her shoulders; she was smiling. He tried to remember where he was and what had happened. Last night? Last night? She held a cup of the apricot-tasting drink to his lips, leaning so close to him that one breast brushed his arm.

After his drink, Pasque shook his head and rubbed his eyes, pretending that he was just beginning to figure out where he was. He tried to pretend not to notice that she was sitting there in her nightgown. Pasque moved his neck as though he were stretching a kink out of it, and he sneaked a look at the door. It was closed.

"Now I see how you got wounded," she smiled, "letting people creep up on you while you sleep." Her laugh was light and happy. "But you are fortunate. I am not going to shoot you. I am only going to hold you prisoner until you heal."

204

"Guess you got me," Pasque answered. "Seems like a fair deal, too, just as long as you don't want to shoot any arrows in me." He took the cup from her hand and had another sip from it.

"Anything else?" she asked.

"What?"

"If I don't shoot arrows into you, I can do anything else?" Her eyes teased him.

"Guess so. Like you said, I'm your prisoner." He looked around the room. "I ain't got a single gun in sight, either."

The lady leaned close to him again and ran her cool hand over the exposed part of his chest. She touched his lips with a single fingertip, very lightly.

"How bad is your wound this morning?" she asked in a low, whispering voice.

Pasque coughed and cleared his throat. That stirring feeling under the covers was starting up again.

"Not bad," he said, "but, when your husband comes in that door and finds us here, I think I'm gonna have some new wounds to worry about."

She pulled back a little, and laughed again. "Oh, that! He left early this morning to go hunting. I imagine he'll be gone all day."

"Well, all the same," Pasque said. He put his hand under the covers to touch the bandage around his leg. "Not to change the subject or anythin', but this piece of sliced ham is startin' to leak blood again. I'd be grateful for a clean bandage . . . this one here's gettin' soggy."

"Of course," she said. "I'll have Constance bring some fresh wrappings." The lady slid off the bed with a rustle of silk and smiled back at him. "She and I will wash your wound and dress it. Just as we did yesterday."

And leaving Pasque to let that bit of information sink in, she opened the door and glided away down the hall.

He was able to keep his modesty, thanks to the loose covers that he could wrap around his hips. It didn't feel too bad at all, when the two women sponged his leg with warm water and wrapped it, as long as he didn't look at what they were doing while they were doing it. Afterward, left alone, he managed to crawl down off the bed long enough to use the chamber pot, and then he fell back on the deep pillows to sleep.

Pasque had planned to get up and get dressed and be on his feet, when the man of the house got back from his hunting trip. But he passed out in his first attempt to stand. He woke up again a long time after sunset, and found Constance standing by his bed with a bowl of beef soup. After eating, he slept again.

That night's dreaming was full of softly rounded hills in the sand, of arroyos that curved down in V-shaped shadows of summer warmth. He dreamed of water flowing silently in an *acequia*, and it reflected a pale blue sky through over-hanging branches of manzanita. He saw Don Diego on a gigantic horse, smoking a cigar and nodding in approval as Pasque turned away from a woman who had long curls of dark hair and, instead, held out his arms to Elena. He saw a river. A picket rope ran along it, with ghost-like skeletal people tied to it — Pasque knew that they were the souls of all the

Indians and Spaniards and Americans who had ever died for the sake of a piece of ground. Other souls were drowning in the river, screaming out for revenge against their enemies while their mouths filled with water. He searched among the lost souls for the faces of Link and Moore, but they weren't there. And somehow it didn't seem to matter to him any longer.

A scent of small roses drifted to him. Pasque came out of his sleep and felt the cool smoothness of a woman's hand pressed against his forehead. Elena. Her room of the house, the sprawling adobe ranch house. Elena. He did not open his eyes at once; instead, he lay there and drank in the odor of roses.

Adobe rooms have a hushed feeling; any sound you hear in them is gentle and without echo. The air in an adobe room has an even temperature — the temperature of the earth, the old people used to say — without drafts or pockets of cold air. Behind the fragrance of the roses, he could smell the clean smell of adobe walls. It must be Elena's room. She had said that she loved roses. Some day in the summer, she had told him, when he returned to her, she would show him her roses, and he would help her collect the petals. These she would crush, and then she would soak them in very light oil to make a perfume.

He should not be here, in her room, but the scent of roses, the luxury of the deep bed, the warmth and the quiet made him want to stay. *Have to get more awake,* he thought, *have to get out of here before something happens.*

He opened his eyes. Winter sunlight was pouring through the window. A tray was on the table, and on it was a steaming mug and a covered plate. The thick pine door was closed, just like before. This time the woman was in the bed next to him, sharing the pillows with him. Her legs lay alongside of his; he could feel the whole length of them through the single blanket and through her silk nightgown. This time her nightgown was silver-grey, and clung to little curves that the red one had missed. Around her shoulders she wore a thin, silver-gray bed jacket.

Pasque tried moving his tongue around his dry mouth, but it was like pulling a wooden spoon out of last week's oatmeal. The woman took a cup of water from the table and held it to his lips. "Mmmm," he said. "*Gracias.*"

"I have your breakfast here," she said. There was a new coolness in her voice. "That is, if you have enough strength to eat."

"Plenty," he said. "Fact is, I feel good enough to get up and get dressed."

"Later, perhaps. You seem weaker to me. I would say you had no strength at all. But, at least, try a little of your breakfast. My husband shot a fine antelope yesterday, and Constance made a delicious hash to go with your eggs."

Pasque started to take the plate and fork from her, but she pulled them away from him and fed him, as if he were helpless. It was a good breakfast, no doubt of it. Awful good. So was the coffee, which she let him sip from the mug as she held it. The attention she gave him was appreciated, too — almost as much appreciated as the view he had of her silk-covered legs and the peek-a-boo valley beneath that flimsy little bed jacket. But this stuff she was saying about him still being an invalid was something he didn't understand.

"I'd just as soon hold the plate an' fork, if you'll let me," he said. "Wouldn't want the man of the house to bust in and find us . . . like this." Pasque tried to laugh, but it sounded pretty nervous.

"Oh, no!" she replied, placing another bite between his lips, "you are not up to it. My husband would see right away that I'm in no danger from *you!* Besides, he and two of the men have ridden down toward the flats today . . . they went to hunt buffalo. A good slice of buffalo liver would give you your strength back."

Pasque said no more, but let the woman feed him until the plate was clean and the coffee was gone. He leaned back and stretched, stiff from sleeping and staying in bed so long, careful to keep the blanket well up around his chest. Her body next to his was making him nervous, but, otherwise, he felt very good this morning. Even his ankle had stopped throbbing.

The lady was strangely quiet, and did not smile very much.

"Want to tell me what's the matter?" Pasque said.

"Oh, nothing," she replied. Ever since Eve, women have had that way of saying "nothing" so that it really means "everything."

"Unh-huh. Well, what makes you think I'm worse off this mornin', then? Look more puny than yesterday, do I?"

"Well," she said, "I might be mistaken. I thought that you were one of those dashing, gallant cowboys that one hears about. You know . . . the sort that would kiss a woman and sweep her up in his arms and carry her off? Yet, here I am on your bed, and the door is bolted, and you don't even have the strength to kiss me."

With that, she turned and sat at the foot of the bed, out of arm's reach. Pasque didn't quite know what to think. He had seen men who could not be aroused by a woman as beautiful as this, but all of them had been in pine boxes with their boot toes pointing up. And a kiss wouldn't be all that much trouble. The minute he thought about kissing her his heart gave a skip and his mouth went dry again.

She was pouting. "Of course," she said, "it might be that you don't think I'm attractive enough to waste your strength on."

Oh-ho! So that was the game she was playin'. She figured that his next move would be a buck-naked jump down across the bed at her. Well, he *had* thought about it. He believed her story about her husband's being away. But after having been around Gwen and Art, and having had Don Diego trust him with Elena, this just didn't seem right. Even if he wasn't in love with Elena, it wouldn't be good manners to make love to his host's wife.

So, Pasque thought, he might start a little game of his own here. Kind of like poker. Maybe he could bluff his way out of this situation.

"Well, ma'am, I don't lie much, except when I'm sellin' a horse or playin' cards, and I can honestly say that you're as pretty a woman as I've ever seen in my whole life. Just lookin' at you there makes me feel like I could fight off another fifty or sixty Apaches."

He reached over and got himself another drink of water. She was smiling, a little.

"And as a matter of fact," Pasque went on, "I've been thinkin' I'd like to try to kiss you, ever since I first seen you. But it ain't safe."

"Not safe?" the lady said, making her eyes wide with pretended amazement. "Don't you believe me, when I tell you that we're here alone?"

"Oh, sure, I believe you" Pasque said. "I wasn't talkin' about that. But it's been over six . . ." — he looked at the ceiling and counted on his fingers — "no, maybe eight months since I kissed a gal." It was a lie, but he needed it to make the story work. "Last time, I'd let it go for three months. Been deliverin' cattle, three months on the trail to Nebraska. Kissed a gal in Omaha, and by the time we'd finished with that one kiss her lips was all blistered, and we'd got so excited that we whirled and bucked around yellin', and purty soon all her parlor furniture was broke, and th' fire brigade turned out to see who was crankin' the siren. And that was just after three months had gone by. I'd hate to think what I've got stored up in me after *eight* months!"

She was laughing now, covering her mouth with one hand and holding the front of her bed jacket closed with the other. Pasque was getting into the swing of his yarn-spinning.

211

"Why, if I was to come down to that end of the bed right now and start in to kiss you . . . and I'd sure like to . . . I s'pose it would end up that we'd bust the furnishin's, and then the walls would come tumblin' down like that town in the Bible, and all the livestock would run off, and one of us would be howlin' . . . I won't say which one . . . loud enough to scare off that herd of buffalo, and then your husband would come up here and cut the livers out of both of us.

"I don't think we oughta make him do somethin' that in-hospitable. Later on, he'd get to feelin' so downright bad about butcherin' me that it'd spoil his whole day. A man who owns a ranch in this country, he just shouldn't let it get around that he's that poor of a host to people."

The lady, still laughing, stood up and came to him and gave him a very light, friendly kiss on the lips. The scent of roses was there again.

"You win," she said. "I hadn't realized the destruction that it could cause, releasing all that power. You just rest now, and, perhaps later, you'll feel well enough to dress yourself and come to supper in the dining room. And," she smiled widely, "I'm going to let you feed yourself this time!"

She started to leave the room, then turned back to indicate a tall pine cupboard that stood against the wall. "Your things are in the *armario* there," she said. "Constance washed your clothes and mended your trousers for you. Oh . . . and you'll find your Apache arrowhead in one of your pockets. Rest well."

212

Pasque curled down into the depths of the featherbed, the covers all the way up to his nose, and relaxed into drowsiness, and then into sleep. He could not remember when a clean, warm bed had felt so good.

CHAPTER
FOURTEEN

Hochland's Secret

When Pasque woke up, the sun was going down, giving the room a soft half light. He lay quietly there in the gloom, listening to the silence. *The sun goes down early this time of year*, he thought. *It always does in late December.* He wondered what day it was, and whether Tallak Hochland had gotten tired of waiting for him. Pasque knew that it must be close to Christmas, or New Year's, one way or the other, but this household didn't seem to prepare anything for the upcoming holiday. No one had so much as mentioned it.

The door opened, and Constance came in with a mug of hot chocolate and a thick robe for him. She pronounced her Spanish carefully so that he would understand her: she had prepared a bath for him in the room across the hall, if he would care to bathe and dress for supper. She opened the doors of the *armario* to show him that his clothes were there, then left him alone.

The bath was a luxury. There was a big copper tub that a man could sit in, and a pipe running to a wood-fired heating tank so that he could have all the hot water he wanted. There was a sharp razor and

214

shaving soap and a mirror lying on the tray that went across the bathtub in front of him. An indoor bathroom was sure worth all the trouble it would take to build it, and as soon as he built his own adobe ranch house, he was going to fix up a rig like this. Elena would love it. He could picture her sitting in a tub, just like this one, sipping hot chocolate and smiling. It made a very nice picture.

It felt good to have clean clothes and polished boots. He felt lean and strong again. He walked tall and straight, when he went down the hallway to the dining room. His ankle gave him a few twinges, and his thigh was still swollen, but, all in all, he felt fine. Sort of like a condemned man all dressed up for his own execution, but still fine.

The lady of the house was waiting in the dining room. Constance was also there, and a wrangler who was just finishing his plate of food. The wrangler didn't say anything, except to excuse himself to the señora.

Pasque's thick venison steak was buried in chili with some kind of corn or hominy alongside; sopapillas and tortillas were in the center of the table, kept warm on an oven-heated plate covered with a cloth. Pasque ate as though he had been starving for weeks, when, in fact, he had eaten pretty well between his long naps for the last few days. Or week. He didn't know how long it had been. Between mouthfuls, Pasque asked the lady about her husband.

"Oh," she replied, "we don't expect him tonight. He has ridden out onto the plains, where he stays at the casa of some friends. It is so far to ride home in the

215

same day . . . besides, he enjoys visiting. Our friends often put him up, when he and his men ride out that far."

After supper, Pasque felt full and contented, but he didn't feel sleepy. He had slept enough for a couple of months, and, now that his energy was coming back, he felt restless. Constance stoked the piñon log fire that was burning in a big corner fireplace, and then she smiled and excused herself from the room, leaving Pasque and the lady all alone to drink their after-supper brandy together. That was another thing that Pasque planned to do, if he lived through this New Year's rendezvous with Hochland: he had heard that Santa Fé still had a Spanish winery that made brandy and that the old mountain men used to ride all the way from the Tetons to Taos just for a taste of that brandy and a glimpse of a Mexican *señorita*. Now he knew why.

She offered him a slim cigar, which he accepted, and, when he looked around for a match, she took a length of straw from a jar on the mantle and bent down to light it in the fire. The firelight from the blazing piñon logs danced and shimmered on her green, silk dress. The flare of the straw as she held it to the tip of Pasque's cigar flickered across the soft beauty of her face. Something about her — her face, her voice, the inviting body that her dress emphasized — was making Pasque pretty warm, and the brandy or the fire sure weren't helping matters much. He and the lady were just making small talk, so far, but Pasque knew what he was thinking about, and he had a good idea she was thinking about it, too. It was time to change the subject.

216

"Tell me somethin', Missus . . . Ama, is it?"

She laughed, and he saw the firelight now dancing in her eyes. "You heard Constance call me that," she smiled, "but it is not a name. It is Spanish for 'lady of the house,' . . . a sort of title. But what is it that you wanted me to tell you?"

"I, uh . . . I understood from Don Diego . . . at the Godinez Ranch where I stayed a while . . . that somebody here could show me where a fella named Hochland lives. Tallak Hochland?"

"Yes," she said. "I've been waiting for you to ask about him. His place, as you may call it, is not far from here. If you feel strong enough, I can have a man take you there tomorrow. It is a ride of perhaps two hours. Not far. You could be there and back before noon, I would think."

Pasque stared into the fire until it began to hurt his eyeballs. Suddenly his thoughts were not on the woman, or on anything in particular. Knowing that he was so close to Hochland clamped down on his mind like a huge hand. For many minutes he just stood there, gazing at the flames as his cigar went out. He finally found his voice again.

"This place of his . . . it's a ranch, then? Like this one?"

"No," she said carefully. "Not like *Siempre Verde*. He doesn't have anything like this over there."

"*¿Siempre Verde?*" Pasque said.

"Always green. It is this valley, you see. This valley is the greenest place in the region. The Indians used to

217

say that the sun came here in the winter to rest, before beginning its spring trip northward."

"I see. So this Tallak, he doesn't have a ranch. Just a house, then? A trading post, maybe?"

"Oh, he has a large *rancho*. But he will be awaiting you at his other house. No, not a house, really. I would not call it a house. Hmm. Now that you have asked," she smiled, "I don't know what word I would use. We have always just called it Hochland's place."

"And one of your men knows where this place is and could show me?"

"Oh, yes. As I said, less than two hours away."

There was that feeling again, like a fist clenching in his mind. It must have shown on his face.

"What's wrong?" she went on. "You look worried. And so quiet! Not very good company, are you?" She was teasing him now, trying to lighten his mood. "You haven't even taken notice of my dress this evening."

That wasn't exactly true. He had noticed it because of her hair. Her hair had just a suggestion of red in it, like cherry wood looks when its curves catch every gleam of the lamplight. The color of her hair was perfect against the emerald dress she wore this evening. It was a dress of silk with a full skirt that swirled with her slightest movement, a tight waist no more than the span of a man's two hands, a bodice that was almost too daring. Her shoulders would have been bare except for the little emerald jacket that she wore. Yes, he had noticed. He might be dead tomorrow morning, but he sure wasn't dead tonight.

218

Her question made him realize how his mind was wandering, split between two places. Part of it here, talking to her and looking at her, but there was a fuzzy echo to their words, as though he wasn't really present. His other part was already out on the trail, figuring what would happen when he got to Hochland's place. That part of him couldn't see things too clearly, either. Her question brought him back to the present again.

"Ma'am, that dress could ruin the whole Keystone Ranch, where I come from. Yes, it could."

"And how is that?" she laughed, lifting her brandy glass to her perfect lips.

"Well, if I was to go home an' tell the boys how beautiful you look in that dress . . . providin' I could do justice to it, that is . . . why, there'd be a stampede of cowpokes down here to see for themselves, and the ranch would be left high and dry with nary a single hand left on it. Except the boss. He'd want to come, too, but he's married. Ol' Lou, he wouldn't come. Married, too. And besides, he's lame. Yes, ma'am, I would call that particular dress a definite threat to the cattle business, all things considered."

She laughed again, and began to chat about how far she had to travel in order to buy clothes, and how seldom she had a chance to wear her best things, and how glad she was to have him there so that she could show them off, although it *was* too bad that he had been wounded. And the conversation drifted along that way, here and there and back again, until Pasque thought of the other favor he had to ask of her.

"You only have to name it," she said. "Whatever I can do for you, I will."

"I was thinkin' I'd ride over there to Hochland's tomorrow, if your man's free. Got a little business there, sort of unfinished. Might as well get it over with."

"Yes, I understand. How can I help?"

"Well, to be really honest with you, I don't think I'm comin' back. He and I got into this little game of showdown, back at the Keystone, and, when it came my turn to ante, the stakes turned out to be a little bit higher than I'd figured. Got into a situation where I've gotta let him shoot me."

"Shoot you?" she said. Her tone of voice did not seem surprised. She did not even seem surprised when he told her about putting two bullets through the giant man and, then, watching him laugh and ride away afterward.

"Well, that seems to be it," Pasque said. "But what I'd really like you to do for me is keep my horse and my stuff here at your place. Maybe you'd loan me a horse that your man could bring back with him. Just in case . . . you understand. If you could, I'd like you to keep my things and, maybe, if John ever comes by, he could take 'em back to the *Hacienda* Godinez. He'll likely be goin' that way, and might not mind trailin' my horse back. He could give my gear and the horse to Elena, there, at the ranch. Tell her what happened. It's pretty important to me for her to know."

"Ah!" she said. "I thought there was another woman! That's why you've been able to resist me so easily. Isn't it?" She leaned a little closer to him and swirled her brandy and looked into his eyes.

"Well, yeah, that's part of it. That, and with your husband bein' away and all, it doesn't seem right to take advantage. Bein' a guest and all."

"But shouldn't a guest be able to do as he likes? And a good guest never refuses an offer of hospitality! And since I'm your hostess, shouldn't you do what I want?"

Pasque studied the end of his cigar carefully. Then he turned his attention to making a close examination of the way the adobe fireplace was built, and took a sudden interest in trying to kick a stray coal back into the fire.

"It's all right," she smiled. "No need to feel embarrassed. You are right. And who knows? Perhaps we will see each other again some day, after your meeting with Tallak Hochland."

"Well," Pasque said, "I sure hope so."

Part of him did hope to see her again. The other part, the part that was thinking about Hochland, was just hoping to see another day.

Pasque woke up to memories. The dim first light of the December dawn was starting to eat away at the shadows in the corner of the room across from the window, and Pasque lay there with his hands behind his head, thinking about what a long time it had been since he had been back at the Keystone. He remembered charging into the bear with nothing but his fists, and how scared he had been for Gwen, but not for himself. He remembered coming across the branding iron at the Kathy Fork cabin, and how it had made him think that there was a shooter behind every tree and rock as he rode home.

He remembered the cold winter — could it have been the same year as this one? — and all the death he had seen. And the death he had caused. When he thought about the mountain lion, he imagined it asleep beneath the rocks and snow, but not dead. He remembered going out in April and finding the strange, big blacksmith, forging chain in the middle of nowhere. And the muleskinner, back in the mining country. What the heck was his name? All of these memories seemed to belong to somebody else. His whole life seemed to be back with Elena and here, too, just a few hours away from Hochland.

Pasque got up from his bed in the early gloom, and went to the *armario*. He pulled on his pants, and then he took the Colt from its holster. He opened the loading gate and shucked out each cartridge onto the bed, then carefully examined each one and polished it clean with his bandanna and put it back in its chamber. He took a sixth cartridge from his gun belt and slid it into the last chamber, the one he usually kept empty under the hammer. This done, he took out the Winchester and went through the same careful process. He unloaded it, checked each cartridge, and reloaded.

He had just eased the hammer down and had set the rifle against the wall, when the door opened very quietly, as though someone were silently peeking in to see if he still slept. A head appeared around the edge of the door. Her hair was darker in this early dawn light, without its flashes of cherry wood, and it was soft and tumbling over her shoulders.

She smiled beautifully and whispered — "Good morning." — as though seeing him was the best thing that could happen to her whole day. She stepped in and closed the door. She skipped lightly across the room and jumped onto the bed, telling him that the floor was cold on her bare feet. She showed them to him, along with a nice bare curve of leg, by lifting her thin black gown. She offered to let Pasque feel how cold they were.

Pasque touched the extended foot carefully, agreed that it seemed chilly, and offered her the blanket from the bed. She declined.

"Are you still thinking of leaving today?" she asked. "Will you be going over to Hochland's place?"

"Might as well," he said. "Must be gettin' on toward Christmas, and that's when I said I'd be there."

"Christmas! Christmas is . . ." — she put her lips into a very pretty pout and looked upward as she counted on her fingers — "just five days away."

"Five days," he said. "Well, my mother always said that I was in such a hurry to grow up that I'd probably show up early for my own hangin'."

Pasque looked at the Winchester and then at the way the gray light was beginning to shine on the mountains beyond the window, and thought about his home back in Kansas, when he was a boy. He sat down on the edge of the bed and found himself telling the señora about Christmases from his past — ones he remembered from his childhood and about the big parties at the Keystone. Pasque and the lady made quite a picture,

223

the two of them in that bedroom: a lean young cowboy, sitting shirtless and shoeless on a very large bed in a dim room, next to a strikingly pretty woman wearing nothing but a black nightgown with a wispy black rebozo thrown across her bare shoulders. And all he was doing was talking about Christmases he remembered.

She was patient with him, waiting until he had finished talking, and then she slid close to him and took his arm and put it around her waist. "May I have a kiss?" she asked. "As a going away present? Or we could call it a Christmas present. But as my husband would tell you . . . it is the custom here to exchange gifts with guests. And since you have so little with you . . ." — she looked at the narrow *armario*, which easily held everything Pasque had that was of any value — "I'll settle for a kiss."

But still he sat there, hardly reacting at all to the feel of his bare arm around her waist or to the nearness of her lips. He seemed still to be back in the past somewhere, his mind oblivious to the present. Something was distracting him, and it was not she.

"What's the matter?" she asked.

"What?" Pasque looked at her as if he had just noticed her.

"You seem far away," she smiled. "I think that I asked you to kiss me, but the idea doesn't seem to interest you very much."

"Sorry," he said. "I guess I've got this Hochland thing on my mind."

She moved away a little, and looked at him with a steady, studying gaze. She seemed to be considering something.

"Don't move," she said. "Just wait."

She left Pasque alone there in his room, and, when she came back, she was carrying a cloth bundle. She put it on the bed beside him.

"What's this?" he asked.

"Hochland's secret," she said. "The secret of invulnerability. If we are going to exchange gifts, I will give it to you."

"You have . . . ?" Pasque started. "You've got somethin' that he uses? That's how he can get shot and live through it? Mebbe the boys back at the Keystone were right. They said he had a trick of some kind. An' you got it here in the bundle?"

"Yes," she said. "Believe me. I will give it to you, but only in exchange for a kiss. Or two kisses. You will need it. I know you can't turn me down, not *this* morning."

"I know it ain't polite to ask," Pasque said, "but where did you get it?"

"From a locked chest in my husband's room. He doesn't know that I have a key."

"And where did your husband get it? Is he another one of these *hombres* that Hochland's played his game with? And what the heck is it?"

"Trust me," she answered. "If you are wearing this, when you face Hochland, he will not be able to kill you. Now . . . do we have a bargain? Or would you like me to put it away again, and you can have your breakfast and be on your way?"

A year ago, Pasque would have kissed her without a minute's hesitation. And he would have laughed at the idea of some kind of magic that could turn a bullet. But

225

that was before he had met the wandering blacksmith. Before he had met the priest who appeared from nowhere and went back to the same place. And before he had seen the huge stranger laugh and ride away. A year ago.

But she was the wife of another man. And it looked like she had stolen this cloth thing, whatever it was. Pasque might be on his way to getting killed, but he still believed in Art's ideas of honor and trust and faithfulness. One kiss could lead to a lot more than kissing — although even one kiss would prove he could be tempted. On top of that, if he took this thing, it would be an admission that he was scared. But he had every right to be scared. In a few hours, he had to stand in front of Hochland and let him shoot him. Three times, unless the first one did the job.

He weakened. Hell, if he lived through it, he didn't need to come back to this place called *Siempre Verde*. He could just light out for Elena's place. Nobody would know what happened, once he was away from here. If he didn't live through it, it didn't matter anyway.

"OK," he said quietly. He tried a smile. "You got yourself a bargain."

It was when she reached out her hand and took his and drew him to his feet that he noticed the cold. Up until that moment he had been comfortable without his shirt and boots on, but now he felt a chill running all over his bare back and up along his ankles, as if someone had thrown a door open to the outside air.

Her arms slid around his bare waist; one of her warm hands moved up his spine, pressing him firmly, reaching the wide muscles between his shoulders, pressing even more firmly until he bent forward. Her head was thrown back, her long hair brushing his arm at her back, her lips moist as they waited.

For an instant, neither of them moved. He felt everything stop — his breathing, her breathing — and a tension rising along his neck and a hard lump in his throat. The kiss was moments away from happening, and they both paused as if they wanted to keep the anticipation of it.

When it came, he could not keep his eyes from closing, and she could not keep a murmur from escaping her throat. His arms crushed her, and he could not release her. Her nails were sharp in his back, and the sharp pain intensified the feeling in his lips. Their kiss went on and on, and she murmured again and again, sometimes with her lips insistent, sometimes with the lightest little brushing sensation, like a feather.

When it was over, she held him tightly and rested her head on his chest, and they stood warm and motionless together as the sun's rays moved down the wall.

When they finally drew apart, she went to the cloth parcel on the bed and carefully unfolded it. It was a shirt, just a homemade, old, white cotton shirt like his mother used to make out of flour sacking. The only difference was, this one had been painted. The big circle painted on the back of the shirt was divided into four sections, each one a different color. On the front there were pictures of what looked like buffaloes and some horses and stick figures of men, riding and carrying bows and arrows. They seemed to be coming out of a cloud.

"A ghost-dance shirt," she said. Her voice was low and trembled a little. "I don't know how long you have been in the Southwest country, but I have been here many years, and I have seen many strange things. I have seen Indian healers cure rattlesnake bites and deadly fevers. I have seen sand paintings and rituals bring rain to the crops. *Curanderas* among the Mexicans perform magic . . . good magic . . . to cure all sorts of illness. They have been known to make the dead walk.

"The ghost dancers came into this country about two years ago. Strange men, and the strangest of them was a mystic warrior, who was showing all the tribes the power of such shirts as this. The Indians made their own shirts, and he would wash them with special powders. And then, if they wore the shirts and danced in the way he taught them, they would become bulletproof. More than that . . . the buffalo would return, and the white men would begin to die."

Pasque let her slide the shirt over his head. "Where did your husband get it?" he asked.

"That will cost you another kiss," she answered, and, without waiting for his reply, she again put her arms around him, and her moist, warm mouth again made its own kind of magic on his lips.

When he had regained his breath, Pasque sat on the bed while she helped him with his socks and boots. As he put on his vest and coat, she went on with her story.

"The Indian mystic, Tavibo, came here to our *rancho*. He had carried the ghost dance religion across the mountains clear to the big river, the Arkansas, and beyond. His sky-grandfathers told him that his work was finished. They told him he must find the place that is always green, and die there. And so he did. He slept here for over a month, near the stream where the Indians built him a small lodge. They took his body . . . we don't know where it is buried. And they left the ghost-dance shirt with my husband."

Pasque buttoned his own shirt and vest over the ghost shirt. With that and with his Colt strapped on, he couldn't feel any of that old spine-tickling fear that had been with him for all these long months. The cloth wasn't bulletproof, of course, but something about the shirt was special. Now that he had it on, he knew that he needed it.

He was ready. She took him to the kitchen for a simple breakfast of hot chocolate and a steaming, meat-filled pastry, while Constance went to see if the wrangler was ready to go.

The señora came up behind him as he sat at the table and leaned around and kissed him once again. "A third kiss," she said. "To release you from any obligation. As soon as you are away from *Siempre Verde*, you must lose all thoughts of me. Whatever happens, our time is over with this kiss."

She must have known that it would happen. As he rode away on his borrowed horse, following the wrangler, Pasque turned to look back at the ranch house. He tried to remember the excitement of those mornings and the thrill of her kisses, but all he could think of was Elena and his invisible host, the mysterious man he had never seen at *Siempre Verde*. He had been a traitor to Elena and to the woman's husband and to

229

himself, and not once, but three times. Maybe it was for the good in the long run. But right now he just felt like an ordinary saddle tramp.

Sir Pasque, Gwen Pendragon had called him.

"Shit," he said as he spat.

He unbuttoned his heavy coat so it would swing open just in case he needed to get to his Colt in a hurry. He tipped his Stetson a little lower across his eyes. He squared his shoulders. He sat up ramrod straight in the saddle. To Hochland's or to hell. Whichever one, it didn't matter much.

CHAPTER
FIFTEEN

Hochland Finishes the Game

They were riding in circles. The *vaquero* from *Siempre Verde* led Pasque south, up onto a flat mesa, then turned onto a trail going west. After an hour, he left that trail and doubled back south again as though he wasn't sure where he was going. Either that, or he wanted to mix up his tracks. And the whole time he never said a word. He finally pulled up. He pointed toward a brushy, overgrown cañon below. It was a gigantic crack down through the mesa, a hidden place protected from intruders. It even seemed protected from the winter cold, and Pasque could see green cottonwood trees among the pines. He saw a thin column of smoke rising.

"That the place?" he asked.

The *vaquero* nodded. He pointed to a dim trail, winding down through the mesquite and piñon and motioned that Pasque should go on alone. Obviously this was as far as he was going, and Pasque couldn't blame him. The narrow cañon was dark. The undergrowth down the trail was thick enough to slow up a stampeding longhorn. Everything was green, even the grass, but it was a spooky color of green. And the green place looked dark and dangerous.

A few hundred yards down the narrow trail into the gloomy cañon Pasque turned in his saddle to look back, but the *vaquero* from *Siempre Verde* was gone. Pasque turned and rode on, watching the thin line of smoke rising above the trees, and in a few minutes he heard the gunshot.

It echoed up through the trees and faded away over the mesa. It was followed by another boom. Then another. Still, nobody was shooting directly at him, at least not yet. The sound of the gunshots didn't seem to move around; it was more like somebody having target practice. Target practice. Pasque thought about Elena and smiled. It was the first time he had smiled that morning.

Pasque rode on down toward the smoke and the sound of the gun going off. Three more shots came bouncing up off the cliffs. They had a *whumph* sound to them, like a big, old, black-powder rifle. Or pistol. It wasn't a single-shot gun — the shots came too close together. After six shots, several minutes of silence followed, broken only by the steady clop of the horse's hoofs and the underbrush and tree limbs scraping against his chaps. Then the shooting started again. Three shots, a few seconds apart. *Percussion revolver,* Pasque thought to himself. *Took him four, five minutes to reload six chambers. Reckon he fires three times, waits for the smoke to clear, shoots the other three. Then reloads.* He rode on, forcing his way through the tangled undergrowth.

When he finally got to his destination, the place didn't amount to much. Just a skinny creek and a patch of pasture, some tall, green cottonwoods and willows, and a corral made out of poles lashed to the trees. The smoke was coming from the tin chimney of a dugout. It looked like somebody had started to dig a mine tunnel in the side of the cañon, then decided to make it a root cellar, and finally figured it was a house. All Pasque could see was the stovepipe and an old mossy door in the hillside, with a grimy window next to it. If this was where Hochland lived, he must have to stoop over double to get through the doorway.

A horse in the corral nickered to Pasque's horse. It was the big one. It was a good four hands taller than any saddle horse he'd ever seen. The same horse that Hochland had ridden into Art's dining room last Christmas. Pasque dismounted and put the borrowed horse in the corral, the reins looped over the horn. In a lean-to shed against the back of the corral he saw the heavy Spanish saddle he remembered from that Christmas night, the saddle with the two pistol holsters, one strapped on either side under the horn. Now both big holsters were empty.

Pasque didn't see any point in unsaddling his own horse — either he would be leaving again soon, or somebody else would take care of it. He unlashed the rifle scabbard. Besides the clothes he was wearing, the Winchester and his Colt were the only things he had brought with him from *Siempre Verde*. That, and the bulletproof medicine shirt, which was beginning to scratch him.

Whumph. Whumph. Whumph. Three more shots came from down the creek. Pasque slid the gate poles

233

back into place. He looked down at himself. Under his coat and vest and shirt, the ghost-dance shirt was hidden. Pasque eased the Colt in its holster and started toward the sound of the shots.

Funny what went through a man's mind in less than a second. He heard the trickling of the small creek, the tinkle of his spurs, the sound of his own breathing, and the sound of the blood rushing in his veins. He felt warm sunlight on his face in the cool air, and his eyes felt gritty as if he hadn't blinked since starting down the trail into the cañon. He thought about the stiffness in his gun hand. He thought about the gunman waiting for him. Real soon, he and Old Buffalo Coat would see each other. Everything else was a blur of green, a background of faint, fuzzy noises.

During the long ride from the Keystone and through all those days and nights at the *Hacienda* Godinez, Pasque had had plenty of time to think. Sometimes, even when he was with Elena and they were laughing together, he would get serious thoughts. Mostly he thought about death and life and the way things ought to be and the way they had of turning out wrong. Even as a kid, Pasque had worried about the way things should be. If one of his brothers took something or said something bad, Pasque knew inside him whether it was right or wrong. He had never said much about it, and he hadn't always done the right thing himself, but he had known right, when he had done right, and wrong, when he done it.

Now he found himself south of the Purgatory, alone in a lost cañon where a giant waited to shoot him with his antique pistol. Pasque stopped walking and listened for some sound of the other man. He knew Hochland had to be close. As he took in his surroundings, Pasque observed that the brush offered good cover. He could sneak off the path and up around the cottonwoods and just ease the Winchester out around the trunk of a tree and have the drop on Hochland. After all, why fool around with a man that big and that dangerous? He studied the trees and brush, picking the best way to go so it would be quiet.

Doubts filled his mind. *What if Hochland saw me, or heard me? And what if I did get the drop on Hochland, what would I do then? The giant would probably walk right up to the rifle muzzle and laugh. Then kill me. It'd be better just to bushwhack him, just cut the crazy hombre down like a diseased wolf or a wounded bear. Nobody around to see, nobody to care. Shoot him, bury him here, ride on out. If I could get to that one big cottonwood there, I could probably drop him with the first shot.*

A shot rang through the cañon. After a few seconds, another shot came. Then another. Hochland had gone back to his target practice. Three more shots, and then he would be busy reloading, and those few seconds would offer Pasque his best chance to sneak up behind him.

But Pasque still hesitated. *What could I say, when I get back to the Keystone? That I had decided to ambush Hochland and shoot him in the back? Or should I make up some story about the giant man taking three shots at me, missing each time? I might*

235

even tell them about the medicine shirt and claim that it had saved my life, and that I had returned it to the lady at Siempre Verde. I would be alive, and that's all they would care about.

Except truth. Art was always honest with his neighbors, even if he wished they were neighbors to someone else. And what had the blacksmith told him? That the old West was changing? Six-gun justice and using a Colt to "look out for yourself" was a way of life that had to end. Surely, Thompson wasn't talking about this here situation. What the hell would he say, if he was down here in the cañon with this crazy *hombre*, carrying a hand cannon? Let Hochland shoot him to show that six-gun revenge and personal justice were a thing of the past? Thompson and his puzzles. Him and his medicine directions. If the whole picture was supposed to be here at the end of his journey, Pasque just couldn't see it.

Those miners up in the high gold camps, they hadn't heard about the new West. They were still stealing and killing to get enough money and supplies for a few more feet of digging, and there was no law around to stop them. Ugly life. What a difference the priest was. To him, nothing was worth shooting another man for.

Nothing is worth shooting a man for. Pasque wished he had thought about that a year ago, back at the Keystone, when he let himself get bluffed into shooting Hochland. But the priest wouldn't know, if he ambushed Hochland, and Elena and her father wouldn't know, either. Didn't he owe it to them to come back alive? And bushwhacking Hochland was

236

probably the only way to do it. Why had Elena let him go, anyway, unless she knew that he'd manage to come back again?

Maybe it was all a big puzzle. Maybe this woman at *Siempre Verde* was the last piece of it. He was supposed to do something, but what? Kill Hochland and go back and lie to everyone? Get killed himself? Or . . . play the hand. Play it like he had an ace in the hole, keep a straight face, and maybe he would even come out of this alive. That's probably what Art would do. But if he was going to bushwhack Hochland, the time to do it was now. If the chance passed, it would be too late.

Pasque felt the shirt scratching at him under his vest. His ace in the hole. It might not stop a bullet, but, if he could just force himself to believe that it would, it might give him the edge. If he could manage to look like a man who knew the whole thing was a trick, who knew he was not going to die, he might just bluff his way through this. Maybe it really was just some kind of game. What if he ambushed Hochland, and then found out that's all it was?

The feeling came back strong: playing out the hand was the right thing to do. He walked on until he came to a wide clearing. Tallak Hochland was there, waiting.

Glaring sunlight seemed to be dancing around the giant. He still wore the dark green, old Stetson. The silk bandanna drawn up to hide his mouth was the color of kinnikinic. Under the heavy, buffalo-hide coat, his shirt was the same color as tarnished old copper rivets. The

237

sulphur smell from burning gunpowder hung in the air. He was holding a Walker revolver.

Pasque's eyes looked straight into Hochland's, and neither man blinked. *At least this feels right*, Pasque thought. *Ambushing Hochland wouldn't have felt right.* Pasque was looking his own death right in the face, and he was strangely unafraid. It was the right thing. Like the Apache warrior, he knew that the time had come to gamble with his death, or with his life. And there would be no cheating either one.

"Well," Hochland boomed in his big voice, "so the Keystone Ranch *does* keep the faith after all!"

The Keystone! That was what made this feel right. Pasque hadn't come all the way down here just to shoot some overgrown *hombre* and then go back to tell lies about it. He hadn't made this journey just to find Elena Godinez. It all had something to do with the Keystone, and he had almost forgotten. The Keystone was bigger than him, more important than all this, bigger than any cowboy. But each man on the place had to act as if he was as big as the Keystone. That's what Art always said. Art believed in building a new country in the West, a country with peace and law in it, and nobody who worked for him could back down from that. If he let them forget it, he might as well turn the range over to the rustlers and the bushwhackers. That's why Hochland was at the ranch that night. That was the game, a game that was a deadly test.

"That's right," Pasque replied. "Hell, there was a dozen men who wanted to take my place. We drew cards for the chance, and I won."

Hochland looked him up and down, carefully, slowly, sizing him up. Pasque felt like he was being measured for a pine box. Then Hochland went to a big, flat rock where a stoneware crock and two tall mugs stood. Hochland filled one and handed it to Pasque and filled the other for himself.

"Well, here's to the Keystone Ranch, and to bravery!" he bellowed. "You followed the trail well." He raised his cup in a salute. "Now, here we are. No one to stop us or see us. You have come far, and you've done well. You could have backtrailed anywhere along the way. Could've shot me in the back. But here you are. The two of us, all alone."

"Sure," Pasque said, downing his drink. It was bitter wine.

The big man lowered his silk bandanna to drink. His beard was a strange dark color. Under the huge mustache his teeth gleamed in a mocking smile. Again he studied Pasque from head to foot.

Pasque was beginning to get nervous. "Let's get to it," he said. He felt the same anger, the same heat in his blood as a year ago when he first shot Hochland and watched him ride away.

"No hurry," Hochland replied. "This is my game, after all. And you have come so far. It would be a shame to have it all be over so soon." Hochland still had his mocking smile as he looked calmly into Pasque's face. "I'll tell you what," he said. "Since it's Christmas season, let's exchange gifts with each other. Then each of us will have something to remember this day by."

239

Pasque thought he would remember just fine. Or he might not have to worry about remembering anything. Hochland seemed to think they were both going to get through his little game alive. Somehow.

"If I'd known you wanted a present," Pasque said, forcing one side of his mouth into a smile, "I'd have stopped off at the store. The way it is, I don't have much with me 'cept my guns. And I'd kinda like to keep those a while longer, if you follow my drift."

"Oh, I think you must have something to swap, young Pasque. Perhaps when you see what I brought for you, it will help you think of something to give me." He reached behind the rock and brought up a pair of saddlebags. They were Pasque's, the ones that had been stolen back on the Arkansas River.

"You see!" Hochland laughed. "I have something to give you that was yours to begin with! The best gift that a man can give, I think, is something that the other had thought was lost. Don't you agree?"

Pasque took the saddlebags. Inside was his money and his shaving kit and spare ammunition and everything else that had been there when the outlaw had run off with it. Even the other Walker revolver was there.

Pasque pulled out the revolver and held it butt first toward Hochland.

"OK," Pasque said. "So here's something that you lost. You'd be glad to have it back, I reckon. I guess it matches that one, lyin' on the rock there."

"No," the giant man replied. "You fail to see the point of our little exchange. After all, I gave you that pistol, and it would hardly be polite of you to return it to me. And as you said, I still have the other one for . . . well, in order to finish our game. No, you keep it. Perhaps you have something else of mine?"

Pasque's eyes went cold. He looked at Hochland, and he calculated the distance to the gun lying on the rock, wondering if Hochland could get to it before he could get his own Colt out. Then Pasque remembered. The Walker revolver hadn't stopped Hochland last Christmas, and his Peacemaker probably wouldn't stop him, either. Hochland was looking straight at him. Although his huge smile was still broad and white-toothed, his eyes were in dead cold earnest. For a long time the two men stood without moving, sizing each other up, each knowing what was in the other's mind and waiting for the next move.

Hochland made it. Breaking the long silence, he pointed at Pasque's boots. "Those are quite the ornate spurs," he said. "Now that would make a suitable exchange, I'd say. A nice memento of our afternoon together. Tell me . . . where did you earn them?"

"Earn 'em? Hell, I bought 'em off of a horse wrangler in Kansas. A friend gave me this here jinglebob."

"You bought them?" Hochland said. "So you merely bought them. Well, isn't that a shame. The old knights, you know, had to earn theirs. One spur at a time, according to some of the legends. Let me think . . . to earn one's spur, or spurs, one had to perform some act of courage or chivalry. Chastity went with it, of course.

241

Not too many cowboys can boast of chastity these days, now, can they?"

"Guess not. So, you've taken a likin' to these old spurs, then?" Pasque had already put one foot up on the rock and started to unbuckle the strap.

"Only one. Only one. We could say that you have earned at least one spur on your long trip to the Picketwire, don't you agree?"

Pasque handed one spur to him. Hochland was becoming absorbed in knights and chivalry and was forgetting about the ghost-dance shirt, and that was all right with Pasque. All of this fancy playing around with words. Hochland knew he had the shirt. And Hochland wanted to get it back without coming right out and saying so. As far as Pasque could tell, that was the clincher. If Hochland wanted the shirt so badly and couldn't come right out and ask for it, then the shirt really did have some kind of secret to it. It could make bullets go around a man. Or if that wasn't it, it sure as hell did something that made Hochland want it.

Pasque wondered. *Maybe the ghost-dance shirt had been Hochland's in the first place. Maybe that lady's husband had stole it from . . . wait a minute! What the hell is the matter with me? Her husband is Hochland!.*

It was Hochland who owned that *Siempre Verde* place and was always somewhere else off hunting. He probably knew how his wife acted while he was away, all her games to get into bed with him. All of it was play-acting, like that shooting game Hochland played at Christmas. Like some kind of stupid test to see what he'd do.

242

Sure. That made sense. Maybe that lady and Hochland had a bet going on the side: there was going to be shooting, and whoever wore this shirt wasn't going to get hurt. If he had made love to her, then Hochland got the shirt. If he didn't, then he got it. No, that still didn't work out right. It didn't matter; he'd sort it all out later. The important thing was that the shirt had some kind of power. He had to keep it, unless Hochland was going to push the issue.

Hochland took the spur Pasque had handed him and set it on a rock. He picked up his revolver. Pasque backed up a few steps, holding the rifle scabbard and saddlebags in his left hand. He needed to keep his right one free.

"Time to do it, I guess," Pasque said.

Hochland smiled on. "If you'll just stand right where you are," he said, "I'll stand over here. That makes it about the same distance as before, doesn't it? And what did we have, three shots?"

Three shots. Pasque suddenly thought of something that might even the odds.

"Hold it," Pasque said. "If you want t' make this a square game, you oughta use this other gun."

Hochland looked puzzled, but went on smiling. Pasque pulled the other Walker from the saddlebag.

"This one," he said. "Same as I used on you."

Hochland came and got the revolver, then went back to his position. The Walker Colt was a gun that most men found heavy and awkward, the biggest hand gun of its day. But it looked small in Hochland's huge hand. He examined the cylinder. "Three chambers are still

243

loaded," he said. "At least they appear to be loaded. And the caps are still in place. But," he went on, "the gunpowder in these three chambers must be more than a year old. So are the percussion caps. And I daresay the barrel was never cleaned after you shot me. The odds are that this gun will not fire. And depending upon the soot and corrosion that might be in the barrel, if it does go off, it could blow up in my hand."

"Back at the Keystone, did I ask you if the gun worked? Did I ask you if it would blow my hand off?"

"No, you did not. However, I do recall that you tested it by shooting a milk bucket."

"Feel free to test it again, then," Pasque said. "Fair's fair."

"Very well."

Hochland lifted the revolver, pointed it straight at Pasque's heart, and thumbed back the hammer. Pasque heard the small click of the sear as the weapon went to half-cock. Then he heard a bigger click. Full cock. He set himself and swallowed hard. He saw Hochland's finger tighten on the trigger.

Pasque flinched to one side. The blast left Pasque's eardrums ringing. Through a cloud of sulphur smoke he saw the outline of the giant like a ghost, standing in a fog. Hochland had pulled the pistol at the last minute, sending the lead ball harmlessly past him.

"Well!" he laughed loudly, so loud that Pasque heard it through the ringing in his ears. "Not so brave, after all? I must say that I'm disappointed. I thought you had ridden to this cañon to take my shot like a man, without flinching. When you shot me, didn't I stand solid?"

Pasque's hand was itching for his Colt, and the blood was rising into his face. He glowered at Hochland, his pale blue eyes steady and dangerous.

"Well, you'd better not miss the next one," Pasque said. He had his nerves and his gun hand under control. His mind was working fast. Maybe he had this deal figured wrong again. All that palaver about swapping and stolen things, maybe there was something to that. His thoughts were flying off in all directions like being on top of a sun-dancing wild bronc', but his sense of how things should be was coming back to him. That lead going past him had scared it up.

Hochland had the revolver pointed again. Slowly he thumbed it to half cock, while he sighted down the barrel.

This damn' shirt don't mean nothin', Pasque thought. *Besides that, it belongs to him. Here I stand wearin' it, tryin' to pretend I don't know anythin' about it. And I know it ain't gonna turn a .44 load.*

Hochland smiled, enjoying the suspense. He pulled the hammer to full cock so slowly that Pasque could see the cylinder turn. *Wait a minute,* Pasque thought, *this isn't right . . . ,* and Hochland's finger tensed again, and the hammer fell.

There was silence. The little creek went on bubbling under its banks, and somewhere a hawk cried, and a lost breeze rattled some dry leaves that were caught in a wild rose, but the rest was silence. There was a faint click, when the hammer crushed the copper percussion

245

cap, but nothing else. Maybe the cap was a dud, or the gunpowder was damp, or the nipple was plugged. Something had kept the Walker from firing. Pasque stood there. He stood solid, without flinching, sweat beading up on his brow, and his fingers trembling.

There were no words until Hochland thumbed back the hammer for the third and last time. Then Pasque spoke up.

"Hold it," he said, unbuttoning his vest with his shaky fingers. "This ain't right."

Pasque opened his vest and shirt and showed Hochland that he was wearing the ghost-dance shirt.

"I thought pretty good of myself," he said, "managin' to keep my hands off of that lady these past three days. But then she offered to let me steal somethin' to get me through this shoot-out of yours, and I did it. And I ain't proud that I tried to hide behind it, neither."

The giant man lowered his revolver, silent. His smile was still there, but it was a smile that said nothing.

"Just let me get this shirt off," Pasque said, "and you can shoot your last shot. Maybe it's magic and maybe it ain't, but I didn't come by it honest, and I don't want to die in it. And," he continued, "you can go ahead and use your gun with the fresh loads in it, if you want."

He started to pull off his coat so he could get to the vest and shirt, but Hochland ordered him to stand still. "Stop!" the big voice roared. "It's too late. You chose to take my shirt. You chose not to return it at your first opportunity. Nor did you mention it at the second opportunity. Now we will determine whether or not it works."

Hochland pulled the trigger. The revolver blast ripped a ragged hole in the December stillness. At Hochland's words, Pasque had turned, and then, frozen in his tracks, he reached for his Colt, when he was hit in the side and spun back and seemed to trip and fall to the ground. For a minute he lay there, dazed and surprised as though he'd been bucked off a horse and had the wind knocked out of him. When he was finally able to get propped up on one elbow, he saw a long gap torn along the side of the ghost-dance shirt. Blood flowed from a furrow under his ribs. It felt warm.

The shirt was just a shirt. He was just flesh and bone. And he was still alive.

CHAPTER
SIXTEEN

The Return

Tallak Hochland used his green scarf to bind up
Pasque's wound. He folded the ghost-dance shirt and
put it away among his own belongings, along with
Pasque's spur. He offered Pasque another cup of
wine to ease the shock, when the pain of the gunshot
began to set in.

"You did well," Hochland smiled. "You see? You
failed only one test. You yielded to that one single
temptation. You accepted the shirt. And, of course, your
fear of me caused you to keep it a secret. But, in the
end, you dealt square with me. So here you are, hardly
wounded at all. Other men have done far worse."
Hochland looked past the crude dugout toward the far
end of the meadow where the ground rose and fell in a
series of low, regular mounds. "Yes," he said, "others
have done worse. And now," the big man continued,
"you must come back home with me. We will enjoy a
few days of good food and drink. You can spend
Christmas with us. What do you say?"

Pasque got to his feet. His side burned with pain.
But, at least, his ears had stopped ringing, and his
muscles had stopped twitching.

"If it's all the same to you," Pasque said, "I'd just as soon make tracks early tomorrow mornin'. There's some folks waitin' to know if I'm alive or dead."

"I do understand," Hochland said.

Pasque went behind the cottonwoods to relieve his bladder. The wine had caught up to him. But pain and dizziness caught up to him, too, and he had no sooner buttoned his fly than he was reeling and weaving. He hugged the tree, slid down it, and passed out on the ground.

He slept a long time. When he finally came to, the sun had moved on down the sky, and his wound had settled into a dull, throbbing ache. He got up, held onto the tree until the world stopped revolving, and made his way back to the creek. Hochland was gone. Horse, belongings, everything. Pasque's borrowed horse stood in the corral, and his Winchester in its scabbard was leaning against the bottom rail. The only proof that Hochland had ever existed was the blood-stained scarf wrapped around Pasque's ribs. And the missing spur. The dugout was empty, its stove cold. Pasque listened to see if he could hear hoofbeats going up the trail out of the cañon, but heard nothing except the mumbling of the creek and the whisper of the breeze.

He swayed on his feet and wanted to lie down again, but more than anything else he wanted to get out of this cañon. The way it squeezed its dark shadows in on him reminded him of a long, rocky grave. It reminded him of death. Less than an hour ago, he had been certain that the cañon would be his grave. When he was looking down the muzzle of Hochland's gun, Pasque had felt a deep sadness about the death that was about to happen, like it was someone else about to die while he stood and watched. Right at that moment he felt something more than fear, something that lay on top of the fear. It was a deep grief about his past, sorrow because his whole lifetime had been such a wandering trail.

High in the late afternoon sky, an eagle screamed. Pasque looked up. *You got the right idea*, he thought. *Stay up there. I need to get above it, too. Get high enough to see where I'm goin'.*

In spite of his pain he got himself into the saddle. He rode out of the corral and across the creek to the trail, leading to the top of the mesa. He did not put the gate poles back up, and, as he rode away, he did not look back.

When Pasque rounded the last turn in the trail and came out on the flat mesa again, he found his own horse and a fresh pack horse tied to the tree where he had last seen the *vaquero*. He had not expected to find his horses there, but, in a way, it didn't surprise him. He was bone weary, and he hurt too much to worry about it. He got down and shifted his scabbard and saddlebags to the saddle horse, then opened up the top of the pack horse's load and looked inside. It contained his cooking gear and his spare clothes and his bedroll. Someone had added a flour sack full of groceries — flour, soda, bacon, coffee, salt, cans of beans and cans of tomatoes, a few pounds of pintos. A man could ride quite a few days with this. Someone had filled his big canteen. He took one of the cans of tomatoes and opened it with his knife. It had been a long time since he'd had any, and they were wet and good. He drank the juice and tied up the pack again.

The polite thing would be to take the borrowed horse home and thank his hosts for the supplies and pack animal. He could make camp near *Siempre Verde* or even stay overnight at the house, like Hochland had said. Pasque tied the horses into a string, mounted up, and went on along the trail. Up here on the rimrock he could see sky everywhere. He could feel the sun warm on his back, and he could smell the piñon and juniper. He could even smell the sand and the rock.

Pasque saw black dung beetles that stood on their heads when the horse approached them. He noticed small lizards frozen motionless on the sun-warmed stones. He saw seedling pines, hardly taller than a man's finger, growing in impossible cracks in the rock. He saw the track of prints that a mouse had made crossing the trail, and once he thought he saw a young cougar, watching him from the cover of a scrub oak on a ledge.

The trail was clear and easy to follow, even though it kept winding and turning. Within an hour or so, it brought him to where the mesa overlooked the valley of the Cimarron River. Pasque thought he had gotten himself confused, because down there where he should have seen the ranch house and buildings, he saw nothing except brush and trees and rocks.

For another hour, Pasque rode back and forth along the edge of the rimrock mesa, looking for signs of

Siempre Verde. He kept riding until he saw, in the distance, the place that looked like the one where the Apaches had attacked him. He took a bearing on the spot and backtracked, attempted to follow the route the old mountain man, John, must have taken with the travois. But Pasque still couldn't see any ranch. It was getting late — the sun was going down behind the far-off mountains, and the chill evening air was starting to make his wound throb. Ranch or no ranch, he had to make camp soon.

Pasque decided to give it up for the night. He took the horses down over the rim of the mesa as soon as he found an easy slope. He wanted to camp where a cooking fire wouldn't be visible all over the territory. Near a snug little overhang under the rock he found a good place to tie the horses. There was a flat patch of clean sand and a place where the cliff face would reflect the heat and hide the glare of a fire.

Pretty cozy, Pasque decided, as he pushed the sizzling bacon to one side of the frying pan and poured in a can of beans. *Pretty cozy*.

After breakfast the next day, Pasque packed and stiffly climbed back on the horse and resumed his ride along the rim of the mesa, watching the valley for *Siempre Verde*. Finally, after scrambling up one slope and sliding down again and then up another, he came out on top of the next mesa to the north. Below him he could see mile after mile of the Cimarron River, shining in the sunlight. But not a sign of a ranch or a house. Just flat-floored valleys, the silvery morning river, and stair-stepped Fisher Peak that looked like a castle. Not knowing what else he could do, Pasque cut the borrowed horse out of the string and set it loose, figuring it would find its own way home. He could have taken it with him, at least as far as Raton Pass, but he just didn't want it around. It was bad enough that he owed Hochland one horse.

Pasque turned west again, staying high on the slope so he could see more of the valley. He touched the scars on his hand where the ball from John's old Hawken mountain rifle had ripped it full of slivers. He checked the tightness of the wrapping over his ribs where Hochland's .44 Walker Colt had left a furrow big enough in which to plant corn. In the pocket of his chaps he felt the Apache arrowhead. It might be tough riding up on the crumbly slope, but it sure beat riding down where he could be a target again.

When Pasque got to Raton Pass, he didn't even consider a wide detour which would avoid Dick Wooton's toll road. The wages from his job at the mine were still in the saddlebag Hochland had returned, so he had plenty of money for the toll and a night's lodging.

In back of Wooton's place in a lean-to wash house there were a couple of tubs and a boiler, another of Wooton's "luxuries" for the traveling trade, so, after seeing to his horse and eating, Pasque set about cleaning up himself. By tomorrow, he figured, he would be seeing Elena again.

When Pasque looked into Wooton's shaving mirror, he saw a stranger. His hair was a lot longer than he remembered. His eyes were darker than before; little creases crept out of the corners, and there were new lines under his cheekbones. "Gettin' old," he muttered, scraping whiskers away. "Maybe too old to go chasin' after that Godinez girl." But he grinned and whistled a tune while he went over his chin twice with the razor and splashed on plenty of the stinging bay rum.

By the time Wooton's other lodgers were having breakfast the following morning, Pasque was already several miles down the road. The morning was clear and cold under a dark pre-dawn sky, when he set out, but before long the sun came climbing over the rim of the horizon and peeked down into the cañon to take the chill out of the air. It didn't get warm enough to go without gloves, and it was cold enough that Pasque kept his heavy coat buttoned up, but it was a perfect day for riding. Even the saddle horse seemed to feel it. He danced and kicked until Pasque was tempted to run him up the side of the hill a few times just to settle him down.

Horses and rider came out of the cañon, left the wide road, and took a trail that skirted the edge of the Trinidad settlement. They found a ford to cross the river and rode on. They rode through the piñon and juniper brakes covering the wavy apron of sand slopes on the sun-swept side of the mountains and rode on. They drank at an *acequia*, where Pasque smiled at certain memories, and rode on. They stopped at an open clearing in the piñon where the horse grazed and the man ate bread and jerky and washed it down with a can of tomatoes. And they rode on.

254

The sun went up the sky and across, then began the long slide toward winter twilight. It was getting ready to drop onto the tips of the Sangre peaks, still throwing fierce slants of light across the range and through the trees, when the horses and the rider pulled up. Below them, low adobe walls were golden in the evening rays of sun. Smoke rose from four chimneys. It was the sprawling *hacienda* ranch house of Don Diego de Tovar y Godinez. And Elena.

Pasque put the saddle horse into a fast jog, dragging impatiently on the pack horse's lead rope, his eyes on the adobe house for signs of movement. Someone opened a door and came out. At a distance, it looked like Felipe. The tiny figure spotted him coming and rushed back inside. In a few more moments, the door opened again, and this time Elena stood in the door frame. She was a long way off, but there was no mistaking that slim figure running toward him, long hair flying. She was calling to him, and even across the distance he could hear her laughing from pure joy.

Pasque dropped the lead rope and kicked his horse into a ground-eating run, and Elena ran on toward him. Her shawl floated behind her, tangling in her long, streaming hair. Her skirts molded to her legs as she came. Her arms were outstretched, her face glowing, and then she was so near that he could see how her eyes were laughing. He could hear her calling his name over and over.

With a pull on the reins, Pasque nearly set his horse down on its haunches, then leaned forward and swept her up with one arm, gathering her into his arms as if

255

she were weightless. Her arms hugged his neck hard, and she kissed him on the mouth while her hands caressed his face. She kissed his face and touched his lips with her fingers, while her throaty voice whispered: "*Alma, querido.*" She kissed him with her hands holding tightly to his shoulders, then wrapped her arms around his back to hug him hard. He winced; she was pressing against his wound. She pulled back to look into his face, her quick dark eyes flicking over him with concern and curiosity, and, when he smiled to show that it was all right, she put her arms around his neck again and went back to devouring his mouth.

The saddle horse moved more slowly than before, but not because of the slight added weight of Elena, sitting sidesaddle, on Pasque's lap. Even at that gradual amble, however, the lovers arrived at the house much sooner than they wanted to, long before they could bring the excitement in their faces under control. When Felipe held the horse, he discretely looked the other way as Pasque lowered the *señorita* to the ground and then dismounted. He helped Pasque untie his saddlebag, and then he walked out to get the pack horse, doing everything in slow motion to give the lovers the time they needed to calm down. They needed to put on their formal faces now.

When Elena and Pasque had stopped breathing heavily and the color in their faces was back to normal, she took him inside, where her father was waiting. The don bellowed gleefully to see Pasque again and clasped him in his arms like a long-lost son. But his energetic embrace didn't come close to having the same effect as Elena's. If anything, it was embarrassing.

Father Nicholas was there, too. Elena vanished into the back of the house, probably to fix her hair, leaving him at the mercy of the two older men. These two had been having a glass of wine before dinner, and now they were anxious to have Pasque fill a glass and tell them all about his search for Hochland. Pasque asked for a glass of whiskey, instead of wine, and with Father Nicholas translating into Spanish for Don Diego he began the story. There was nothing else he could do. The two men were amused to see how Pasque kept glancing down the hallway.

At dinner Pasque was still answering questions and recounting the fight with the Apaches and the meeting with Hochland. For now, he wasn't going to mention Hochland's lady or the strange tale of the medicine shirt. Even without those parts in it, his story sounded like something a bored cowboy might make up to entertain his bunkmates during a long winter evening.

"You know," Pasque said, "I feel kinda like a wrangler we had back in Kansas. The man told some real stretchers. No respect for the facts whatever. Had a greenhorn in camp once, listenin' to old Mic's stories, and our foreman leaned over to this greenhorn and whispered . . . 'He's lyin.' 'How kin y' tell?' the greenhorn asked. 'Well, for one thing, his lips is movin'."

Father Nicholas laughed. "And you think we see you as a man who stretches the truth, then?"

"Maybe," Pasque replied. "After all, if a cowpoke was to tell me some of this stuff, especially if he'd been drinkin' this good whiskey, I don't know as I'd believe him. But I got a feelin' that maybe the *padre* here knows more about this. You feel like tellin' me how the land lies, Father?"

"What did you want to know?" Father Nicholas helped himself to more potatoes. Elena passed him the gravy boat.

"Well, take this Hochland fellow, for instance. How many times has he played this little game of his?"

"I couldn't say," Father Nicholas replied. "It's been going on for a very long time, of course, and each year it takes a slightly different form. Well, I told you about *my* encounter with him. My theory about the man . . . and it's only a theory . . . is that he himself has had some sort of experience with death and violence. An experience that changed his life. He apparently goes about reminding men that they do not have the right to take the lives of other men. He gives them one of his lessons."

"Seems like a funny way to go about it, one man at a time," Pasque said. "Kinda like settin' out to fill a wagon with corn by puttin' in just one kernel at a time."

"Ah, Pasque. You don't see the whole plan. In my case, he created a spokesman who will preach the word of brotherhood and respect for life . . . until I am gone to my own grave. In your case, you will spread it by telling others, by your influence. Before long, every man at the Keystone will be spreading your story across the Wyoming Territory." The priest paused. "That is," he continued, "if you intend to go back north." He looked at Don Godinez as if asking a question.

"Don't see any way out of it," Pasque said. "My Uncle Art and his wife, they're goin' to be worried about me, until they see me in the flesh. Of course, that doesn't mean I couldn't find my way back here again. Anybody want this last biscuit . . . what do you call 'em?"

"*Sopapilla*," Elena smiled.

"Oh, yeah. *Sopapilla*. Anybody want this last one?" Pasque smiled at the way her eyes kept smiling at him.

After supper, the four of them retired to the *sala* in which the fire was blazing in the corner fireplace and in which the bottle of Spanish brandy and glasses waited on the hewn pine table. Pasque sank into a comfortable chair where he could gaze at Elena seated on the other side of the fireplace. She picked up a small guitar and softly strummed through the chords of a love song.

"And so, when would you start north?" Father Nicholas asked. "The weather can be quite unpredictable this time of year, once you get beyond the Arkansas River and the mining camps."

"I've been thinking of that," Pasque said. "Maybe I'll ride over to Santa Fé, or wherever there's a telegraph, and send word to my uncle that I'm all right. Kinda roundabout, but maybe a letter or a telegram message would get there before I could."

Pasque sipped his brandy and kept watching Elena. When she was brushing the cords on the guitar, she had a way of tilting her head so that her long, black hair fell down across her shoulder and over her breast. He loved it.

"I was wondering," he said, addressing Don Diego, "whether a man like me could find any land to lease, maybe buy, if the terms were right. Around here, I mean."

Don Diego's eyes came alive. *At last*, he thought. *At last!* After four hours of conversation, the young man had finally opened the topic of settling down. It could only mean that he intended to marry Elena, and it meant also that his grandchildren might be close at hand when the two lovers built their *casa* somewhere nearby. He spoke to Elena, who translated the Spanish.

"There are several ways to acquire land in this territory of *Nuevo Méjico*," Don Diego explained. "One can marry a wealthy widow, for instance, who may have been left to struggle with a large *hacienda* alone. Or, one might ask the territorial governor for permission to settle upon some of the unclaimed land, where with much hard work one might eventually scrape out a living."

"Any chance of just gettin' some kind of grazin' lease on some good land? Those other options of yours don't sound too attractive."

"There is dowry, of course," Don Diego said, taking a deliberately casual sip of his brandy and walking over to toast his backside by the fire. He was blocking Pasque's view of Elena. Elena was blushing as she translated.

"Sometimes, especially in a family whom God has seen fit to bless with a daughter but no sons, a man who marries that daughter could find himself in ownership of some very good land, indeed. Such as, for instance, all of that land to the south and east that you can survey from the high hill out beyond my corrals."

"Sounds better than marryin' a widow or tryin' to make a range out of rocks and cactus. About how long do you think it might take to do it that way?"

Elena choked and coughed. Pasque chuckled. *Caught her on that one*, he thought.

Don Diego looked at Father Nicholas, who took the hint and ventured an answer to Pasque's question.

"Well," the *padre* began, "presuming that some kind of . . . agreement already existed between the couple in question, and presuming that they had the permission of the bride's father, there would be a period of formal courtship, perhaps two months, and the necessary announcements and arrangements with the Church. Then the wedding. The men would want to ride into Santa Fé for wedding clothes, as would the ladies of the household. And food, and invitations . . . oh, it would take a month at least."

"So, about four months is what you're sayin'?" Pasque said.

"Yes. It could be done in that amount of time."

"Well then," Pasque said, rising from his chair to get a cigar from the humidor on the table, and looking straight into Elena's face at the same time, "I guess we'd be heading north along about April or May."

Both Don Diego and Father Nicholas could feel the hush between Pasque and Elena, as if both of them were holding their breath and afraid to let it out.

261

"*Mañana*," Don Diego said at last, looking at Pasque with both amusement and interest, "I think you and I might take a ride together, and I will show you the land which I mentioned. And we can have a talk. A long talk. But for now, I am suddenly feeling sleepy. And I see the heaviness in the eyes of Father Nicholas. We will talk *mañana*, but now these two old men must find their beds before they both fall asleep in the *sala*."

It was proper and expected that Elena would also excuse herself at this time. With a quick "I love you" glance at Pasque, she said her good nights and floated down the long, dimly lit hallway toward her room, the one with the small window looking out into the walled garden.

"I'm not quite ready to call it a night, I guess," Pasque said. "I think I'll just get my coat and take this cigar out into the patio for a quiet smoke."

CHAPTER
SEVENTEEN

Link!

Standing in his stirrups, Pasque was a solitary silhouette on the ridge. His horse cropped at little green shoots of grass that were just beginning to show up in the clumps of last summer's dry stems. Toward the south Pasque could just make out the distant outline of Pike's Peak, sitting out in front of the range like a sentinel. Beyond that, if he strained his eyes and imagination, he could see the jagged purple skyline of the Spanish Peaks. Weeks ago, down along the Arkansas and Purgatory Rivers, he had been looking at those same mountains from the other side. That country to the south seemed ages away from him, now. It seemed as remote as a half-forgotten dream, like a place he had imagined.

He turned in the saddle to look northward. Today, or the next day, they'd be crossing the North Platte River. They had made a wide swing to the east, keeping far out on the high plains to avoid the chaos of the Denver City and Cherry Creek settlements, and they had made another dogleg around the railroad's end-of-line camp. They also had skirted Fort Tyler on the Bijou. Pasque had heard stories about soldiers from such posts. Some roamed in gangs, looking for wild game and anything else that they might take a fancy to. People said that the soldiers were worse than the railroad roustabouts, and the roustabouts were worse than the Indians.

Pasque didn't mind the extra time that these detours had cost him, but, now, he wasn't sure how far he was from the Platte. From the high divide it looked like there was a major river valley a few miles north. He could see the line of trees, still leafless this time of year but dark against the tan of the prairie, coming down from the mountains and meandering far out to disappear over the eastern horizon.

Springtime was creeping north along the high plains, leaving buds of leaf on the sage, tender shoots of grass in the dead groundcover. All over the prairie there was a general haze of green with fingers of light green stretching up into the valleys and cañons of the foothills. The sky was a clear deep blue, a colder color than the skies down in the southwest. Colder and clearer.

Pasque turned to look south again. He remembered the wedding and the month of preparations beforehand. He remembered riding into Santa Fé with Don Diego and spending hours at a tailor shop, getting fitted into a stiff black suit. Don Diego joked about it being a good suit for a funeral, but Pasque didn't think it was that funny.

When they had come back to the *hacienda*, they had found the women transforming the sprawling adobe house into a gigantic wedding cake of white bows, white wreaths, white satin hangings and drapes, white candles, and white flowers they had made from silk. And laughter. Pasque had never heard so much female laughter and chattering as those women, putting up decorations and planning banquets.

After his ordeal with Hochland it was a pure joy each day to wake up and find himself and the whole world alive, but that four-day rodeo of a wedding had been almost more life and hilarity than he could take. Almost. People had come all the way from Mexico and God knows where else, and they had acted as if they had just been next door and had heard about the party. Pasque had shaken hands with every back-slapping, hugging *ranchero* and *vaquero* in the territory, and had been kissed on the cheek by every giggling *señora*.

He had danced with a dozen *señoritas* every evening. He had told the men every story he could think of, every campfire, cowboy, tall tale he could remember, and those that he couldn't remember he embellished with his imagination. Half his audience couldn't understand English, but it didn't matter. He was the bridegroom, and everything he said in those groups of men turned out to be the funniest thing they had ever heard. And to the women he was never less than the most charming *caballero* who ever wore a tight black jacket and embroidered, black sombrero.

There on the ridge, sitting relaxed in the saddle, Pasque could remember how angry he had been when he crossed this country, heading south. Angry because Link had gotten away from him and because Uncle Art had protected him. Angry because Old Buffalo Coat had sidetracked him from going after Link and Moore. Angry at himself for letting them do it to him.

The anger seemed a long time ago. A long time ago. Thanks to Elena. And Hochland. Here he was, sitting a ridge, wondering how far it was to the Platte and how far beyond that it would be to the Keystone, and it just didn't much matter to him. If he reached the Keystone in a day, or in a month, it would all be the same. If an antelope or a deer came along, and he wanted venison, he might hunt it, or he might decide not to. It just didn't matter much, one way or another.

Any anger he still had in him was 'way below the surface now, harder to reach down and get hold of. Getting hit with Hochland's bullet had gotten rid of his need for more revenge and more killing. It was like that old bottle of iodine that Pat kept in his tack room. Stung like hell on a barbwire cut, but afterward you felt better. Getting shot was sort of the final part of the circle that Thompson had talked about. It completed the circle. Rustlers had shot Jim and Chris, and their killing had given Pasque a crazy mad thirst to go after them and kill them. Then he had shot Hochland and had had to ride south so Hochland could shoot him. Now north again, back to the place where it began. But what would happen if he ran into Link again?

Elena seemed to be part of this medicine idea, too. A lot of the reason he felt better this spring was because of her. With soft seductions and smiles when he spoke, she drew him into talking about Link and Moore and his murdered brothers. But she softly held him away from his anger. She understood his feelings; when he was talking and his mood moved toward revenge and rage, she stepped between him and his thoughts. She put her arms around him and held him until the fury cooled and slipped back down inside somewhere, and, after a while, he couldn't find it.

Elena could make him smile, too. And grin. Instead of glowering through the day, he now found himself smiling at almost everything.

Pasque's ridgetop meditations were interrupted by hoofbeats, coming hard. It wasn't long before he saw the rider's hat appearing and disappearing behind each rise and fall of the ground, coming straight toward him. He called out as she drew nearer.

"Looks like you got it worked out," he said.

"I hope so! He is one jumpy devil this morning. I ran him for a mile or more, until he quit fighting me," Elena replied, drawing rein next to him.

"Don't know why," Pasque said, "but some ponies just seem to get a burr in their . . . under their saddle every time you get on 'em. Got a couple of'em at the Keystone. It's like a rodeo almost every mornin' for the cowboy who draws one of those snakes."

"Perhaps they take their example from you, my dear husband? Some mornings they feel more frisky?"

A rush of hot blood went across Pasque's face. Several days after setting out on this honeymoon trip, they had had a pretty wild morning in the blankets. Luckily, on the day before this particular episode, he and Felipe had been talking and wondering how far it would be to the North Platte River.

"Perhaps, *señor*," Felipe had said, "since the *señora* prefers to do the cooking and Felipe is not needed, I might take some of the pack horses and ride on ahead. I would be glad to scout and leave markers for you to follow. Newlyweds, I think, do not need the chaperón."

A courteous *vaquero*, Felipe. Don Diego had insisted on sending him along to help with their animals and do camp chores for them, but it was awkward as hell. When Elena wanted to wash, or change clothes, Felipe had to find a reason to leave camp. Sometimes Elena and Pasque wanted to be alone together, but there was no way to tell when their helper would come back.

It was the first morning they had their camp to themselves. Pasque woke up just as the red ball of the rising sun was showing itself above the piñon grove. He pushed the heavy blanket down so he could stretch his arms. It was the coldest morning they had seen so far. There was frost on the saddles, lying near their bedroll.

Pasque's movements woke Elena. Her long, dark lashes opened, her deep, dark eyes danced to see Pasque next to her, and that wonderful smile instantly spread across her lips. She turned and raised herself on her elbow to kiss him lightly on the mouth, and then sat up and stretched her arms into the crystal-blue sky above. The blanket slipped down her nude body, and she seemed not to notice. She closed her eyes tightly and smiled at the new sun, washing over her face. She tilted her head back. Her long, black hair hung down behind, and she ran her hands through it. Her breasts pointed at the sun with nothing on them except the

268

wine-red light. Her nipples jutted out stiffly in the cold air.

Pasque could only stare at her. Before reaching for her to pull her down to him, he had to catch his breath and squeeze his eyes tightly shut once or twice to shake himself out of the spell. Nowhere in the world was there a man with so beautiful a wife. He embraced her gently, lovingly, his heart made tender by the sight of her. He became aware of the deep morning quiet all around them and the scent of sage and piñon in the chilled air. The blankets were warm and deep.

Elena had other, more urgent thoughts. Whispering in Spanish — "My love, these breasts need your mouth, your hand must warm them." and "Quick! Now touch me here." — she grasped his hand hard and directed it where she wanted it — "And here. And here." She seized his shoulders, raked his back with her nails, seemed to be beneath him one minute and atop him the next, demanding more and more of him, until they were both breathless and moaning in the language of passion.

Afterward, they lay very still in each other's arms. While the sun rose gradually to lick the frost from the pines and from the saddles, Pasque remembered Felipe.

"Thank God Felipe wasn't sleeping near here," he said aloud.

"Why else did you send him ahead to look for the Platte River?" Elena said, laughing.

Felipe continued to stay a day ahead of them. Pasque figured he was either looking for a river crossing or was already across the Platte and searching for Keystone landmarks. His tracks were easy to follow. He had used stones or sticks to make arrows on the ground, pointing the way around a concealed arroyo or a bog. The country was mostly rolling hills, but every so often there would be a deep draw or gully wandering and twisting its way through the hills. Many of them had steep high banks, and long detours had to be made.

The bride and groom loitered along, taking the detours as they came, sometimes quietly holding hands as they rode, sometimes chasing each other in wild horse races. Pasque always lost to Elena, usually because he had to keep the pack horse with him. He didn't mind. It was well worth it to be in the rear where he could enjoy the sight of Elena's fair figure in the saddle.

Then, one morning, they spotted a haze moving ahead of them like the spurts of dust made by spooked antelope. Pasque led the way into a shallow draw, then up the bank again to get into a position behind some scraggly junipers. He peered through the branches as the dust got closer. Riders were coming.

It looked like four or five, maybe six. Hard to tell at that distance. Pasque and Elena had been riding almost due north, and these horsemen were quite a way off to the right of their route.

"Better stay here till they're gone," Pasque said. "Another couple of minutes up there, and they'd've spotted us."

"Who are they?" Elena asked.

"No tellin'. Might be just cowboys from some ranch, lookin' for stray stock. Could even be from the Keystone, dependin' on whether that's the Platte out there, and how far up it we are. Or they could be outlaws."

"Should we not ride out and ask? Perhaps they will know how far it is from your Keystone." Elena smiled at him sweetly to show that the decision was all his.

Pasque dug into his saddlebag for the small, brass telescope. Once he got the lens adjusted, he could count seven riders. They were spread out in a line and riding as if they were searching for something.

He dismounted and handed his reins to Elena, then steadied the telescope on a cedar branch to take a better look. Two of the riders had a third rider between them and were sticking close to him, as though he were their prisoner. The horse was a light buckskin, almost white. Felipe's horse.

Pasque's mind raced. Felipe must have run afoul of a bunch of range rustlers. Now they were following his back trail! Spread out the way they were could mean that they'd lost it and were looking for it. Felipe had had two pack horses with him and enough luggage and gear for three people. These rustlers must've seen Elena's clothing in the packs, as well as her jewelry and the presents they had been bringing to the Keystone. The outlaws might be figuring that Felipe's back trail would lead them to even more loot.

Pasque looked to his left. A lone rider had broken off from the end of the line closest to them and was making a wide swing. If he kept coming the way he was heading, he'd be certain to cut Felipe's trail. It would lead him right to them, since they had been staying in Felipe's tracks all morning. Too close.

Pasque mounted up and led Elena back down into the draw.

"One of 'em's comin' this way," he said. "Six others are stayin' off to the east quite a ways."

He drew his Colt and checked it, then loosened his Winchester in its scabbard. Finally Pasque leaned over and pulled out Elena's rifle to make sure it was loaded and ready to use.

"You got that little *pistolita* of yours in your saddlebag?" he asked.

Elena twisted around and opened the leather flap. Her .38 Smith and Wesson was in a holster on a belt, but, since it was a nuisance to wear while riding, she kept it in her right-hand saddlebag on top of her folded poncho. She buckled it around her waist and checked the .38's cylinder.

"What shall we do now?" she asked, holstering her gun.

"Let's work our way along this draw, keep movin' toward the mountains. There's only one of 'em ridin' our way. If we can get the drop on him, we'll try that. Find out who they are, maybe. Could be just ranch hands from somewhere."

Pasque didn't want to scare Elena, so he didn't tell her he was almost certain he had seen Felipe being escorted between two of the men. If she would stay calm and quiet, there might be a chance of getting this lone rider out of sight of the others. If they could capture and hog-tie him, they might bargain for Felipe.

They rode a few hundred yards before Pasque changed his mind about taking Elena along with him to confront the lone outrider. A deep washout led into a steep-sided gully. It looked like it ran straight north and then took a turn toward the east. It might be a way for her to sneak clear around that bunch of *hombres* and make a break for it.

"This is close enough," he said softly. "Now I want you to get down in this arroyo here, and keep the pack horse with you. If there's shootin', ride like hell. Stay out of sight as long as you can. Try to be quiet about it, but get goin'. Cut the pack horse loose. Just light out of here, away from these riders. If you can get around 'em without bein' seen, then swing north and keep headin' north. Keep the mountains on your left, and you'll find the Keystone, maybe a day or two from here. Probably, you'll cut a road sooner or later. Take it north or west, and you'll get there."

"Should I look for Felipe?" she asked.

Pasque hesitated. Then he saw what a calm courage was looking out at him from those deep brown eyes. "They've got him," he answered. "Now get on along the arroyo there."

Pasque swung off his horse and cautiously led it up the slope until he could take a peek over the top. He heard hoofbeats, somebody coming slow just past the next rise. He lifted the telescope and waited for the rider to come out into view. Moments passed. Pasque had just decided to go back to Elena and sneak away, when the rider reappeared again. Pasque looked through the telescope.

"My God!" he said, under his breath. "Link!"

No doubt about it. It was Link. Straight in the saddle, dark Stetson tilted down in front, black mustache, fancy, tooled vest. He didn't seem to be expecting trouble, since his Colt was holstered, and he didn't have a saddle carbine with him. He was just riding along, eyes fixed on the ground.

Pasque studied the terrain, while he figured out where Link might be headed, then slid back down out of sight. The distance was two hundred yards, maybe. He could crawl or walk scrunched down, stay low, stay in the arroyo until it petered out, till there was only about fifty yards of open ground. That is, if Link kept going in the direction he was headed. He had to get the drop on him where they'd be out of sight of the others. But it was a risk — one shot would bring the whole outfit on the run.

He looked back in the direction Elena had gone. He couldn't sneak away from this, not now. Her only chance to get away would be to draw the gang into following him in the wrong direction. Or maybe pin them down with his rifle until she was long gone. And taking Link alive might be a chance to get Felipe back.

Link! Pasque had pictured this moment in his mind. He had always seen it the same way. He would get the drop on him and give him one chance, and only one chance, to tell the whole story. At the first sign he was lying, Pasque would wade into him and batter him to the ground. He would shoot him, or beat him to death.

It wouldn't matter. In his mind, Pasque had practiced the insults he was going to use to get Link good and mad, to make Link start a fight that Pasque would finish. He was going to give him more of a chance than the back-shooter had given his brothers, but he was still going to kill him.

But try as hard as he could, Pasque now found that he couldn't rouse up his anger. Not the anger he had felt before. He might be able to coyote his way up the draw and cut Link off from his outfit, but then? Without the rage, without his anger, he might not know what to do when they were face to face again. Might not even know what to say.

But it had to be. Chris and Jim were dead, and Link had something to do with it. It had to be finished. He thought of Elena, trusting in him and riding around the gang, believing that he would catch up to her, and he knew now that he was taking a chance. This could leave her alone, a widow in a strange northern land. He had to think about that. But the thing had to be finished. It was part of his life from before she had been in it, and, if he rode away from it now, it would be a question forever standing between him and their future. It had to be now.

Pasque tied his horse to a sagebrush and went ahead on foot, crouching over and moving quietly. The Winchester swung heavily in his hand. He smelled the new sage leaves and the damp spring earth, and then he was aware of the odor of his own sweat. In spite of the cool air, a drop of sweat under his shirt rolled from his armpit in a cold line down his side. He shifted the rifle from hand to hand so he could wipe his palms on his jeans.

He was fifty yards from his horse, when he heard Link coming. But then the sound of hoofs stopped; Link had pulled up to look around. Pasque had to get closer. If he could make it to the end of the draw, he'd be able to get behind Link and get the drop on him. Ten more steps got him into the clear. There was his man, sitting on his horse, looking off into the distance, unaware that Pasque was coming up behind him. Close enough for the Colt. The Winchester would be too clumsy at this range. Pasque quietly set the rifle on the ground and started to creep ahead.

But his foot caught under a sage root. Without thinking, he jerked it loose, forgetting about the jinglebob. The silver tinkle of the little bell on Pasque's spur was just loud enough to make Link turn around. He shouted and grabbed for his gun. His horse twisted and reared, while he dragged his Colt out of its holster and tried to get a steady bead on Pasque's chest. The horse kept dancing and tossing its head, and Link cussed him. Pasque stood steady and calmly thumbed back the hammer of his Colt and took aim at Link.

And hesitated. He did not know why he hesitated, but he knew it meant his death. As surely as he knew anything, he now knew that Link could kill him. Pasque had his gun pointed at Link the whole time, but his finger was paralyzed on the trigger. He saw every detail of Link's surprised face, from the oiled, black mustache to the pockmark on his cheek, and it was not the face of the man he had been waiting so long to kill. It was the

276

same man, but the face was not hard and evil as Pasque had imagined it all these months.

Link did not shoot, either. He ran, just as he had done the last time they met. He got control of his horse, turned it away from Pasque, and took off as fast as the animal could gallop, not looking back.

"Well I'll be god-damned . . ." Pasque said.

He grabbed up the rifle and ran for his own horse. It was going to be close, but he still had a chance of catching up with him before he got to the main bunch. Pasque glanced backward as he started the horse into its run. At least, Elena was out of sight, headed out around the trouble, if she had any sense at all. In the meantime, he would keep these buckaroos occupied. He would hold their attention, and she'd make it.

He pounded up over the hill, leaning forward, whipping the pony right and left with the rein ends, and he saw Link far ahead of them, already halfway to the group of riders. One of the riders separated from the group and started out to meet him. Then the whole line swung and headed straight for him.

Pasque was close enough to use the Winchester. He no longer had any hope of catching Link alone, but at least he could make the bunch hunt for cover. He reined his horse to a stop and levered a shell into the chamber. He would try to pick off one of the men guarding Felipe, give the *vaquero* a chance to run for it.

When Pasque sighted along the rifle and swung it to bear on the group, the horseman he thought was Felipe was riding free. Pasque could see the broad sombrero and the outline of the big Spanish saddle, and Felipe was waving like he was excited about something.

There was something familiar about that other man near Felipe — something familiar about the way he sat in the saddle.

Pasque cradled the Winchester in his arm and rode on at a trot. No point in running the horse any farther. He didn't have much of a plan at this point, except to parley with these *hombres*, if they wanted to parley. And if it came to threats and guns, he thought maybe he would turn and ride full out for Elena. If he could catch up to her, the two of them could find some kind of cover and maybe hold out until dark. Between her rifle and his, they still had a chance. After it got dark maybe they could sneak away. Felipe could follow them, if he were loose. Not much of a plan, but it was the best he could do right then.

As soon as the riders got closer, all of Pasque's plans vanished like dust. He knew who the men were, now. Drawn up in a line, facing him, were Link and Felipe and Art. Bob Riley and the Pinto Kid and two other boys from the Keystone were coming up behind them.

"Hullo, Pasque," Art said. "Been looking for you. Your man, Felipe, here rode into the ranch yesterday morning, so we decided to ride out and meet you."

"Good to see you," Pasque said. He kept the rifle cradled in his arm so that it was trained on Link as he spoke. "What are you doin' with this *pendejo* here?"

Link looked pale, but kept quiet.

"Link, I don't know what you think you're up to, ridin' out here like one of the boys," Pasque went on.

278

The chill was coming into his voice. The anger was down there, somewhere, and rising. "But I'll tell you one thing. That brand on your saddle and the way you keep runnin' from me tells me that you killed my brothers. Or you know who did."

"Now, Pasque, just a minute . . ." Art said.

"I don't think so, Art." Pasque replied, keeping the rifle trained on Link. "I think me and Mister Link here might just walk off into the brush a ways and settle this. And he'd better have the caps on that old Colt of his, this time."

Art had not become the most respected man in the territory by letting anyone take charge that easily, not even if he was a nephew, so now it was his turn to act. He nudged his horse up to Pasque's, and reached out in a matter-of-fact way and took the Winchester from him. He just wrapped one large hand around the receiver, gave a twist, and had the rifle.

"A .44 rim-fire?" he said. "You left the Keystone with a center-fire."

"It was a present," Pasque said. But he didn't say "wedding" present. "The center-fire's on the pack horse."

Art carefully lowered the hammer, but now the rifle was aimed in Pasque's general direction just in case his nephew decided to go for his Colt.

"You've got some explanations coming," Art said. "But there's not going to be any gun play. We're all going to step down now and make some coffee and have a bite of lunch. We'll cool off, and then have a talk. Bob!" Art called out, not taking his eyes off Pasque and

279

Link. "You want to unpack that coffee pot and fix us up a little cooking fire?"

"Just you get Link's gun, then," Pasque said. "I don't trust him any further than I could throw him. You see that he stays put, and I'll listen to these explanations of yours. And Felipe ain't my man, by the way. He's a *vaquero* from the *Hacienda* Godinez. Link is my man, and he's sittin' on that horse beside you. He ain't goin' anywhere, until I settle with him."

Link handed over his Colt. Pasque noticed that none of the cowboys was moving, in spite of Art's order to fix a fire. They were just sitting on their horses, facing Art and Pasque, frozen in place, keeping their hands away from their side-arms, all of them looking at something behind him and Art. Pasque looked around to find out why. And find out he did.

"Art," Pasque said, as calmly as possible, "I think you should hand me back my Winchester. And make it easy-like. Muzzle pointin' straight up. Right now."

"Are you sure I want to do that, Pasque?"

"Damn sure. That rifle's part of a matched set, and the other one's aimed right at the middle of your spine."

Art looked at Felipe. Felipe, sitting next to Pasque, nodded. Art turned a little to look at Bob. Bob nodded, too, and used his chin to point the direction of the other .44 Winchester that had just been dealt into the game. Art handed the rifle to Pasque and then turned around.

About fifty feet away was the prettiest *señorita* he had ever seen, and she was holding a bead on him with another Winchester. A .44 is already a big caliber, and looking down the muzzle end makes it look a hell of a lot bigger.

Pasque smiled at the lovely ambusher. He wanted to be mad at her for not riding away like he'd told her, but he was proud that she managed to sneak up behind them that way.

"Art," he said, "I'd like you to meet my wife. And the first thing you want to know about her is that she don't do anything you tell her to do. I told her to get north of here as fast as she could, but I guess she decided to help out instead."

"Can she shoot that thing?" Art asked.

"Taught her myself," Pasque smiled.

"Then I'm damn' glad she has a better temper than you. With your hair-trigger brain, you'd've shot me by now." Art turned back toward his riders. "OK, boys," he barked. "Get that fire going. Pasque says that the lady probably won't shoot you."

The Keystone hands had their coffee and bread and jerky, then each found himself a scrap of shade. Before long they were napping, hats over their faces and legs stretched out as if this were just another nooning on a cattle drive. Having retrieved the pack horse, Felipe also lay down with his sombrero over his face. Pasque, Elena, Art, and Link sat on the ground near the small fire. Link made his explanations.

"To start with," he said, "Moore and I didn't have anything to do with killing your brothers. Like I told your uncle, we went to work for a trail-cutting outfit, and we thought they were on the up and up. We heard about trail drovers getting killed, mostly rumors we'd pick up when we went to a town. But we never saw any murders. Anyway, our outfit got ambushed by a big trail herd crew, and Moore and I got away.

"Ended up, after a while, at the Keystone. And you showed up, and, as God's my witness, that's the first time I knew our Oval Cross bunch were murderers. I don't even know if your brothers were shot before or after we ran away from them."

Link turned toward Art, hoping he would go on with it from there.

"I believe him, Pasque," Art said. "You remember that telegram? Bob Roberts saying he was still tracking the bunch? Link and Moore agreed to go out to the Republican Crossing and see if they could identify them. And they ended up helping catch them, too."

Pasque looked at Art, then at Link again. "So you found 'em?"

By his tone, Art could tell that Pasque wasn't convinced yet.

"Yes," Link said. "We found out that they'd headed toward Kansas again, after being scattered in that ambush. In fact, they joined up right in the same place where we'd met them. We knew where they held the cattle, too." Link helped himself to more coffee. "That's where we caught them," he went on, "and we had a posse of almost forty men. We cornered the gang down around Cottonwood Springs in an old trapper's cabin they'd always used. Had to shoot it out with them. We like to never got them out of there."

"Dead?" Pasque asked.

"Yeah. One of them gave up, after we shot the others to pieces. He was new to the bunch. Didn't have anything to do with your brothers, but some of the boys showed him a new rope they'd brought along, and he started telling everything he'd heard. He said a couple of them bragged about shooting a couple of men, guarding a herd. I'm pretty sure they were the back-shooters who killed your brother. And they're dead and buried out there, now, and they aren't buried any too deep."

A silence followed. Art made some polite conversation with Elena, and Elena asked Felipe if the equipment and luggage were safe, and the talk drifted back to Link again.

"So you and Moore are goin' to be with us a while," Pasque suggested. "I suppose we can get along all right without Art havin' to send us all over the territory on his errands."

"As a matter of fact," Art said, "the McLauchlins decided to pull up stakes, so I bought that place of theirs, up north. Not too far from the line cabin on Kathy Fork, but lots prettier country. I figure I'll put some man up there with maybe three, four hands. Run it like a separate ranch."

"Good job for you, Link," Pasque said.

Art stood up and kicked some dirt on the fire, then dumped the wet coffee grounds into the coals. "We'll talk about who goes where later," he said. "Now that I know you two aren't goin' to kill each other, we can see about getting to the Keystone. Gwen is going to be mighty glad to see you, Pasque. And, Elena, my wife will be thrilled to death to meet you. I can see already that you're going to be real good friends."

"I think we will," Elena replied. "We have already one thing in common, you know. We both know what is best for this Pasque *hombre* here!"

CHAPTER
EIGHTEEN

A Patch of Lavender

Gwen reached into the picnic hamper and brought out the rhubarb and wild apple pie, one of Mary's specialties. She cut it and used the flat of her knife to lift the pieces onto plates which she handed to Elena, Art, and Pasque. Elena was sitting on a log, her poise and posture as perfect as if she were in her own drawing room. She was in her riding skirt and white blouse, with her sombrero hanging at her back by its chin string.

Art and Pasque were sprawled on the ground nearby in nearly identical postures, each supporting himself on one elbow as he put his fork to the pie.

"I just can't get over the change in Pasque," Gwen said to Elena. "When he left here, he always seemed to have a little dark cloud floating over him. Honestly! Why, do you know, I'm not sure that I ever saw him laugh. And now look at him. He seems so much older, somehow, but not nearly as dark. Not so gloomy."

"Comes from bein' married," Pasque said. "A man couldn't be too gloomy with a lady like this to look at all the time."

"Whatever it is, I'm glad," Gwen replied. "I don't think a foreman ought to be grim. He should be serious, of course, but not grim. Art and I were talking about it . . ."

"Well, Pasque," Art interrupted his wife, "this story of yours about the man Hochland . . . and the priest and that blacksmith's stuff about going off in four directions . . . sure is a tale for those long winter nights."

Art wanted to get to the foreman question, but he didn't want to ride straight at it. A man needed to work around a question like that, talk about other things, until the time seemed right to bring it in.

"And you never found out if that ghost shirt was magic?" he continued. "Probably wasn't. Me, I'm not much of a believer in magic stuff."

"What about that axe story of yours?" Pasque asked, smiling at his uncle. "Can't tell me there wasn't somethin' magic about you gettin' the blade outta that stump."

Art just laughed. "Son," he said, "you gotta learn two things yet. One, stories are stories. And whether it's this yarn about a giant man who goes around getting himself shot and then coming alive again, or about a man who could lift a loaded wagon off a injured man, a story tends to stretch in the tellin'."

Elena smiled at Art. "Your nephew told me of the great axe and the stump," she said. "But how did you do it, if not the way it is told?"

"Tricks to everything. That's the second thing you've gotta learn. When you drive an axe into a fresh stump that's full of sap, it's like glue. Trick is to grab the handle right away, out at the end, jiggle it to keep the sap from hardening. And then you push down on the end. You don't try to pull up on it. You've got to use your weight and use the heel of the blade as a kind of prop, like levering a rock outta the ground. Leverage and gettin' to it before it cools down . . . that's the magic. There's tricks to everything."

Pasque helped himself to more coffee, and Gwen helped him to another slice of pie. Then Gwen stood up and asked Elena if she would like to go for a walk.

"I think Art wants to talk business with Pasque," she said. "Shall we leave them alone to do it?" And the two ladies strolled off up the streamside toward the foothills.

"Probably the two best-lookin' women in the whole territory, right there," Art said, watching them go.

"No doubt," Pasque said.

"Tell me something," Art said.

"Sure."

"Are you gonna ever get yourself a new pair of spurs? It's kind of curious to see a man wearing only one."

"Well," Pasque said, "you don't need but only one. If you get one side of the horse runnin', the other side sorta goes along with it." He grinned. "And if people ask about it, well, I got a story to tell them. My way to spread the word that the old, rough days are over with."

Art took off his own left spur and tossed it toward his saddlebag draped over the log.

"I didn't get around to telling you," he said, "but I appreciated the way you faced up to that Hochland *hombre* last Christmas. I think you saved the Keystone reputation in a way. From now on, I'm going to wear

287

one spur, too, as a reminder. Hell, it might get to be a Keystone trademark."

"Speakin' of reminders," Pasque replied, "when are you goin' to remember to ask me about bein' foreman?"

Art laughed and set his plate aside, then rolled over onto his back to look up into the limitless blue sky overhead.

"Now's as good a time as ever," he said. "The point is, me and Gwen agree that you've earned the job. But I had a better idea, especially since I don't want to take that job away from Bob Riley. What I'd like you and Elena to do is take over the old McLauchlin spread and run it. You know how nice it is up north there. Maybe someday you could end up ownin' that part of the Keystone."

Pasque sat, quiet, thoughtful, pushing a crumb of pie crust around his plate with his fork.

"It's a good offer," he finally said. "But I've had about enough of the north. Don Diego promised us a place of our own, by way of a dowry. Dowry's a big tradition down there, and a man has to take it real serious. It would insult him pretty bad, if I turned it down. And he'd never get over it, if I made Elena move 'way up here and away from him. Might be grandkids and all that. Besides, I like that Picketwire country. Warm. Good people. So, all things considered, I guess we'll head on back south this summer."

"Enough said," Art replied. "Maybe you'll get a good herd goin' down there, and you and I will end up swappin' some livestock one of these days."

"Wouldn't be at all surprised," Pasque said.

The two men had time for a smoke; Pasque had introduced Art to Don Diego's thin cigars, a large supply of which had been among the wedding presents. When the ladies returned from their walk, the two men were sitting side by side on the log, finishing their cigars. Each one had a stick in his hand, and they were drawing brand designs in the dirt at their feet. If Pasque was going to have a ranch and a herd, they would need to figure out a good brand.

Elena was in a merry mood. She was carrying her riding hat in both hands in front of her as she came skipping and running to Pasque.

"Look, my love!" she bubbled. "See what I have found! They are growing all over that hill back there!"

Pasque looked into her hat. It was full of pale lavender flowers, some almost purple, some nearly white. He looked up the hill where she had pointed. There in the springtime sunlight a lavender haze spread through the new grass under the rabbitbrush and sage.

"Your flowers!" Elena exclaimed. "Everywhere! I was so happy to find them! And Gwen is right . . . some of them, like this one and this one, even match your eyes, my husband. Just look how beautiful! I knew you would like them. I know that you are happy to be here again, with your friends, where the pasque flowers tell you it is spring."

Pasque took Elena in his arms and hugged her while the hatful of flowers dangled from her hand. He couldn't tell whether his heart was smiling harder than his face, or the other way around.

"You're somethin', you are," he said, laying his cheek onto her soft dark hair. "But I tell you what . . . next time, let's leave 'em growing where they are. You and me, we'll come here together, once in a while, and just look at 'em."

About Author

James C. Work was born in Colorado where his family had lived for three generations. His mother's grandparents were in Leadville and Cripple Creek during the gold rush days, while his father's forebears were pioneer farmers on Colorado's eastern plains. He grew up in Estes Park and attended Colorado State University and the University of New Mexico, and holds degrees from both. He taught literature at Colorado State University. Work has received awards from the Western Literature Association, the Colorado Seminars in Literature, the Charles Redd Center for Western Studies, and the Frank Waters Association for Southwest Writing. He is the editor of the classic textbook, *Prose and Poetry of the American West*, and, in addition to writing Western fiction and editing Western literature, he has published a collection of essays titled *Windmills, The River and Dust: One Man's West*. His expertise in English and American literature merged with his interest in Western history to produce the Keystone Ranch series of novels, beginning with *Ride South to Purgatory* (Five Star Westerns, 1999). Here history mingles with allegory, myth finds foundation in fact, and the ancient tales of King Arthur's knights find new life as Work shapes them into chronicles of the Keystone Ranch. Each novel in the series takes a unique approach to the West of the later 1800s, yet every novel is grounded in historical research and flavored with archetype and myth. For fans of the mystery genre there is Work's other series in which a professor at a Western university solves murder cases through his knowledge of literature, and include *The Tobermory Manuscript* (Five Star Westerns, 2000) and *A Title to Murder* (Five Star Westerns, 2004). Work lives in Fort Collins, Colorado. Additional information concerning his works may be found on his website: www.jameswork.com